Gilly shrugged. "I get a bit carried away sometimes."

"I'd say," Gavril said. "But I love it. Wouldn't want it any other way."

Gilly gave him a strange, shy look, and it was then that Gavril realized he'd used the *L* word. Although he hadn't actually said the words "I love you," it had been close enough to give her pause.

"Good," Gilly finally said. "I'm glad you like it. 'Cause I only come in one color."

"What's that mean?"

She stopped and gave him a long, soulful look. "It means, Mr. Gavril Hyland, that when it comes to me, what you see is what you get."

"And that's supposed to be a bad thing?"

"It's been known to get me ⬛⬛⬛⬛⬛⬛⬛⬛ time to time."

"Good," Gavril ⬛⬛⬛⬛⬛⬛⬛⬛⬛⬛ after my own hear⬛⬛

Deborah LeBlanc is an award-winning, bestselling author from Lafayette, Louisiana. She is also a licensed death scene investigator and a private investigator, and has been a paranormal investigator for over twenty years. Deborah is currently the house "clairsendium" (clairvoyant/sensitive/medium) for the upcoming paranormal investigation television show *Through the Veil*.

In 2007, Deborah founded Literacy Inc., a nonprofit organization dedicated to fighting illiteracy among America's teens.

For more information, visit www.deborahleblanc.com and www.literacyinc.com.

Books by Deborah LeBlanc

Harlequin Nocturne

The Wolven
The Fright Before Christmas
Witch's Hunger
The Witch's Thirst
Witch's Fury

WITCH'S FURY

DEBORAH LEBLANC

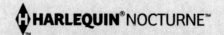
HARLEQUIN® NOCTURNE™

**Recycling programs
for this product may
not exist in your area.**

ISBN-13: 978-1-335-62955-5

Witch's Fury

Printed in U.S.A.

Dear Reader,

Thank you for choosing *Witch's Fury* to add to your library. I hope you enjoy reading it as much as I enjoyed writing it. Occasionally, it's difficult to add a strong plausibility base for the creation of a new creature. It's a little like writing about love, unconditional love. The quality is so rare that oftentimes only our imagination can create the vastness of such love—which is why we read romance novels. :) May this book bring you the prickle of excitement of new creatures and most of all may it give you a nodule of hope for the unconditional love we all seek.

Deborah

TO MY FAMILY FOR THEIR LOVE AND PATIENCE.

Chapter 1

Over the past three weeks, Gilly François and her sisters, Vivienne and Evette, had been living a nightmare that the triplets couldn't seem to wake from. The sisters, known as the Triad—a special set of witches—were at a loss over all of the strange and unusual events that had been occurring lately. Each sister was responsible for otherworldly creatures known as the Originals, the first of their breed. Gilly took care of the Chenilles, the original zombies, Viv the Loup-Garous, the original werewolves, and Evee the Nosferatu, the original vampires. Lately, however, no one seemed capable of taking care of anything or anyone.

Chenilles had been slaughtered, just like Loup-Garous and Nosferatu. Even worse, many of the members of their Originals factions had simply disappeared, leaving the safe haven created by the Triad years ago.

Although the sisters had cast additional protection and boundary spells over their assigned territories, more times than not, the spells appeared ineffective. The killings continued.

Feeling at a loss and hopeless, the Triad were nearing their wits' end when four men showed up on their doorstep: Nikoli, Lucien, Ronan and Gavril Hyland. They'd said they were cousins, known as Benders, and had been sent to New Orleans to help the Triad. Whatever they were, there was no denying they were all tall, muscular and drop-dead gorgeous.

Along with their arrival, the cousins brought unsettling news. They revealed that the local deaths of the Triad's Originals were not due to infighting among the factions as the Triad had first suspected. According to the cousins, the deaths were coming by way of creatures known as Cartesians—massive, monstrous creatures with long, razor-sharp talons and teeth. Their bodies were protected by inch-thick scales that hid behind a heavy matting of fur. Their job as Benders, a special generational group of men ordained by the Church centuries ago, was to destroy the Cartesians.

Gilly and her sisters had heard of the Cartesians before but only in folkloric tales. According to legend, Cartesians were an invisible lot, only revealing themselves occasionally. They fed on other-worldly creatures, anything whose life force exceeded that of an average human, which, of course, included the Triad.

Although it had taken some time for the Hylands to convince Gilly and her sisters that the men weren't a few cards short of a deck, the Triad was eventually convinced. So much so that they'd decided to split up into three groups with the Benders to cover more territory in search of their missing Originals. Viv worked with Nikoli, Gilly with Gavril and Evee with both Lucien and Ronan.

Sadly, in the midst of a surprise attack on Evee, Ronan, whom Evee knew had a crush on her, had rushed over to save her and had been gored in the head by a Cartesian's massive talons. The Cartesian had then disappeared with Ronan into another dimension. Evee and Lucien had witnessed it all; Nikoli had contacted the family back home and notified them of Ronan's death.

Gilly had been sure that after that horrid event, the Benders would be off to their homeland to help console their family and help with Ronan's memorial service. Instead, they'd chosen to stay in New Orleans. It was evident to Gilly that the Benders met their commitments and finished their missions, no matter what.

The Triad had even set up an elaborate feeding system in Algiers, across the river from New Orleans, using cattle as their feeding stock, so the Originals were always satiated: the Nosferatu fed on the blood, the Loup-Garous on the meat and the Chenilles on the bone marrow. But despite the appearance of the Benders and their offer to help, things had started to take a turn for the worse, and quickly. Word from the Triad's Elders was that some of the missing Originals had already moved out of New Orleans proper and murdered two people.

In the midst of all the chaos, the Triad met with their Elders—Arabella, Taka and Vanessa—to ask for their advice, help and understanding.

Unfortunately, not only were the Triad's powers beginning to wane, but the Elders' powers were, as well. Everything from binding to comehither spells worked, didn't work, or barely worked. The last two symptoms became more dominant each day. The only advice the Elders had to offer was to possibly speak to the three sorcerers who lived in New Orleans, in hopes they might be able to break through this spell malaise.

While meeting with the Elders, it was discovered that Viv and Evee had already been intimate with their Benders—more than once. The revelation came by way of the Triad's familiars, all three of which snitched on their mistress for what they thought to be the greater good. Appalled, the Elders demanded that they no longer have any intimate contact with the Benders. Triad members were forbidden to marry or live intimately with humans. If so, they'd lose their powers completely, and the Originals they were there to protect would run amuck, killing humans at will.

Evee and Viv tried to deny that they had been romantically involved with the Benders. But to the Elders, what else explained why things had taken such a severe turn for the worse? It had to be because Gilly's two sisters had sex with their search partners, and the reason their powers were waning Although Gilly had spoken to her sisters about that hypothesis and they had agreed that it might be a possibility, neither Evee nor Viv seemed to regret their actions.

So far, Gilly was the only member of her Triad who hadn't had sex with a Bender, and it wasn't for lack of desire. Every time Gilly saw Gavril, the only thing that crossed her mind, no matter what else might be going on, was kissing his full bottom lip. She wanted to stare into his violet eyes and run her fingers through his collar-length, ginger-colored hair. She could have wrapped up her emotions in one huge, lust-filled package, but it didn't explain why her heart ached when he wasn't near. As much as she longed for him, she supposed guilt played a part in allowing it to go any further. After the Elders had found out that Viv and Evee had been intimate with their Benders, they'd confessed their senses of guilt to Gilly. They worried about the role their intimacy played in making things worse. But despite worry and guilt, however, they both declared that the drive, need and love for their men kept them going back for more.

"Fifty bucks for your thoughts," Gavril said, as they walked to St. Louis I cemetery to check on the remaining Chenilles.

She gave him a sideways grin. "Isn't it, 'a penny for your thoughts'?" The Benders had been with the Triad for a little over two weeks now, and the longer they stayed, the more Gavril tugged on her heart strings. His looks were one thing, but she so admired his drive and determination, his caring, thoughtful manner, and his do or die attitude when it came to accomplishing any task.

Gilly and Gavril had been searching incessantly for her missing Chenilles. By last count, twenty-five had gone missing. If her brood wasn't found before feeding time, chances were extremely high that they would start attacking humans for food. The police were getting involved, and that scared Gilly to death.

The last thing Gilly would admit to anyone, however—especially her sisters—was how badly she wanted Gavril. So badly, in fact, that it wasn't unusual for her to have wet dreams about him. She felt a bit guilty about that. Viv's entire troupe of Loup-Garous had vanished, as had Evee's lot of Nosferatu. She should be thinking of them, of helping them, while keeping track of her own Originals.

She and her sisters had spent their lives working hard to fit into the social day to day of New Orleans so as not to draw suspicion that they were witches. They were also ultra-careful in tending to their Originals, keeping them out of the way, in safe zones, so humans wouldn't find them. They lived in the Garden District and made sure to play nice with the neighbors at all times.

"So I'm a big spender. Besides, you haven't said three words to me since we left Evee's café to come to the cemetery. You looked so lost in thought, at times, I was sure you'd run headlong into a lamp-post." Gavril stopped walking and took hold of her arm gently, stopping her movement and turning her toward him. "I know things are crazy right now, but aside from that, are you okay?"

Gilly sighed. "Yes and no. I wish I could be more help to my sisters, but I know I have my own Originals to look after."

When she stopped speaking, Gavril studied her face. His eyes pierced hers, looking for more answers than what she'd just given him.

Gilly bit the corner of her mouth, unable to resist the questions in his eyes. "And I'm scared. So much has gotten out of control that I don't know if we'll ever know normalcy again."

Gavril ran his hand up and down her arm with a soothing touch. "All we can do is the best we can do. You can't explain why some of you and your sisters' spells aren't working, or if you know you haven't told me about it, and I have no idea why the scabior canopies are failing. I mean, this has never been done before, not to my knowledge, but it should react similar to our scabiors, which never just go out."

The Benders had assured the sisters that the Cartesians were not fictional creatures but real, vicious monstrosities that were determined to be the sole power in the netherworld, a three-dimensional place that held vampires, elves, djinn and other supernatural creatures. They had also dispelled the myth that Cartesians moved under the cloak of invisibility. It only appeared that way because Cartesians were able to slip in and out of physical dimensions in the blink of an eye.

The Hylands were able to track Cartesians by their scent, which was a noxious odor of sulfur and clove. They'd been taught, as were their fathers and grandfathers before them, how to battle the giant hellions in order to protect those who lived in the underworld. They did so by using a special weapon called a scabior—a six-inch rod of steel with a bloodstone attached to one end—which was handed down from generation to generation.

Not long after the Benders had arrived, in order for them to find the missing Originals and keep the ones they had safe, they'd created a scabior canopy, an electrical shelter that hovered over each safe zone. No Cartesian would be able to drop in through that crisscrossed electrical current.

"But they did go out. One of them, anyway— Evee's, the one Lucien set up in the catacombs for the Nosferatu. Remember? He told us he'd had to recharge the current. Then, before we knew it, it was completely out, and all of the Nosferatu that were inside disappeared."

"I know."

"How could that happen?"

Gavril frowned and shrugged. "It's as much a mystery to me as it is to you. What's stranger still is that the canopy was still intact over the north compound, where Viv kept her Loup-Garous, yet all of them disappeared."

"Yeah," Gilly said. "Explain that one."

"I wish I could, but I have no answers. The canopies were something that had never been done before, just a brainstorming idea that seemed to make sense, so we really don't know their power or capabilities. As for the Loup-Garous going missing with the shield over the compound still operational, it's beyond me. The only thing I can figure is that they purposely chose to leave."

Gilly shook her head. "That doesn't make any sense. Their food is there. Safety is there."

"That may be, but if they've never known anything else but the safe zones, they have no way of knowing what they face once they escape it."

Gilly lowered her head reluctantly. She didn't want to break eye contact with Gavril. His gaze consumed her, no matter the topic of conversation. The rest of him was nothing shy of downright hulk, bulk and sexuality. He exuded all three.

Although Gilly had never asked his age, Gavril appeared to be in his mid-thirties. He stood at least six foot four and had a body and face built for *GQ*— wide shoulders, biceps that looked like he could lift an elephant one-handed and, even from the black T-shirt he wore, the ripples in his abs were evident. His violet eyes were accented by a short, red beard, an aquiline nose and a cleft chin. His hair, the same color as his beard, sat just below shoulder length. His lips were always something Gilly worked hard to avoid looking at. Average upper, thick bottom, a mouth made for kissing. For deep, passionate kisses, not only on her own lips but all over her body.

When she looked back up at him, his eyes were still on her face. "Right now, our best move is to make sure your Chenilles are okay in their safe zone and lead them to their feeding. Once that's done, you bring them back here, and we keep hunting for the ones that're missing."

Gilly watched his lips as he spoke, feeling warmth spread through her body. She had to concentrate hard on his words as they were damn near lost to her need for him. So much of this felt odd, yet wonderful to her. It had been at least a year and a half since she'd dated. Since a committed human relationship was forbidden, she'd kept her dates limited, never with the same man twice.

With a feeling of reluctance, Gilly felt Gavril release her arm. "We're almost at the cemetery. I'll wait across the street near the voodoo shop, where it's darkest. Once you have them on their way to the docks, I'll follow but at a distance."

Gilly nodded. "No heroics, okay? Remember, the Chenilles are going to be ravenous by this time. If they see you before I can get them on the ferry and across to the compound, we'll be the ones contacting your family about your death." Gilly regretted her words the moment they came out of her mouth. A cloud of sorrow and depression crossed Gavril's face, and she was sure he was thinking of Ronan. What an insensitive ass she was.

"I mean—"

"I know what you mean," Gavril said, the light returning to his eyes. "No worries. I'll be careful."

Knowing that the François family ferry was waiting at the dock for her Chenilles, Gilly signaled Gavril to go into the shadows. Then she went into the cemetery to round up her brood.

As the Chenilles exited the cemetery—following Gilly's lead Chenille, Patrick—Gilly stood by the cemetery gates and took count as they went by. Ten more short than the last count, and as best she could tell, the scabior dome was still intact and operational. Being led by Patrick, the Chenilles followed in pairs. Their tall, thin figures bent over at the waist slightly, their beautiful faces intent on the Chenille before it. It was feeding time, and every Chenille knew it, which was what kept them from breaking formation and made it easy to walk them through the shadows and alleys to the dock.

Not having time to stop and give Gavril the news, she hurried over to Patrick's side and led her Originals to the docks, winding through side alleys and behind buildings to remain undetected.

Once they were loaded onto the ferry, Gilly got on. As the boat began to move, Gavril came out of the shadows and watched her, and she watched him. With the distance between them growing, Gilly could have sworn she saw Gavril give her the smallest wave goodbye and then lay his hand over his heart. If she was right and hadn't mistaken the gesture for some odd shadow, the thought of him making that heart tap made her heart feel full to the point of bursting. It took a lot of will power for her not to return the gesture. But what if she'd been mistaken in what she thought she saw? What would he think? That she was having a heart attack and attempt to get to her? Or would he see it for what it was and think she was making a move on him?

Deciding to play it safe, Gilly faced forward, glancing occasionally at the water lapping on either side of the ferry, and forced her mind to focus on business.

With Viv's Loup-Garous and Evee's Nosferatu both missing, her clan would have to use their screw-like incisors to drill down hide and meat to get to the bone. Marrow fed them, and they were used to having fresh bone to suck from when brought in for a feeding. Usually the Nosferatu had drained the cattle of blood, and the Loup-Garous had eaten the meat from the same. This left only the bone for the Chenilles to deal with. Now that wouldn't be the case, however. She didn't have any idea how they'd react to this change.

Viv was waiting for her on the Algiers side of the river, as was Evee.

"The cattle are in the feeding area like always," Viv said loudly so her voice carried over the ferry motor. "Lead them down the feeding shoot like usual. We'll be waiting for you here, behind the trees, over there, while they feed."

Nodding her understanding, Gilly moored the ferry to the dock and saw her sisters in her peripheral vision hurry off behind the grove of trees nearby.

Gilly unlatched the back gate of the ferry, led her troupe down a winding path, and once they came

to the front of the feeding shoot, no more direction
was needed. The Chenilles took off at a dead run,
all of them ravenous and anxious for the food awaiting them.

In the distance, Gilly heard a few Chenilles whine,
while others grumbled, obviously displeased over the
fact that they'd have to do so much work to get to
marrow. Once all had quieted down, and the only
sound she heard was the crunch of bone, Gilly went
back to the dock to meet Viv and Evee.

"Any issues?" Viv asked.

"Some whining, a few sounding pissed off," Gilly
said. "But at least they're eating."

Evee let out a shaky sigh that sounded very much
like she was close to tears. "What are we going to
do? We can't keep running around the city looking
for our Originals. We've run out of time. With so
many Nosferatu and Loup-Garous missing, human
deaths are going to become the norm—every day."

"We can't give up," Gilly said. "If we do, we're
already defeated."

"I'd call losing an entire troupe of Originals
pretty much defeat," Viv said. "I have no idea why
my Loups left. The north compound was their home.
Why would they just walk away from it?"

"*If* they walked away from it," Gilly said. "We really don't know what's happened to them."

She suddenly looked up and about as if just re-
membering something. "Where the hell are Nikoli
and Lucien? They're supposed to be with you, protecting you. Or did they forget that those ugly sons

of bitches determined to kill all of our Originals intend to kill us, as well?"

Viv held up a hand as if to stop Gilly's tirade. "Nikoli's still back at the hotel, dealing with his family about Ronan's death. Lucien went to check on him."

"To check on him?" Gilly huffed. "The man's six-four, if he's an inch, and built like a tank. What's to check on?"

"Emotions," Evee said. "I know you're worried about us, Gilly, but you can't forget that these men, no matter their size, have hearts. And right now they're mourning the loss of a close cousin."

"Yeah, whatever," Gilly said. "So is that the excuse I use if one of you gets chewed up by those sky assholes?"

"Chill, okay," Viv said. "We're fine. We'll leave here as soon as you get the Chenilles back city side, and the ferry makes it back here."

"I don't like it," Gilly said. "You're too out in the open. If something happens to one of you...well, it ain't gonna be pretty for Nikoli and Lucien. That's all I've gotta say."

With small shakes of their heads, Viv and Evee cocked an ear toward the feeding area.

"Sounds like they're about done," Gilly said. "Patrick will lead them back here, so go hide behind a tree or something, will you? The last thing I want is for one of my own to get to either of you."

Doing as they were asked, Viv and Evee ducked into a grove of trees just as Patrick led the now satiated Chenilles back to the ferry. They boarded lethargically, all of them seemingly overfed.

Once everyone was on board, Gilly closed the back gate of the ferry, kicked the motor on and steered the ferry to city side, where she knew Gavril would be waiting. She wished the ferry had a throttle, wanting it to go faster. All she cared about right now was seeing his face and getting her sisters back from the compound safely. But there was no throttle, so she had to tolerate the chug-chug of the engine and snail crawl of motion until they reached the other side.

After unlocking the back gate, Gilly motioned for Patrick to take her troupe back to the cemetery and make sure they were hidden in old crypts that had been busted open by vandals or in between any open mausoleum slots.

Patrick nodded and, with a grunt, motioned for the other Chenilles to follow him, which they did. Their steps were lumbering, as if trying to balance oversized bellies as they walked.

When they were well out of sight, Gilly uttered an incantation that sent the ferry back to Algiers for Viv and Evee to board. She waited at the water's edge, nervously biting her nails, her insides shaking. Her nerves were already shot with all that had been going on, but thinking that her sisters might get hurt by a stalking Cartesian en route made her nerves so bad, she thought she'd vomit.

"They'll be fine," a man's voice said behind her. And it took a nanosecond for Gilly to recognize it as Gavril's. He put his hands on her shoulders and leaned closer to her ear. "I promise. They'll be fine. And as soon as they return, they'll have Nikoli and Lucien at their sides at all times. That I assure you."

"But what if—"

"You can 'what if' until the cows come home," Gavril whispered into her ear. "But the key is to think positive. Visualize them back here safe and sound. Nothing will happen to them."

Gilly turned toward him, Gavril's hands still on her shoulders. "Nobody can know for sure. Crap happens, you know?"

Gavril let out a chuckle. "That's one thing I like about you, Ms. François. You do speak your mind, no matter what crosses it."

"It's not funny," Gilly said. "They're alone out there and—"

"Look," Gavril whispered and turned Gilly around. There in the distance was the ferry, already headed city side. From the light of the moon, Gilly easily made out Viv and Evee, both standing near the landing gate. She let out a breath of relief she didn't even realize she'd been holding.

Instinctively, Gilly reached up and covered one of Gavril's hands with her own. The spark of electricity that went through her when they touched shocked her, and Gilly quickly removed her hand. She thought of the Elders' warning not to be intimate with the Benders, as doing so might be their undoing. Yet she couldn't help but think of Evee and Viv. Both had received the same warning but continued their relationships with Lucien and Nikoli.

Gilly helped maneuver the ferry into its slip and hugged each of her sisters as they walked off the ferry.

"What's with the mushy stuff?" Viv asked with a laugh. "We only saw you a few minutes ago. You're acting like you haven't seen us in a year."

"Mushy stuff, huh?" Gilly huffed. "Just glad both of you are safely here."

"Me, too," Evee said, with a worried expression on her face. "Me, too."

Gavril watched as Gilly greeted her sisters, and felt his heart swell. As tough and independent as Gilly might have come across to the rest of the world, Gavril had been fortunate to see more. He'd seen how hard she could love, how deep her loyalties ran, her tenderness when the moment called for it.

Simply watching her interact with her sisters now, Gavril could not deny the fact that he was falling for Gilly and falling hard. This filled his heart and took him aback at the same time.

Gavril had dated more than his share of women over the years, but not one of them had affected him the way Gilly did. This had him walking in unfamiliar territory, which made him a bit nervous. He didn't want to move too fast or too slow, and knowing either with Gilly was a hard call. Aside from that, he had to keep his mind on the matter that had brought him here in the first place—the Cartesians.

Worrying about how to approach Gilly with his feelings had to come second. His first order of business had to be protecting the Triad and the remaining Originals from the Cartesians. The problem was, every time Gavril saw Gilly, his mind took a hard left without permission, and all he could see or concentrate on was her.

Regardless of how he felt, he had to gain control over his emotions and focus on protection. He'd tried comforting Gilly earlier by telling her to focus on Evee and Viv returning on the ferry safe and sound. The whole time he'd been trying to convince her that they would return safely, he'd been worried about their safety. Both Evee and Viv had been out alone without a Bender to protect them from Cartesians. And having a Triad member out alone when the Cartesians were after them along with their Originals was like teasing a catfish with a fat, juicy worm.

He was just as grateful to see them return safely as Gilly had been. Now, however, things had to change. No more outings without a Bender in tow. And no matter what it took to make that happen, even when it came to feeding the Originals, Gavril would make sure it did.

Chapter 2

"What now?" Gilly asked as she, Gavril, Viv and Evee walked away from the docks.

"More hunting," Gavril said. They crossed a broken piece of sidewalk, and Gavril placed a hand on the small of Gilly's back to maneuver her around it.

"Our hunting skills suck," Gilly said.

"Yeah," Viv said. "All we've gotten out of hunting for our missing Originals is more missing Originals. There has to be a better way to tackle this."

"I think it's time to hit our Grimoires," Evee said, referring to their book of spells. "Read through them to see if there's not a spell we've missed or one we can alter slightly that might help us."

"You can't just alter a spell," Gilly said gruffly. "You change it, and it changes the outcome."

Evee frowned. "It was just a thought."

"And a good one," Viv said. She gave Gilly a warning scowl, and then she laid a hand on Evee's shoulder, trying to reassure her. "It wouldn't hurt for us to look at our Grimoires. I vote we go through them…just to be sure."

"Well, if that's the case," Gavril said. "I'll walk the three of you home, then go to the hotel and meet up with Nikoli and Lucien to make sure the arrangements are set up for Ronan. Knowing Nikoli, the details have already been set in stone, though."

"Then why go?" Gilly said and then felt embarrassed for asking.

"Support," Gavril said. "Everyone can use some from time to time. The three of you look through your books, and we'll go back to the hotel and wrap up a few things regarding Ronan with our families. Let's say the six of us meet up in front of St. John's Cathedral in a couple hours."

"Sounds good," Viv said.

"Fine. Two hours," Gilly said, and the she turned on her heels and started for home. She made sure she stayed at the lead as she didn't want Gavril to see the disappointment on her face. She didn't like the fact that he was leaving—for any amount of time.

"Slow down, will you?" Evee said as they neared the Garden District. "We're not running a marathon."

Gilly tsked and glanced over her shoulder at Evee. "No, but the sooner we're off the streets, the better."

When they finally reached home, Gilly unlocked

the front door and marched into the foyer. She heard Viv reiterate to Gavril that they'd meet in front of the cathedral in two hours. After closing the door behind her, Viv turned on Gilly.

"What the heck's wrong with you? He only offered to walk us home, and you'd have sworn he carried a contagion the way you stormed ahead."

Gilly pulled off her T-shirt in the middle of the kitchen and started making her way to the stairs in order to shower and dress. "I wasn't storming ahead," she declared. "Just because I walk faster than you, it doesn't mean anything else."

Gilly heard Evee let out a giggle, and she stopped and glared at her sister. "What's with that? I don't find any of it funny."

"I know why you were acting weird coming home," Evee said.

"Oh, yeah, Smarty? Why?"

"Because you like him," Evee said. "You didn't want Gavril to leave."

"Aw, that's bull-crap," Gilly proclaimed, and she walked into the foyer and started stomping up the stairs to her room.

"No, it's not," Evee said. "Admit it, Abigail François. You like Gavril Hyland."

"Stop acting like a pubescent teen," Gilly shouted down at her. She hated when anyone used her full first name. It made her sound like a wuss. "I'm going to shower."

By the time Gilly made it to her bedroom, Elvis,

her albino ferret familiar, was stretched on her bed. He greeted her with a big yawn.

"She's right, you know," Elvis said.

"About what?" Gilly asked, stripping out of the rest of her clothes.

"You liking that Hyland guy."

"Oh, for the love of peace, would you stop already? I'm getting enough crap from Evee about that, and it just isn't true."

"But it—"

Naked, Gilly spun about on her heels and faced Elvis. "One more word out of you, and I'll dunk you in cold water, got it?" Elvis hated to have his body immersed in water, much less cold, which Gilly had done to him by accident a year ago. She'd been holding Elvis while filling a tub with water. Before the water temperature had crawled to warm, as it often took the time to do in their big old house, she'd tripped and accidentally dropped Elvis into the tub. He'd howled and shrieked and sprang up on all fours out of the tub, then ran out of the bathroom into hiding. He'd stayed angry with her about the incident for weeks.

Elvis lay his head down and covered it with his front paws.

Once in the shower, and away from Elvis' badgering and Evee's teasing, Gilly relaxed under the hot spray and thought about Gavril. It wasn't so much how he looked that tantalized her, although his Adonis-like handsomeness was nothing to spit at, it was who he was that intrigued her. It was the intensity with which he tackled any project he put his hand to, his gentleness when he touched her and the caring he showed for his family, which seemed as strong as what she felt for her own. She had a strong sense that Gavril felt for her the same way she felt for him. The way his eyes gazed into hers, how they never moved away from her face when she spoke, as if every word uttered held an importance that needed to be understood. Not once had he ever spoken over her. And the most beautiful thing about him, to her, anyway, was the way he seemed to be able to read her mind. To comfort her without her asking. To give her space without prompting. He accepted her for who and what she was. Never showing a hint of disgust or frustration. Not even when she dropped an F-bomb on occasion. In all of her adult years, Gilly had yet to meet a man with all those wonderful qualities.

Oh, and the way he smelled. An earthy scent, a manly scent with the slightest hint of cinnamon. It made her feel like a starving woman ready, needing, to consume all he had to offer.

It was easy to find one or two of these qualities in men, Gilly knew, but she had never known one man to possess them all. It was that and so much more that kept Gavril at the front of her thoughts. How would she ever find another man whom she felt had been so perfectly designed for her? She could only wish and hope he felt the same.

With his looks, Gilly was sure that he could have any woman he desired. All he'd have to do was look her way and smile, and any woman would melt like cream on a hot sidewalk at his feet. The thought of that jumbled Gilly's belly with jealousy, and seemed to turn the water about ten degrees colder.

Scrubbing her face with her hands, Gilly let the thought of other women go down the drain with the dirty water she washed from her body. If anything, she'd discovered in the few days she'd known him that Gavril was as loyal as they came. And jealousy was not her strong suit, anyway, which was another piece of the puzzle that made their match perfect.

Only one square peg refused to complete the picture. That peg was the one the Elders had thrown in their lap by demanding that the Triad have nothing more to do with the Benders. They'd reminded the Triad that having relationships with the Benders would be their undoing, which in turn and in the end, would be the destruction of the world.

As Gilly stepped out of the shower and dried her body, she repeated what the Elders had said verbatim in her mind. Although she easily remembered their remarks word for word, she found them unfair and questionable. If having a relationship with a Bender would be the end of them, then what about Viv and Evee? Both had sex with their Benders but were still around, their powers on par with her own. She was the only one who hadn't experienced hers. She wanted desperately to change that, but what if the Elders had been right? What if more intimacy with the Benders meant more destruction, more discord and more deaths among the Originals and humans in the city? Was she willing to take the chance and find out? The more she thought about it, though, the less sense it made. If the Elders' words of warning were to be taken verbatim, then Viv and Evee would be useless as witches right now. Gilly couldn't help but wonder if after all the centuries of interpretation, their Elders might have gotten something wrong or out of context.

After throwing Elvis a warning glance to keep his mouth shut, Gilly went to her closet, chose a pair of light blue linen pants and a short-waisted white cotton pullover. She pulled on a pair of ankle socks, shoved her feet into a pair of white sneakers and hurried out of the room. She was about to head down the stairs, when she heard Elvis' voice.

"Don't say I didn't warn you!"

"Pfft," she proclaimed and hurried down the stairs.

She found Evee in the kitchen, steeping a cup of tea.

"Where's Viv?" Gilly asked.

"She left," Evee said. "Said she had to discuss something with Nikoli before we all got together, so she headed for his hotel."

A prickle of worry stung the back of Gilly's neck. "She shouldn't be out alone. Maybe we should go and find her. Walk her over there."

Evee glanced at the clock on the wall. "Too much time has passed. She's surely already there, safe and in one piece. We still have an hour before we're supposed to meet up with the guys in front of the cathedral. Whatever Viv and Nikoli have to talk about, I think we should give them that privacy." She held up her cup. "Want some tea?"

"No, thanks," Gilly said and found herself starting to pace the kitchen. "It's still very dark outside. Suppose she gets jumped by some freakazoid."

Evee smiled. "She brought a flashlight with her and the bat we keep in the laundry room. If anyone tries to attack her, I pity them more than anything."

Evee's smile and words usually comforted Gilly, but right now, they did little more than piss her off. They made her feel like she was being treated like a child.

"Look," Gilly said. "I doubt if the Hyland cousins are going to give a rat's ass if we show up at their hotel early instead of meeting them at the cathedral at a precise time. I really think we need to go and check on Viv—make sure she got there okay."

"Okay, okay," Evee finally agreed. "But I'd like to finish up this chamomile tea first, if you don't mind."

Gilly wrinkled her nose. "Chamomile? That crap tastes awful. You just as soon be drinking horse vomit. Why chamomile?"

"It relaxes me. Gets rid of anxiety so I can focus."

"Peppermint tea does the same thing, but at least it tastes good. Besides, chamomile wires me up."

"Yes, but—"

Gilly waved a hand to cut off her words. "Drink whatever you like, but just drink it. I'd like to get going sooner than later."

"What're you so worried about? She'll be with the Benders."

"If she made it there."

Evee gulped down the rest of her tea, smacked her lips and then placed the cup and saucer into the kitchen sink. "Viv's a big girl. She can handle herself."

"You mean like she had to handle herself when a Cartesian attacked and Lucien had to perform a flying tackle to get her out of the way, and Ronan ended up dead?"

"Geez, you don't have to be so brash," Evee said. "I'm done with the tea, so let's go already. Anything to ease that wild-stallion brain of yours."

Satisfied that they were finally on their way, Gilly grabbed a flashlight from the utility room and hurried to the kitchen door to lead the way to the hotel.

"Shall I find another bat?" Evee asked with a grin.

"Don't be stupid," Gilly said. "We only had one. Maybe bring a butcher knife or something like that. Anything to protect us if we need it."

Evee let out a sigh of exasperation. "I will not run around the city with a butcher's knife. Should, and I do mean *should*, something come up, remember we are witches. We'll turn the attacker into a toad or a rabbit."

"I prefer a pile of dung, myself," Gilly said, walking out of the back door with Evee in tow.

"That's because you've got the class of a hyena, sister. You know, everyone claims we're triplets, but really, you could have been adopted."

"Oh, shu…hush up. You're just upset with me because I'm a little wired about Viv."

"A little wired? Abigail, darling, you could light up half the state with your worry wires. She's fine. I'm sure of it. I'll bet you ten to one she's with Nikoli at the hotel, sitting nice and cozy beside him."

It was earlier than they'd originally planned to meet at the cathedral; more than likely, Nikoli and Lucien were still talking to family members about Ronan's death. Gilly knew she should have given them the space they needed to make their family calls, but Viv's heading out there alone made decent protocol appear stupid. She had to make sure her sister was safe with her Bender.

With dawn breaking, and the trolleys still not up and running, Gilly and Evee had to foot it from the Garden District to Royal Street in the French Quarter, where the Hotel Monteleone was located.

Gilly speed-walked the entire way, with Evee occasionally stopping to work out a stitch in her side.

"Slow down, will you?" Evee said to Gilly. "At this pace, you're going to give me a heart attack."

"Witches don't have heart attacks."

"Okay, then my lungs are going to burst. You're faster than I am, so slow it down a notch. Why are you all but running there? We agreed to go to the hotel to make sure Viv was okay, and we're doing that, but you didn't mention speed-walking like a gazelle to do it."

Gilly slowed slightly, allowing her sister to catch up. "Something's wrong," she said suddenly. "I feel it in my gut. That's what's making me so anxious to get there as quickly as possible."

Evee came to an abrupt stop. "What's wrong? Cartesians? Are they around here? Did one of them get Viv?"

Taking her sister's hand, Gilly pulled her forward, not wanting to stop their progress to the hotel.

"I can't quite put my finger on it. It just feels like a fur ball growing in the pit of my stomach. I'm not sure who or what's causing it. The only thing I know is it isn't good."

Evee tugged on Gilly's hand, attempting to slow her down even more. "Is it a Bender? Did we lose another one like we lost Ronan?"

"I already told you, I'm not sure what or who is causing me to feel this way, but there's only one way to find out—get our asses to the hotel and find out."

That bit of information seemed to add new energy to Evee's step. Gilly pushed her speed up a notch. She really wasn't sure how many more catastrophes she'd be able to manage without losing her mind. She might be a witch, but she was still human, filled with emotions and yearnings. Being a witch didn't stop that from happening.

When they finally reached the Monteleone, Evee led Gilly to the elevator bank near the Carousel Bar. She remembered the room number from before and figured it best to go directly there instead of heading to the reception desk first.

Having reached the appropriate floor, Evee led Gilly to the suite shared by the three remaining Benders and then knocked on the door.

Within seconds, Nikoli opened the door and

seemed surprised to see them. His eyes were slightly red-rimmed, as if he'd been crying. Gilly couldn't blame him. Had he not shown some emotion over the loss of his cousin while telling his family, she'd have considered him an asshole of the highest order.

"Are we late?" Nikoli asked, glancing at his watch. Evidently seeing that they were in fact a half hour early, he asked, frowning, "Is there a problem?"

"Is Viv here?" Gilly asked.

Nikoli looked surprised. "No, she hasn't been here since we arrived at the hotel earlier. Why?"

"She was supposed to be on her way here to discuss something with you," Evee said. "At least, that's what she told me."

Nikoli invited them inside and motioned for them to have a seat on the couch in the living area. When they were seated, Nikoli stroked his beard, worry etching his face. "She said she was coming here?"

"Yes," Evee said.

"You mean to tell me she's not shown up here at all this morning?" Gilly asked, getting to her feet.

"I haven't seen her since the feedings," Nikoli said.

"I told you," Gilly said to Evee. "I told you something was wrong."

"What are you talking about?" Nikoli asked.

About that time, Gavril appeared, freshly showered, barefoot, dressed in jeans and a cobalt-blue button-down shirt.

His eyes went wide when he saw Gilly and Evee, and then narrowed. "Is there a problem?"

"I'd say so," Evee said.

"What is it?" Gavril asked.

"The girls are saying that Viv was on her way here to talk to me about something, but she never showed," Nikoli said, nearly shouting. Dressed in jeans and a forest-green pullover, he went over to the desk in the living area, grabbed his scabior and attached it to his belt. Gilly noticed his hands shaking slightly.

Gilly stared at Evee and said, "She's gone missing. Heaven and all the elementals, our sister has gone missing!"

Instead of answering, Evee suddenly burst into tears. "We have to find her! We have to!"

"She's got to be our first priority," Gilly said. "Screw the missing Originals and those damn Cartesians. We want our sister back—now!"

After Lucien belted his scabior to his jeans, they all but ran out of the hotel en masse.

To the patrons of the hotel, they must have looked like lunatics, running down hallways, across the foyer, and all but crashing through the front doors of the hotel.

Gilly had no idea where to start looking. She feared most of all that somehow the same thing that had happened to Ronan had happened to her sister. The only thing that abated her fear was an innate knowledge that all three sisters carried. One knew when the other was hurt. It only made sense that

Gilly would know in her heart of hearts if Viv was dead. And she didn't feel that was the case.

Not dead, but in grave danger.

Chapter 3

Seeing the worry and pain in Gilly's eyes over her missing sister felt like a dagger in Gavril's heart. He would have done anything to remove the pain from her and make her world normal again.

The problem was no matter how hard the Benders had tried to help the triplets, their situation seemed to be getting worse than better. Yes, they'd managed to get rid of more than their share of Cartesians since they'd arrived in New Orleans. But that hadn't stopped Ronan's death, or the death of some of Viv's Loup-Garous, Evee's Nosferatu and Gilly's Chenilles. It was as if all of the Cartesians ever created from centuries ago had zeroed in on this place and were bound and determined to take out every last Original, along with the Triad.

The Benders had traveled the world, fighting groups of Cartesians whenever they appeared to destroy a sect of the netherworld. From Africa to Alaska, England to New Zealand, they'd fought and won each battle they'd been confronted with. Never, however, had any of the Benders faced a situation like this. The more they battled, the worse things seemed to become, and for the life of him, Gavril couldn't figure out why. Certainly it had something to do with the Cartesians discovering the Originals here, but usually, after a battle or two or three, they'd move on to easier territory. This definitely wasn't the case here and now.

Now Gilly and Evee were standing in their hotel room, claiming Viv was missing. She'd told Evee she was coming to the hotel to talk to Nikoli, who knew nothing about the impromptu meeting, but regardless, Viv had never showed up.

Gavril saw the pain in Nikoli's eyes and how quickly his expression went haggard. Viv had been paired with him. His job was to protect her and her Originals, and for all intents and purposes, judging by what he'd seen when Viv and Nikoli were together, it had taken on a whole new course. His cousin was in love with the woman who was now missing, and nothing short of death would stop him from finding her.

So far, all that had happened was the disappearance of all of Viv's Loup-Garous, and now the woman he not only was supposed to protect, but cared for in a deeper way than they were allowed, was missing. Gavril could only imagine how deep the wounds were inside of him. Not only had Nikoli been the one to contact the family about Ronan's death, recounting the tragic tale again and again to various family members, but now he had to deal with Viv's disappearance. How much pain could a man bear without breaking? Gavril could only imagine, for if Gilly had been the one to go missing, he'd have already cracked wide open.

Everyone seemed frozen in place, unsure of what their next move should be. If by some horrid chance a Cartesian had gotten to Viv, they'd never find her. She'd be dead, hidden away in another dimension, just like Ronan. Only there'd be no family to contact, save for the Elders, as Viv's entire family members were her sisters, who were already here.

As if reading his mind, Gilly said, "She'd not dead. I'd know it if she was. But she's hurt."

"What do you feel, either of you?" Gavril asked.

"Danger," Evee said.

"Yes," Gilly confirmed. "It's all around her. I get the sense that she's trapped somewhere and has to stay hidden to stay alive. Wherever she is, she was chased there, coerced there, hurt there. The Cartesians are waiting for her to come out of hiding in order to pounce on her again. They're counting on her doing just that."

"Viv's too smart to let that happen," Gavril said. "If she knows they're waiting for her to come out of hiding, she'll nest herself right where she is until we can get to her."

"I know," Gilly said. "But how long will that be? How hurt is she? She's a prisoner for all intents and purposes. That's no way to live—or die."

"We'll find her," Gavril said. "It may be a good idea to start from the beginning. Nikoli, since feeding is over and all the Loups are missing, anyway, go to the north compound and see if Viv's there. Evee and Lucien, you take the Bon Appétit Café first, and then the two of you head back to your house in case Viv doubled back and wound up being there. I'll take Gilly and head for the St. Louis I Cemetery, just in case she decided to go there to help check on Gilly's Chenilles. After that, if we don't find her at the cemetery, then we'll head to the Elders in case she went there, looking for help."

"Not the Elders," Gilly said adamantly. "I'm certain she wouldn't be there, and telling them she's missing will only freak them out even more."

Gavril laid a hand on the small of Gilly's back. He wanted to wrap his arms around her and never let go. Take her away from this place, from its dangers and heartaches. "We can't leave any stone unturned. From what you've told me, news travels fast among the Circle of Sisters. With all of those witches in your group focused on this, I wouldn't be surprised if the Elders already know she's missing. They might even have a clue as to where she might be."

"You're giving them too much credit."

"They're Elders. We have to allow for all possibilities."

Reluctantly, Gilly gave him a half-hearted nod. "Yeah, no stone unturned."

With everyone assigned a location, they paired together, save for Nikoli, and parted ways, each seemingly carrying the weight of the world on his or her shoulders. They agreed to meet back at the hotel in an hour.

When Gavril and Gilly finally made it to the cemetery, Gavril stayed behind the locked gates, as instructed by Gilly, while she went inside. He hoped against hope she'd find some sign that Viv had been there. He'd never seen Gilly so distraught before, even after all they'd been through so far. He imagined, however, with the Triad being triplets, when one got lost and alone, all of them felt it. He'd heard twins and triplets often felt what their other siblings felt, and he assumed this was no different. Even during their occasional squabbles, it was easy to see how much the sisters adored one another.

By the time Gilly made it back to the cemetery gates, her cheeks were streaked with tears. As soon as she closed and locked the gates, she began to sob. "She's not there. Hasn't been anywhere near here, according to Patrick, her head Chenille. He came up to the gates to find out what I wanted. I hated to tell him because I didn't want him worrying, but I had no choice."

Then, out of nowhere, Gilly's sobs grew louder, and she suddenly pressed a hand to Gavril's chest. He stood fast, placing a hand over hers. Simply by touch he could feel the anger roiling through her.

Not anger toward him, but the situation, for the loss of her sister.

Gavril didn't budge when Gilly released her hand from his chest, turned and punched a light post. He knew all too well how she was feeling, since he'd just recently lost his Ronan, who'd been as close to him as a brother.

As Gilly sobbed, Gavril all but carried her to a side alley off Rampart Street so she could have the privacy he knew she needed to let go completely.

Once there, he pulled Gilly close, attempting to comfort her. She struggled against the gesture, evidently not wanting to give in to the over-the-top emotions she felt.

It didn't take long for her to lose that battle, however. Before Gavril knew it, Gilly finally pressed herself against him and laid her head on his chest. He gently rubbed her back with a hand, whispering comforting words in her ear. "We'll find her, I promise."

Gavril had no idea who moved first, but suddenly his lips were locked with Gilly's, and she was kissing him with the same fierceness she felt regarding Viv's disappearance.

Gavril struggled to maintain control over the kiss, not wanting their intimacy to go further than it already had. He didn't want her to hold regrets for something she did out of sheer emotional upheaval. But her kiss kept his head spinning, his body humming with a hunger he'd never felt before.

Obviously frustrated, and still in tears, Gilly took Gavril's hands and brought them to her breasts. In that moment, it seemed she could have cared less whether the alley was dark or brightly lit. He felt she needed the pain inside of her to go somewhere else, and without question, he knew that the somewhere else was having Gavril deep inside her. He carried the same need for her.

As Gavril tried to hold her back, soothe her with his words, Gilly all but threw him down on a grass mound in the alley. She ripped his shirt open, and then her own. She pressed her breasts against his chest and Gavril groaned, quickly losing resolve.

He felt himself hard against her. She'd obviously felt it, too, because it seemed to make something in her mind click into overdrive. Gilly pressed a hand to his chest, yanked open his belt and unzipped his pants. Gavril opened his mouth to protest, but his body defied all he meant to say. He needed her as desperately as she needed him.

Meanwhile, Gilly worked her slacks and panties off with one hand and, without preamble, settled her wet, swollen self over his hardness.

With a groan, Gavril pulled her toward him, yet Gilly kept her hand on his chest and rode him like her life depended on it.

Gavril felt pain in his groin as he fought to maintain control, but the second Gilly flooded him with her hot, soaking juices, he exploded inside of her like a non-stop geyser that dared defy the laws of physics.

With both of them satiated for now, Gilly lay her head on his chest, and he cupped her head and pressed her closer. The fact that they were out in a public place crept into the edges of his mind, but for now he shoved the thought back. He needed to feel her this way. Needing him, satiated.

Finally, Gilly lifted her head and whispered, "We have to find her, Gavril. She's part of me. If something happens to Viv, part of me will die, too. We have to find her."

Aside from an ultra-explosive orgasm, there was nothing that could make a man go as flaccid as the words she'd just spoken.

Gilly rolled off Gavril, her cheeks suddenly red with embarrassment. She quickly pulled her shirt over her breasts and scurried back into her pants. "I—I'm sorry."

"For what?" Gavril asked, although he suspected the reason.

"For…for acting like this. My sister's missing, we have dead Originals with two sectors completely missing, and all I can think about is having sex with you." She scrambled to her feet, her cheeks still bright pink.

Gavril zipped up his pants and closed his shirt over his chest. He couldn't button it because Gilly had ripped every button from its hole when she'd wanted to get to his bare chest. This brought a gentle smile to his face. He got to his feet and reached for her. She took a step back from him, and the movement pierced his heart.

"Listen to me," Gavril said. "You're a wounded woman who needed something real and alive to keep your world in balance. Sex does that and quite well.

Believe me, if I'd have thought there was any other intention, you wouldn't have reached first base. I may be a guy, but I do have control over my senses and anything below my belt."

"Oh, that you do," Gilly said shyly.

"I wanted you, Gilly, from the first moment I saw you. Not just to have sex with you, but the whole of you. Your spitfire attitude, your willingness to say what's on your mind, even if it involves an expletive or two. Your loyalty to your Originals and to your sisters. Even the way you carry yourself and the way you look. Your pixie cut, beautiful eyes, your tiny nose. It's all of you, Gilly. All of you."

Gilly stood staring at him silently, and for a moment, Gavril feared he had revealed too much too fast. There was no question in his mind that he'd fallen hard for this woman, but she'd yet to voice how she felt about him. Sex was one thing. Feeling another. Matters of the heart went much further, much deeper than sex. He resented the fact that the Elders had lit into the Triad about having relations with the Benders, but he understood. Every group had their rules. Even Benders. While on a mission they were to keep one head in their pants and the other on the task they'd been assigned. So far they'd blown that one out of the water big-time. The last thing he felt about that, however, was regret.

Letting out a deep breath, Gilly said, "We need to head out. It's a decent hike back to the Elders. We'll probably wind up back at the hotel a bit early, but if

Evee shows up first, I don't want her worrying about where I am, as well."

Feeling a stabbing pain in his heart that Gilly hadn't even acknowledged all he'd shared with her, Gavril simply nodded, and both of them headed back to the Monteleone.

By now the trolleys were running, and it would have been easier to hop one and take it down to Canal Street, which crossed Royal, where the hotel was located. But Gavril hoped the walk might give Gilly time to absorb all he'd said and respond in some way.

They'd just crossed Iberville and took a right on Royal, when out of the blue, Gilly reached for Gavril's hand and held it tightly. His heart soared. Her palms were sweaty, so he knew that she was nervous. She probably had no idea how to respond. Although she might not have had the words to respond to him, her taking his hand said more to Gavril than a thousand words would have. Even better, seconds after taking hold of his hand, Gilly moved closer to him. To anyone watching, the two of them must have looked like a couple in love, enjoying each other's company. But sometimes words weren't necessary. Actions spoke more openly and loudly than a thousand syllables strung together.

When they finally reached the hotel and entered, Gilly let go of Gavril's hand and headed to the bank of elevators.

Gavril silently followed, unable to take his eyes off her. He'd known many women in his life, but none so beautiful inside and out as Gilly François. He tried to harden his heart and mind to keep things in perspective, but neither would harden. If only she'd say something about how she felt, aside from holding his hand, he'd be more certain of the direction to head in with her.

Gavril knew of the Triad curse, which mandated that they not marry a human or live intimately with one. Like he needed something else to add to his ever-growing list of things to do—protect the safe zone of the Chenilles, find the missing ones before they attacked humans. And now, everything they'd been working so hard for came to a screeching halt because Viv was missing, and she was a priority. This was something Gavril completely understood.

But somewhere in the middle of fixing this, fighting that, he set it in his mind to find out a way to break the curse that bound the Triad, even if he had to visit their Elders himself. Surely there had to be a loophole; all laws had them. He assumed curses were the same. No one, not even a witch, could remember everything that might cover generations of Triads to follow. Not as far back as the 1500s.

Times and situations changed over the years. Unless the Elders who'd issued the curse were able to see far into the future, they had been only dealing with then, with the times, situations and customs that affected that time period. He seriously doubted they had seen so far into the future. Maybe they had only assumed that the curse they'd set upon the first Triad would hold forever. Or maybe not.

Gavril thought of the Elders who watched over

the Triad now. They were like mother hens to those three women. Even in anger, he couldn't see them implementing a curse that had no end, with no out clause. Anger was indeed anger, and punishment was punishment, but didn't love trump them all? Surely the original Elders had felt some sort of compassion for the first Triad and left a door open that no one had found yet.

Yet. That was the key word.

Once that curse was broken, and if he ever got Gilly to speak her mind as far as he was concerned, his intent was to have her for the rest of her life. Having traveled the world many times over, Gavril had yet to meet anyone as unique, smart, caring and beautiful as Gilly. A man didn't place the largest diamond found in any mine on a shelf, and then leave, hoping it might still be there once he returned. Gilly was his rough-cut diamond, and if it took his entire lifetime, he'd look for a loophole in the curse for the simple purpose of making her his own.

These were words Gavril kept to himself; if Gilly heard them, she'd take off running like a wild rabbit, thinking him mad. What business did a human, who had no concept of the magic they generated, have in messing in witches' business?

And she'd have been right.

But the one thing he did do well was investigate. He'd developed his investigation skills over the years while hunting Cartesians. If somehow he had the chance to read the document that sealed the Triad curse, he'd pick it apart until he found a loophole that worked for them. They'd be free at last, something he knew the Triad had never experienced before.

He wanted, more than anything, to be Gilly's hero.

Chapter 4

"I knew something like this was going to happen," Arabella, the head of the Elders, said when Gilly told them about Viv going missing.

"Well, if you knew, why didn't you warn us about it?" Gilly asked. The last thing she'd wanted to do was come back to the Elders, especially after they'd been royally reamed out during their last visit. The Elders lived only a couple of blocks from the Triad in the Garden District, but coming here again felt like they'd walked the green mile. They'd had no choice. Not with Viv missing. No matter what the consequences might be, they had to let the Elders know.

"Oh, she did," Vanessa said.

"She did not," Gilly insisted.

"Uh-huh," Taka, the third, said. "Remember the

whole thing about Viv and Evee being intimate with their Benders, how it needed to stop. Well, it obviously didn't stop, because now we've got another catastrophe on our hands. They should have listened—that's all I've got to say."

"I wish," Vanessa said.

"Wish what?" Taka asked, frowning.

"That that was all you had to say."

Taka tsked loudly, and then looked at Gavril and said, "No offense meant, Mr. Bender, but witches have rules to live by. If we don't live by them, then all kinds of havoc occur, like now. There are reasons we have leaders, Elders. It's not like the Triad is out there on their own. They have us to bounce things off of."

"So, you're saying that you're blaming Evee and Viv's intimacy with Nikoli and Lucien for all this chaos?" Gavril said.

"I am," Taka said.

"This isn't the time to go into your rant about the Triad members having relations with the Benders," Gilly said. "Viv is missing and that's what matters most. Besides, I think all three of you have this relationship thing wrong or twisted sideways somehow. It doesn't connect or make sense."

"It makes complete sense," Arabella said. "As it was part of the curse set on the Triads since the 1500s. Nothing has changed to refute it. The intimacy you've obviously taken course with regarding these young men has caused nothing but disaster."

"No disrespect meant, ma'am," Gavril said, "but

that's baloney. My cousins and I have tracked these Cartesians around the world. Have been to places where they've taken out an entire species from the netherworld in a city. Humans died, more Cartesians showed themselves. But not once did it have anything to do with me or my cousins being intimate with any female. Witch or no witch."

"But if the Triad doesn't listen, there isn't much we can do about controlling what happens," Taka said.

"Oh, there's plenty we can do about it," Arabella said.

"Like what?" Vanessa said.

"Leave them to their chaos. They asked for advice, we gave it, they ignored it, and now they have to live with it."

"I'd appreciate it if you'd stop speaking about us as though we weren't in the room," Gilly said angrily.

"Hello?" Gavril said. "Did any of you hear what I said earlier?"

"Yes, of course," Arabella said.

"How can you say that when Viv's gone?" Taka said to Arabella. "Mr. Bender said they've been trying to help. Surely you won't attempt to stop them from doing that."

"Please call me Gavril," Gavril said. And Taka gave him a shy smile. "And please give my words some consideration. None of what's been happening was caused by the Triad. The blame goes to the Cartesians."

"Where was the last place you saw her?" Arabella asked Gilly, ignoring Gavril.

"At home. Evee told me she was headed to the hotel to talk over something with Nikoli, her Bender. The problem was that she never showed up at the hotel."

"For the love of stupidity," Vanessa said. "Ever since you three were little girls, your heads were harder than brick and mortar. Now that you're thirty, that doesn't seem to have changed one bit. Arabella told you to stay away from the Benders, and what do you do? Show up at their hotel."

"Talking to someone is no crime," Gilly said. "Especially when we're trying to find Viv. Going to somebody's hotel room doesn't mean sex is involved, Vanessa. People do meet up and talk in those rooms."

"I disagree," Taka said with a smirk. "There are beds in hotel rooms, and where there are beds, there's sex."

"Oh, get a grip," Vanessa snapped at Taka.

Arabella gave Gilly a slow nod. She eyed Gavril, and then looked back at Gilly. "You're right. There's no crime in talking, that's for sure, but let me ask you something." This time she looked Gavril right in the eye before asking Gilly. "Have the two of you been intimate? After I warned you to stay away, did you disobey? Have you been intimate with this man despite our warning?"

"Nothing was her fault," Gavril said. "When she heard about Viv—"

"My question wasn't directed at you, young man," Arabella said. "It was meant for Gilly."

Taka huffed. "You did it, didn't you, Gilly? Was it at the hotel?"

Vanessa shook her head. "A Triad slut brigade, that's what we have on our hands, sisters. They're going to do what they want to regardless of our warnings. How does an Elder combat that? We try and we try to lead them down the straight and narrow, and look, they take the first fork in the road they come to."

"We'll deal with it by allowing the Triad to handle the consequences of their actions," Arabella said.

"Wait a minute," Gilly said angrily. "You're speculating that I've been intimate with Gavril, and because of that, you won't give me any help in finding Viv? What kind of Elders are you? Ever since the beginning, every Triad had Elders who helped them with problems."

"Not all of them," Arabella said. "Or have you forgotten the first Triad? Their Elders didn't change the monstrosities they'd created back to humans. Instead, they punished the Triad."

"So is this what this is?" Gilly asked. "Punishment? You won't help us because of some warped assumption you're making? It begs the same question—what kind of Elders are you?"

"We have tried to help," Arabella said. "Repeatedly. We've even contact the rest of our sisters and asked for help. Something or someone seems to be blocking all of our spells. My only assumption as

to why that might be is, once again, your intimacy
with the Benders. Part of the Triad curse in action."

"And we're smart Elders," Taka said. "I think."
They'd been sitting around the kitchen table, and
Taka suddenly got to her feet, seemingly flustered.
"Anybody want crumpets and tea?"

"Sit down, Taka," Vanessa said. "Now isn't the
time to extend hospitality. We've got to get to the
bottom of this."

"But I'm hungry," Taka whined.

Arabella gave Taka a stern look, which sent her
back into her seat with a pout. "It was just tea and
crumpets."

"You claim your intimacy with your Bender is
our speculation, an assumption," Arabella said to
Gilly. "Is it an assumption? Or did it happen?" She
looked first at Gavril, and then she allowed her eyes
to settle on Gilly. "I want the truth."

Gilly sighed heavily. "Yeah, we were intimate,"
she finally said, and saw Gavril shift uncomfortably
in his seat. She didn't blame him. He was sitting at
a table of witches, any of whom could have turned
him into a frog or turtle with a kindergartner's spell.

"Mr. Bender," Vanessa said, "as you can see, this
conversation is getting quite personal. I think it best
if you leave us to deal with Abigail, who obviously
decided to not heed our advice."

"He doesn't have to go," Taka said.

"It's best he does," Arabella said.

"But he's cute," Taka said. "Easy on the eyes.
And besides, we're not going to be saying anything

he hasn't already heard or known about. If they were intimate, they were intimate. He already knows that. You think we're revealing a secret?"

"I'd prefer to stay if it's all the same to you," Gavril said. "Gilly is not alone in this. And if I may respectfully add, we came here of our own volition. Vivienne has gone missing, and we wanted to see if you'd seen her or possibly know where she might have gone."

"I haven't seen her," Taka said.

"Me either," Vanessa said.

"Nor have I," Arabella added. "Have you tried the compound where Viv kept her Loup-Garous?"

"Yes," Gilly said. "Her Bender is there looking for her now."

"You sent a human Bender into the compound?" Arabella said with shock. "Did you purposely want this man dead?"

"He'll be mauled like ground beef," Taka said, her brows knitting together. "Surely he's not alone there, right?"

"Haven't you heard?" Gilly said. "All of the Loup-Garous are missing."

"What?" Arabella, Vanessa and Taka said in unison.

Gilly nodded. "They were there one morning, and by the afternoon, not one of them remained on the compound."

"Oh, Mother Earth and every worm beneath her," Taka said. "Does that mean they're all loose in the city?"

"I have no idea," Gilly said. "We've each been taking care of our own. I still have Chenilles in their safe zone, but have about fifteen missing. Evee lost all of her Nosferatu. Same thing with Viv's. One minute they're where they're supposed to be, the next, they've vanished."

Arabella got up from the table and began to pace. "You know what this means, don't you?"

"That we're in deep doodoo," Taka said.

"You're not kidding," Gilly said. "With them missing, it means more humans are in danger."

"If more humans start dying at the hands of the Originals, you know what that means, right?" Vanessa said.

"Well, duh," Taka said. "It means those humans will be dead."

"Stop being an idiot," Vanessa told her. She looked over at Arabella. "It means more cops at our door."

"Why are police coming here?" Gavril asked. "How do they know about you and the Originals?"

"I suspect a leak," Arabella said. "And I'm almost certain it's one of the sorcerers."

"I don't understand," Gavril said.

"I'll explain later," Gilly said. "We've got to stay on task with Viv. She's got to be our main focus right now."

"Oh, heck, that's right about the cops," Taka said suddenly. "What do we tell the cops when they come back here to talk to us? Do we not answer the door like before? Ignore them?"

Arabella shook her head. "Not this time. Too

much has gotten out of hand. We've got to let the police know about the Loup-Garous and the Nosferatu. If we don't, the entire city will soon be overrun with dead bodies when those Originals get hungry and need to feed."

"What good will the cops be if they know?" Vanessa asked.

"We'll have to give them information—information we've never given any other human," Arabella said solemnly. "We'll have to tell them how to kill them."

"Have you lost your marbles?" Taka asked. "That means, if they see any Original, attacking a human or not, they'll kill it."

"I know what it means," Arabella said. "But with so many Originals loose, it's come down to a choice. Their lives or the lives of humans."

"We can't let them all be killed," Vanessa cried. "The Triad needs to find them and regain control."

"I wish it was that easy," Gavril said. "But you have no idea what trauma and drama we've gone through with the Cartesians over the last week just trying to find the Originals."

"To hell with the Originals," Gilly said. "What about Viv? We've got to find her. Do you have any idea where she might be? Do you have any spells that might give us some direction as to where she might be hiding?"

"You know we don't use crystal balls," Arabella said with a huff as if Gilly had used a foul expletive. "Our spells are innate, herbs and elemental. But you already know that. What I don't understand is why you've come here to ask us about finding Viv when you and Evee both have natural talents that can help find her. Haven't you thought of doing something with them?"

Gilly looked at her quizzically. "I don't understand."

Taka rested her elbows on the table. "Sure you do. You know how Evee can talk to the dead? Channel them? If she can contact one of the Loup-Garous, Chenilles or Nosferatu, like Pierre, one of them who's already died, they might be able to give her some valuable information. Once she gets that information, you can use your astral projection thing that you do and bring your energy to whatever place the dead might see Viv. Then you'll know if she's there. The dead see more than we do, you know. They're not stuck with two feet on the ground like we are."

"For once, I think Airhead over here is right," Vanessa said, referring to Taka.

"Who you calling an airhead?" Taka asked. "I'm the one who came up with the idea, while you were over there checking for chips in your fingernail polish."

"I was not," Vanessa claimed. "I was listening closely. Just because I'm not looking at your mug doesn't mean I wasn't paying attention."

"Both of you stop bickering," Arabella said. She looked over at Gilly. "Taka speaks the truth. You and Evee have natural talents that don't involve spells that may or may not work. Has Evee tried to communicate with the dead? Have you tried astral projection, since that's your specialty?"

"No, neither," Gilly said. "But…the idea has some promise to it."

"It certainly does," Gavril said. "Not only in finding Viv but locating the missing Originals, as well. I say we give it a shot."

Arabella scowled at him. "It's not your business to say whether or not they attempt to use their powers this way."

Gavril cocked his head to one side and eyed Arabella. "Ever since I walked through that door, you've treated me like I have lice. All I've done since coming here is try to protect the Originals and the Triad. We've managed to destroy many Cartesians while here. What problem do you have with me?"

Arabella held up a defiant chin. "Although we do appreciate what you have done to help the Originals and the Triad, I'm afraid that the attraction you Benders have for the Triad has caused more problems than anything. This entire situation might be solved right now if you would have kept certain parts of your body in check."

"Arabella!" Gilly said, appalled that her Elder had confronted Gavril that way. She got up from the table and signaled Gavril to follow her.

"Taka, thank you for your advice," Gilly said. "We'll certainly give it a try. Arabella, if I were you, I'd do a conscience check. You might be my Elder, but when I see you headed in the wrong direction, as a witch, I have an obligation to let you know. You're way off here. Gavril and the other Benders have been nothing but gentlemen. And, if you remember, you're the one who wanted to get the sorcerers involved, which would have been a far bigger disaster than what we're dealing with now."

"I didn't say the sorcerers weren't getting involved," Arabella confessed.

"You...you didn't go to Cottle with any of this," Gilly said. "Tell me you didn't."

"Cottle? No. But I have spoken to Gunner Stern about it. If you remember, Taka was the one who got him involved in the first place. I simply followed through."

Gilly glared at her. "And?"

"There is no 'and.' He's doing some snooping around. Seeing if there's anything he can do to help."

Gilly shook her head. "Look, as much as we warned you about getting the sorcerers involved, you did as you pleased anyway. You know the sorcerers have always thought us to be an inferior, bothersome species. I'd call that even when it comes to your accusations regarding the Benders. If anything, we owe them our gratitude. You have no idea how hard they've been fighting for us."

With that, Gilly walked out of the kitchen and headed for the front door, Gavril by her side. When they'd made it outside, Gavril grinned. "Really. Do you always talk to your Elders that way?" he asked.

"Only when they're going way off track."

They walked a ways, heading down to the French Quarter to meet up with the others as promised.

Luckily a trolley came to a stop fifty feet away, and they were able to hop a ride on it all the way down Canal. They then got off where it intersected with Royal.

Gavril got off the trolley and held out a hand to help Gilly down the metal steps. She took his hand and made her way to ground level.

As they walked to the hotel, Gavril kept turning to look at her.

"What?" Gilly finally asked. "Why are you looking at me that way?"

"Just think it's cute."

"What is?"

"The set of balls you have is undeniable. You say what you mean and mean what you say. Elder or no Elder. Hell, it could have been the President of the US, and I think you'd have shot him down the same way."

Gilly shrugged. "I get a bit carried away sometimes."

"I'd say," Gavril said. "But I love it. Wouldn't want it any other way."

Gilly gave him a strange, shy look, and it was then that Gavril realized he'd used the *L* word. Although he hadn't actually said the words *I love you*, it had been close enough to give her pause.

"Good," Gilly finally said. "I'm glad you like it. 'Cause I only come in one color."

"What's that mean?"

She stopped and gave him a long, soulful look.

"It means, Mr. Gavril Hyland, that when it comes to me, what you see is what you get."

"And that's supposed to be a bad thing?"

"It's been known to get me into trouble from time to time."

"Good," Gavril said with a chuckle. "A woman after my own heart."

Chapter 5

When they reached the Benders' suite at the Monteleone, everyone was waiting for them as expected.

"You're late," Evee said.

Gavril glanced at his watch. "Only by five minutes."

"Still, it had me worried sick," Evee said. "I feared something had happened to the two of you."

"Well, worries over. I'm here," Gilly said. "I take it, since all of you are here, except for Viv, that none of you had any luck locating her."

"Nothing," Lucien said. "Evee and I searched our assigned territory and more. Not even a sign that she'd been around."

Gilly turned to Nikoli, who sat on the edge of the bed, just outside of the living room area of the suite.

It looked as if he'd purposely distanced himself from everyone in the room. His face looked haggard, his eyes dull.

By the look on his face, Gilly felt stupid for asking, but she had to know. "Nikoli?"

He looked over at her.

"Anything?"

"No," he said, his voice hoarse. "Not even a clue. What about you and Gavril?"

Gavril went over to Nikoli, sat on the edge of the bed beside him and put an arm around his shoulder. "We'll find her, cuz. Somehow, someway, we'll find her."

Nikoli turned to him, a faraway look in his eyes that could be seen by everyone in the room. "She was under my watch," he said. "I screwed up, Nik. She was under my watch."

Gilly went over to Nikoli and placed a hand on his shoulder. "She might have been under your watch, but the bottom line is, stuff happens. I pray to the universe that we find her. I know she's still alive. I can feel her. I just can't feel where she is. If she were dead, there'd be a hole in my heart the size of this planet, and thankfully I don't feel that."

Nikoli looked up at Gilly hopefully. "Did either of you have luck with the Eiders?"

"Well, yes and no," Gavril said.

"What's that mean?" Lucien asked, joining them in the bedroom.

"It's either yes or no, right?" Evee asked, joining

them. "How can it be both? You either got some info or you didn't." She looked at Gilly. "Well?"

"No, we didn't find her," Gilly said, "but the Elders came up with an idea that might be useful."

"The Elders?" Evee said. "All they've done since this started is perform spells that don't work and contact the entire clan of Circle of Sisters for intercession spells, which didn't work either."

"Yeah, I know, I know," Gilly said.

"What possible idea could they have come up with that made you pay attention?" Evee asked.

Gilly looked at Gavril and he gave her the slightest nod of encouragement.

After clearing her throat, Gilly said, "They brought up the fact that you and I have innate talents that don't involve spells that could be used to locate Viv."

Evee looked at her questioningly. "Huh?"

"You have the ability to contact and hear from the dead. I can astral project. The Elders suggested that you focus on one of the Originals that's already dead and see if he has a better view behind the death veil than we do here, stuck as humans. Witches but humans. Once you lock onto one of the Originals, I can attempt to follow its voice and your trance, and astral project to the location it's seeing and attempting to describe."

"Hmm," Lucien said. "Can the two of you do what the Elders claim?"

"Duh," Gilly said.

"Sorry, I didn't mean to question you or them.

Habit to confirm, is all," Lucien said, looking Gilly in the eye.

For a moment, Gilly felt like a stupid schoolgirl. *Duh? Where in the hell had that come from?*

"No need to apologize," Gilly said. "Yes, Evee can contact and speak to people and the Originals that have passed on."

"*If* they're willing to talk," Evee said. "The way it seems to work is, if they crossed over to wherever we cross over to after death, it's less likely they'll communicate. If their spirits are still hanging around on earth, for whatever reason, they're much easier to contact."

"And what's with the astral projection?" Gavril asked Gilly. "Do you just zap yourself to some other location?"

"Not physically," Gilly explained. "My mind goes there, and although my physical body is still in the place where I began, I see myself in my mind's eye when I'm in the place I'm tracking."

Gavril, Nikoli and Lucien frowned simultaneously.

"Think of it like daydreaming," Gilly said, trying to give them a clearer explanation. "In your mind's eye you see whatever it is you're daydreaming about. With astral projection, it's more specific. I can focus that so-called daydream to wherever I want. Only in that situation, I have a *dream* body that goes along with it. I may still be here, but I can see, hear, react, feel in that astral projection state. The only thing I can't do is alter what I see. The best shot we have is if I pick something up while Evee talks to whatever or whomever she connects with. Astral projection will give us more details, so we'll at least know what direction to head in. Make sense?"

"Got it," Gavril said.

"I'm up for it if you are," Evee said to Gilly. "Anything to find Viv."

Gilly nodded and asked Nikoli, Lucien and Gavril to step away so she and Evee had room to concentrate. Too much energy from too many people in one area would tone down what Evee needed to hear.

The men did as they were told, moving to the doorway that separated the bedroom from the living room suite.

Gilly sat close beside Evee and took both her hands into her own. "Ready?"

"As I'll ever be. I'm just not sure who to try and contact."

"Try Chank, since he was a Nosferatu and one of your own. Even in death, given that he hasn't crossed over somewhere unreachable, he should still recognize and respond to his mistress' voice."

Evee nodded and closed her eyes. Gilly concentrated on her sister's face and watched her lips move silently, until she felt she was inside Evee.

After about a half hour, Evee opened her eyes and looked at Gilly woefully. "I'm not picking up anything from Chank. Not one word. I can't even feel him around me."

Giving her head a slight shake to disconnect from Evee's mind, Gilly said, "I didn't pick up anything either. It was like your mind was nothing but a black hole."

"That scares me," Evee said. "Not knowing where he is, I mean."

"I know, honey, but we've got to keep trying, for Viv's sake. What about any of her Loup-Garous, the ones who died in the first massacre? Were you familiar with any of them? Can you bring any one of them to mind?"

Evee stared at her sister, but Gilly knew she wasn't seeing her. She was concentrating on the Loup-Garous that had belonged to Viv.

"I remember Moose," Evee finally said. "A big Loup. Kind of slow, though. You know, in the head. He wasn't at all aggressive like the rest of the pack. He had a gentle spirit about him."

"Okay, then try Moose," Gilly said. "Focus on what he looked like. See if he comes to you."

Still holding on to Gilly's hands, Evee closed her eyes once more. Her lips began to move just as they had before. Only this time, Gilly noticed her eyes moving behind her lids, like she'd entered into some sort of REM sleep.

Gilly concentrated on her sister's face, felt something move in the pit of her stomach. Evee had evidently connected with Moose; only, for some reason, when Gilly tried to connect to their conversation, all she saw was the Mississippi River, wide and winding near the city. She couldn't make sense of it.

With her eyes still closed, Evee said, "Big heads. Lots of big heads. Color, too. Fun colors."

Gilly felt herself frown. What she saw when trying to connect with Evee and Moose didn't make
sense. It was like she'd entered a carnival, and they
were standing, talking in the middle of a midway.
She heard warped music, saw clowns with big heads,
and, of course, every color of the rainbow decorated
the rides that made up the carnival.

"People walking, talking," Evee continued, eyes
still closed and moving beneath her lids. "Surprised
voices. Excited voices. Wheels. Lotsa wheels and
big heads."

Still seeing the same setting, Gilly opened her
eyes, frustrated. She let go of Evee's hands, which
immediately broke the trance her sister had been in.

"Anything?" Evee asked hopefully.

"Nothing that made a damn lick of sense," Gilly
said. "Moose kept saying big heads, colors, surprised
voices and something about wheels. The only thing I
saw when attempting to connect to you and his voice
was a carnival. You know, midway, rides, clowns,
the whole bit."

From the doorway, Nikoli asked, "Are there any
carnivals in town right now?"

"Not that I know of," Gilly said. "But that's not
something I'd usually track. If anyone would know
about a carnival being in or around town, it would
be Taka. She goes to all of them. Sort of like a big
kid. Rides all the rides, eats cotton candy until she
pukes. The whole ball of wax."

"Then we should ask her if she knows of any,"
Evee said.

Gilly groaned. "I've had my row with the Elders already today."

"What?" Evee asked. "Did you get into an argument with them?"

"Kinda," Gilly said. "I told Arabella off."

"Gilly!"

"Well, she'd asked for it. They all did, except for Taka, I guess. She was on the fence during the argument, like always."

"What was the argument about?" Lucien asked from the doorway.

"Nothing that means anything right now," Gilly said and shot a quick look at Gavril, who lifted a brow.

"Abigail François," Evee said with a look of incredulity. "You didn't."

Gilly gave her an innocent look. "Didn't what?"

"You know what. The last time we were all together with the Elders, they reamed Viv and me for being intimate, sexually or otherwise, with our Benders. They warned us that the intimacy might very well be the cause of all the catastrophes we've been experiencing."

"Yeah, and?"

"Don't *and* me," Evee said. She looked from Gavril to Gilly. "The two of you had sex, didn't you?"

Gilly turned away from her sister and threw Gavril a look that said, *No confession necessary.*

"Gilly?" Evee said. "I need to know the truth. It might have something to do with Viv going missing.

The Elders warned us that if we didn't back away from having sex or deep relationships with our Benders that things might get worse. Having one of our sisters go missing is about the second worst thing that could happen."

"What's the first?" Nikoli asked from the doorway.

"Viv's death."

Nikoli took a step away from the doorway and ran his hands through his hair. "I should have kept her in my sights. It's my fault. She'd asked me to wait near the feeding shoot, just in case any of her Loups showed up while she went inside the compound."

"And you let her in there, knowing the scabior canopy was no longer operational?" Gavril asked.

"Yeah," Nikoli said. "Dumb-ass move, I know, but Viv can be strong headed when she sets her mind to something. And I really don't need you kicking my ass about it. Believe me, I'm doing enough kicking on my own. But it turned out okay—she came out. Then we parted ways. I walked her home, then came to the hotel. I shouldn't have let her out of my sight. Ever."

"Is there anyone else you can try to connect with besides Moose?" Gilly asked Evee. "What about the female Viv told us about who was in heat and causing all the ruckus in the compound?"

Evee shook her head. "I don't have a visual to work with. Aside from Moose, most of the Loups looked the same to me."

"Damn," Gilly said. "I refuse to hit a brick wall.

Let's try Moose again, ask him questions. Maybe we can get clearer answers that way."

Evee shrugged. "It's worth a try."

Gilly took Evee's hands back into her own and held tight. When she saw Evee's lips start moving silently, Gilly closed her own eyes and focused on the energy coming from her sister. She felt Evee's hands grow hot and begin to tremble.

"Big heads," Evee said, her voice low as if it had become male. "Lots of color. Laughing. So much laughing. Some scary, too. Clowns. Clowns are scary. Dragons, too."

"Where are the big heads?" Evee asked in her own voice. "Moose, can you see where the big heads and colors are? The clowns and the dragons?"

Still unable to pick up anything but a carnival setting, Gilly opened her eyes, but kept her hands locked onto Evee's.

"The colors are safe." Moose's voice carried through Evee. "The scary clowns are, too. The wheels don't move, though. Not now—it's not time."

"When is the time?" Evee asked, her voice back to its own timbre. "Do you know?" Evee's voice grew deeper. "When it gets noisy. Lots of people. Big heads, lotsa color. Scary faces. Happy faces. Sick people."

Evee opened her eyes and released her hands from Gilly's. "The only thing that comes to mind with his gibberish is some kind of carnival."

"There's only one way to find out," Gavril said

from the doorway. "We'll pile up in our rental car and head out to check it out."

"There's got to be an easier way," Lucien said, standing beside Gavril. "If Taka's a carnival fanatic like you say she is, she'd know about all the ones in town, and probably knows about any outside of the city."

"I've already told you," Gilly said. "We had a bit of a tiff. I'm not comfortable going back there right now."

"So we'll go," Gavril said.

"And get your head chopped off!" Gilly proclaimed. "You guys are the reason they believe we're in so much crap."

"Talking about crap," Evee sad to Gilly. "You never answered my question."

Gilly frowned. "What question?"

"You said we're the reason the Elders believe we're in so much crap. Well, were you intimate with Gavril?" Evee looked over at Gavril, who was looking down at his boots.

"None of your business," Gilly said.

"It sure as hell is my business," Evee said. "If you were, it could be the reason Viv's gone missing. So give it up. Were you intimate with your Bender?"

Gilly looked over at Gavril and rolled her eyes. When she turned back to Evee, she felt sparks of anger flying toward her sister. "Yeah, we were intimate. Satisfied? It's not like you've been Mother Teresa, you know. You can't blame Viv's disappearance on me. You and Viv gave it up to your Benders as well as I did. For all we know, it could be a collective thing, not just something I did. Besides, my escapade with Gavril happened after the fact. Viv was already missing. I didn't cause it."

"The Elders warned us, yet you went ahead and did what they strictly prohibited us from doing. Is it any wonder Viv's missing? You were the last of the three of us to push the lever over too far. You purposely disobeyed the Elders."

"Oh, get a grip," Gilly said, growing angrier by the moment. "Instead of pointing fingers and placing blame, we need to find Viv and fast. Remember the Cartesians? If she's out there alone, she's a moving target for those bastards."

"Viv's not stupid," Nikoli chimed in. "I don't think she's lost. I think she's hiding out somewhere so she doesn't get captured by the Cartesians."

"So how do we find her to help?" Lucien asked. He pointed his chin at Gilly, and then at Evee. "The two of you didn't seem to get very far with Moose. All we have is what he said. We'll have to try and decipher it."

"We've got to find a carnival," Gilly said. "That's what I saw when Evee was communicating with him."

"Fine," Gavril said. "Instead of beating this up to death, let's set up a plan and make it happen. Gilly, since I was with you at the Elders' earlier and didn't exactly earn any brownie points with them, you and I will take the rental car and head to Chalmette. See if any carnivals are up and running in or around the

town. Evee, you, Nikoli and Lucien go and talk to
Taka. Find out all she knows about any carnival in
a hundred-mile radius."

"A hundred miles?" Lucien asked. "Isn't that a
bit far?"

"Not if some of the Originals already infiltrated
Chalmette. They could be anywhere. And wherever
they are, you can bet the Cartesians are on the prowl.
No telling how many Originals we've lost since they
went missing."

"I don't know about this talking to Taka thing,"
Lucien said. "The other two Elders sound like quite a
piece of work. For all we know, they might get mega
pissed because we're there and turn us into turtles
or ants or something."

Evee grinned. "They're tough at times, but not
stupid. Nobody's going to turn you into anything.
Especially when they know you're only trying to
help and find Viv. It'll be a good thing that Gavril
and Gilly won't be around. They were their last two
targets, so at least you'll have a fairly decent shot
at getting their attention, instead of making their
anger flare up."

With that plan agreed upon, the troupe left the
hotel room. Gavril and Gilly jumped into the rental
car, and Lucien, Evee and Nikoli headed for the trolley. It was the fastest way for them to get to the Garden District, where the Elders lived.

As soon as Gavril took off in the rental, Gilly gave
him directions to Chalmette.

"What do you think our chances are there?" Gavril asked.

"Finding Viv, you mean?"

"Yeah."

"Slim to none. Just a gut feeling I have. Not that I haven't been wrong before, but I just don't *feel* her there."

"Maybe it's not about feeling her so much as it is getting information that'll lead us to her," Gavril offered.

Gilly stared through the windshield. "I hope that's the case."

She turned to face Gavril. "I didn't want to say anything in front of Evee and Nikoli because I didn't want to freak them out. But from somewhere deep in my gut, I feel Viv's life force draining."

Gavril shot her a quick look before bringing his attention back to the windshield and his driving. "You mean like you feel her dying?"

Gilly took in a deep breath. "That or something like it. All I know is we have to find her and find her fast. Otherwise, we'll be dealing with another funeral."

Chapter 6

Frustrated with the bumper-to-bumper traffic leading out of New Orleans, Gavril did his best to swerve from lane to lane, but most of the time, he was barely able to push ten miles an hour. Drivers had little mercy. Nobody wanted to wait a moment longer than they had to.

"This is stupid," Gilly said. "At this rate, it'll take hours to get there. Maybe we should have taken a different route."

"We'll make it just fine," Gavril assured her. "This is the fastest. Must be construction holding things up. Once we get past it, I'll push some juice, and we'll be there in no time. We're almost in Arabi, anyway. Chalmette's only ten minutes or so from there."

"Feels like we've been on the road for hours," Gilly said, gazing out of the passenger window. She turned to Gavril. "Do you think we'll find her? Any gut feelings?"

Holding the steering wheel with his left hand, Gavril laid his right hand on Gilly's cheek. "I'm not like you and Evee. I can't pick up signals from the dead or transport myself metaphysically to other places. But I can tell you, I have hope. If you say you still feel her alive, I trust in that. She's still alive." He hoped his words brought her some peace. He'd do anything to take the worry from her eyes, the pain from her heart.

Gilly pressed her hand against Gavril's. "Thanks for the encouragement. Sadly though, like I said earlier, I feel her energy waning."

"Does that mean you think she's been hurt?"

Gilly nodded. "Hurt enough to possibly kill her if we don't find her fast enough."

Gavril grit his teeth, angry that anyone, especially the Cartesians, would hurt someone so innocent. As long as he'd known the Triad, which was but a couple of weeks, all he'd seen was them trying to help, either each other or their Originals.

Anger rushed through Gavril like someone had turned a gas burner up to high heat. To make all of this go away, to protect the Triad, the rest of the Originals, those who made up the rest of the netherworld, he had to find out who the Cartesians' leader was and locate him or it. Cut off the head of the dog, and the rest of the body dies.

The problem was, he didn't have the slightest idea as to where to locate him. In fact, he had no idea what he even looked like. Did he have the same huge body, talons and razor-sharp incisors that his band of Cartesians had? Or did he...or she—he couldn't leave anything on the table by assuming the leader was male—look like a human, hiding among the rest without a care in the world except to accomplish this mission?

Knowing the Benders had to get to the leader to stop the massacres gave him nightmares. It was all he thought about. In his dreams, he'd see an elusive shadow darting in and around corners of buildings, inside houses, and the harder Gavril tried to chase him down, the more elusive the creature became. The dreams were always worse when he felt himself only inches away from seeing the face of the creature, even in shadow. Then it would turn into a huge puff of smoke and disappear right before Gavril had a chance to lock in on him.

With both hands on the steering wheel now, Gavril gripped it so tightly, his knuckles turned white. The traffic had come to a complete stop, all three lanes locked up bumper to bumper.

Gilly laid a hand on his right thigh. "I can feel you deep in thought. Aside from how frustrating this traffic is, care to share what you're thinking? Anything's better than this absolute silence. I'm jittery enough that it's taking us so long to get to Chalmette. Talking might help."

Gavril laid a hand over Gilly's. "Just thinking

about the leader of the Cartesians. I've got to find the bastard. Was thinking that you chop off the head of the dog, the rest of it dies. The problem is I have no idea if he looks like a Cartesian or disguises himself as a human. For all we know, he could be walking around New Orleans like any Tom, Dick or Harry, and we'd never know. He could own a tobacco shop on Canal, disguise himself as any nationality, and we'd never get a bead on him. The only way we have to track him is by going through one Cartesian at a time, and hope that one is him." Gavril squeezed Gilly's hand, and then moved her hand back to her own lap.

Gilly looked at him quizzically.

"Even with all we're facing right now, so much seemingly impossible, your hand on my thigh creates a huge distraction. Hard to concentrate with a woody."

Gavril glanced over at Gilly, who now had her hands folded in her lap; her cheeks were bright red.

"I didn't mean to offend," Gavril told her. "It's just, you have that effect on me. Even having you in the same car makes my mind start to wonder from time to time."

"I—I'm sorry. I didn't mean—"

"Stop," Gavril said with a shake of his head. "I know you didn't mean to create the distraction, but let's face it, Gilly, I'm over-the-top attracted to you. Your touch drives me crazy. It makes me crave more. Armageddon could be in full swing right now, and

I'd feel your touch, and in my mind, Armageddon become a secondary issue. Don't you get it?"

She cocked her head, eyeing him questioningly. "What am I supposed to get?"

"I'm beyond attracted to you. All of you. So when you touch me, I don't just feel your hand—I feel all of you, and I crave it more than I do food and water."

Gavril saw Gilly do an abrupt about-face so she faced the windshield. Her cheeks were now fire-engine red. He wanted to kiss them.

"Does that offend you?" Gavril asked.

"No," Gilly said, finally looking him in the eye, as his attention went from her face to the road ahead, where cars were still at a standstill.

"I'm not offended because I feel the same way," Gilly said. "It makes me feel guilty, though. With all that's been going on with the Nosferatu and Loup-Garous missing, and now Viv up and gone, you'd think that was the only thing that'd be on my mind."

"It isn't," Gavril said. "Is it?"

Gilly shook her head. "No. I feel the same way you do. I'm going to put myself on a line here, some-thing I've never done before. You can either accept it or crush it. I'm a big girl and can take either."

"What is it?"

"Every time I see your face, I need you. When you touch me, even we're talking about the direst situations, my body races to white hot, and if I had my way, I'd take you then and there." She sighed and stared back at the windshield. "Sounds ridicu-lous, even to me. Makes me sound like a slut. My sister's missing, and I'm talking about how much I always need you."

Gavril took advantage of the two inches of space between him and the car in front of him, and then turned to Gilly. "Look, I know you don't like to be told what to do. You're independent and often hardheaded—in a good way. You're more woman than any man could possibly think of handling, except me. I see you. I hear you. I understand you. And I want to see just how far you can tolerate me before you kick me to the curb."

"The curb?"

"You know, shove me out of your life because I'm too much for you."

"That'll be the day," Gilly said with a smirk.

"Accident," Gavril suddenly said, jerking his chin toward the fast lane a half mile ahead. "Cops everywhere. That's what caused the slow down. Shouldn't take us long once we get past them."

"Rubberneckers," Gilly said. "That's the slow down. People in the standard lane slowing to a crawl to see the carnage." Suddenly her voice hitched and tears rimmed her eyes.

It didn't go unnoticed by Gavril. "What's wrong? Surely you've seen an accident before."

"It's not that," Gilly said, and then she quickly wiped away a tear that had slid down her cheek. "It's when I said 'carnage.' I hope to all that's in the universe that isn't what we find when we locate Viv."

Gavril didn't comment. He knew that although Gilly could feel if her sister was alive or dead, he had to let her feel, period. He remembered all too well how it felt when they'd lost Ronan. Yes, there'd been a job to do in protecting the Originals and Triad from the Cartesians, but it was difficult to stay focused on a responsibility when your feelings were swamped with grief.

Traffic broke up about ten minutes later, and it took Gavril another fifteen to get to Chalmette. He drove through the center of town, looking for any sign of a carnival. All he saw, however, were people going about their daily jobs. No signs, no banners, no indication that a carnival had been or would be coming to town.

He saw a Denny's up ahead and turned to Gilly. "Hungry?"

"Not really," she said, still staring straight ahead.

Gavril knew she hadn't eaten that day, since they'd been together for most of it. "Tell you what. I'll go in and grab us a couple of burgers. We can eat them while we drive around town and check things out."

Not looking at him, Gilly nodded, and Gavril had the feeling that he could have said anything and she would have nodded the same way.

Gavril went into the restaurant, intending to get more than a couple of burgers. If anyone knew about a carnival being in town, it would be a waitress. Carnivals meant hungry people, so it only made sense that the restaurant would fill up more than normal.

"How ya doin', hon?" an elderly woman with short grey hair and a yellow uniform said when he walked inside. The name tag over her left breast pocket read

Reba. "Place is pretty empty right now, so help yourself to whatever seat you'd like."

"Thanks," Gavril said, "but if you don't mind, I'd like a couple of burgers and two Cokes to go."

"No problem," Reba said. She then wrote up his order and stuck it on a spinning rack for the short-order cook.

"Heard traffic was tied up real bad out there," Reba said. "Construction or accident?"

"Accident, unfortunately."

Reba tsked. "Everybody tryin' to get somewhere too fast, that's the problem. That and textin' on those doggone phones instead of watchin' the road."

Gavril nodded in agreement, and then figured it was as good a time as any to hold Reba's attention.

"I heard you guys had a carnival in town," Gavril said. "Is it still up and running, or did they already break down and head out?"

Reba frowned. "Hon, I don't know who told you about any carnival, but I ain't seen one around this town for nearin' ten years."

"So no carnival or circuses, nothing like that, huh?"

She shook her head. "The only clowns we got around here are some of our regulars. Now I wouldn't tell them that to their face, you hear what I'm sayin'?" She twirled a finger near her right temple, indicating someone with a screw loose in the head. "But it ain't hard to tell they ain't quite right. As for real clowns, like in a circus, no, hon. Same as with the carnivals. Ain't seen one around in more years than I can count."

"What about in a town near you, like Arabi, places like that?"

Reba raised one of her penciled-on eyebrows. "No. Not there either. You know, you're mighty curious about carnivals, circuses and the like for a man your age. Wanna tell me what you're really looking for?"

At about that time, a bell rang, and the cook behind the counter all but shouted, "Order up."

"Aw, well, ain't my business no how," Reba said. "Your burgers are ready." She grabbed the bag of burgers, brought it to Gavril, and then took two Coke cans out of a glass fridge and placed them in a plastic bag. "Here ya go, hon. That'll be twelve ninety-five."

Gavril grabbed his wallet out of his back pocket, pulled out a twenty and gave it to Reba. "Keep the change," he said with a smile. Then with burgers and Cokes in hand, Gavril hurried out of the restaurant before Reba could ask any more questions.

When he reached the black Camaro Nikoli had chosen as their rental, he noticed the passenger door was open and no Gilly.

Gavril tossed the food and drinks into the car, fear causing his heart to pound against his ribs so hard it hurt.

"Gilly?" he called.

No answer.

Gavril all but raced around the gas pumps, hoping she was standing on the other side of one. Nobody around but an elderly bald man filling up a battered blue pickup.

"Gilly!" Gavril called louder, turning in circles, hoping to get sight of her.

"You looking for that pretty, black-haired woman who was in your car?" the elderly man asked.

Gavril sucked in a breath. "Yes. You've seen her?"

"Sure. Don't see how you didn't. She walked right into the restaurant not long after you did. Figured she was either going to pay for gas or had to go to the john."

"Thank you," Gavril said, and took off at a near run, back to the restaurant. Just as he opened the door, he almost collided with Gilly.

"Jesus!" Gavril said, feeling like he could breathe for the first time in minutes.

"What's wrong?" Gilly asked. "Did you find out anything? Did you talk to anyone? Anybody that might have seen Viv?"

Gavril took Gilly by the shoulders, pulled her toward him until the doors to the restaurant closed behind them, and then pulled her close. "I couldn't find you," he said softly. "I thought I'd lost you."

Gilly pulled away slightly so she could look him in the eyes. "A girl's gotta pee sometime."

Gavril shook his head and grinned with solid relief.

"Any word on a carnival?" Gilly asked. "I saw you talking to that waitress. I was hoping she might have known something."

"Nothing," Gavril said. He let go of Gilly's shoulder, took her hand and led her to the car. "Burgers and Coke in the front seat."

"Nothing as she didn't see anyone who looked like Viv, or nothing on a carnival?"

"No carnival. In fact, the waitress claimed there hadn't been a carnival or circus in this area or the surrounding towns in quite a number of years."

Gilly grabbed the bags of food and slid into the passenger seat.

When Gavril settled into the driver's seat, instead of turning the engine over, he simply sat and gazed out the window.

"What now?" Gilly asked. "What the hell do we do?"

Gavril didn't look at her for a moment, thinking. Finally he glanced over at Gilly and said, "You know how you and your sisters have special sounds you make when it's time to change Originals at feeding time? You know, take out the Nosferatu and bring in the Loup-Garous?"

"Yeah."

"Have you tried calling Viv like that? You and Evee, I mean. Maybe if the two of you try, she might hear you, or more importantly, you might hear her."

"It doesn't work that way. What we do is not a mating or come-hither call," Gilly explained. "It's just an animal noise we copy to let the others know it's their turn."

Gavril chewed on his upper lip for a second, almost fearing the repercussion that might come with his next question. "Have you and Evee tried doing a come-hither spell? Do you even have one of those?"

Gilly frowned at him, anger flashing in her eyes. "Of course we do, but it's for those we command or for something we need. It's not used to call one another. It wouldn't work."

"Have you ever tried it before?"

Gilly narrowed her eyes, and then turned to look at the dashboard. "Actually...no."

"Then how do you know it wouldn't work?"

Taking a deep breath, Gilly sat back in her seat. "Fine, I'll talk to Evee, see what she has to say about it."

Gavril turned the engine over and headed out of the parking lot. "Don't be angry with me," he said. "I'm just trying to think of anything, everything possible we can do to try and find Viv. Even if it means using a spell that's never been used for that purpose before."

"Easy for you to say," Gilly said. "You're not a witch. Things can go wrong if you use spells that aren't used for a specific purpose. Every spell has one. And every spell has a consequence tied to it."

"So you think it might put Viv in even more danger since you've never done it before?"

"Hell, I don't know," Gilly said and slapped the dashboard. "Just get us back to New Orleans. I'll talk to Evee. If it's a go for her, I'm game. If she refuses, it's a no go. We'll have to try something else."

"Like what?" Gavril asked.

"Praying."

Chapter 7

Instead of following Highway 46 back to New Orleans, Gilly insisted that they head east, in order to check out the smaller towns near Chalmette. Since they were out this far, anyway, she didn't want to miss the chance that some carnival had gone through a small town, even if only for a weekend.

Along the way, they made stops at cafés, dollar stores and gas stations. Sometimes, depending on the location, Gavril would get out and ask about carnivals in town. Other times, Gilly had been the one to leave Gavril in the car while she questioned clerks or waitresses. They drove from Chalmette to Meraux, and then to Poydras, where Gilly got out of the car and went into an old convenience store, its shelves nearly bare. She thought about grabbing a bag of chips for a snack, but then checked the expiration date. April of last year. Knowing she was being watched by the clerk behind the counter, she held back an "Ugh!" She then went over to the small man with dark skin and eyes. Not once did a smile light his face.

"Excuse me," Gilly said, trying to act nonchalant. "We heard there was some kind of carnival or circus in this area. Have you heard of it? Do you know where it might be?"

"You buy something?" the clerk asked frowning.

Gilly grabbed a pack of Juicy Fruit gum near a display case by the register. "Just this," she said.

"One dollar, forty-two cents," the clerk said.

Gilly gave him a double take. "A dollar and forty-two cents for one pack of gum?"

He nodded. "You pay or put it back, please. I keep my store very clean, as you see. Everything must have its place."

Infuriated by the price gouging, Gilly pulled two bucks out of her pocket and tossed it on the counter. She waited while he slowly counted out her change.

"So do you know of a carnival or circus around here?" Gilly said.

The clerk handed Gilly her change, made sure she'd only taken one pack of gum, and then shook his head. "No. We have no such thing here. You want party, you go to New Orleans. They always have party in that city. We have party only one time a year."

Gilly's ears perked up. "When?"

"What do they call Fat Tuesday here?"

"Mardi Gras?"

"Yes, that would be the party. It's chaos, I tell you. People fill up all the towns near here. They steal from my store. I know this to be fact. Last year, I found boy with a beer can in his pants. He tried to leave the store, but I caught him. Caught him and called the police. He must go to jail, I tell the police. He must go to jail."

Gilly's expectation bubble deflated. Mardi Gras was still five months away. No carnival. No circus.

"Anything?" Gavril asked when Gilly returned to the car with the pack of gum, which she abruptly threw out the window. For all she knew, it might have had an expiration date of May 5, 1909.

"Nothing but some pain-in-the-butt guy. Wouldn't even give me information until I bought something from his damn store."

"You talking about the gum you just pitched out the window?"

"Yeah. Everything in that place was so old, the gum probably carried botulism."

"So, I take it, gum or no gum, he doesn't know of any carnivals or circuses."

Gilly shook her head. "The guy said the only party they had in town was during Mardi Gras, and that's five to six months away."

Gavril laid a hand over the steering wheel and sighed. Gilly laid her head back on the seat, closed her eyes for a few seconds, and then she opened them and stared at nothing.

"I just can't figure it," Gavril said. "Why would Moose talk about things that sound like they're from a carnival, yet we can't find one that's happened around here for months?"

"Hell if I know," Gilly said, looking straight ahead.

"What now?" Gavril said as he shoved the gear into drive. "Hmm, other than rain."

As if waking from a dream, Gilly looked over at him, and then followed his gaze to the windshield. Black thunderheads had rolled in, and beyond them lay a heavy sheet of gray. The wind had already started to pick up, threatening to rock the Camaro from one lane to another.

By the time they hit Meraux again, the windshield wipers were going at full speed, but were seemingly as useless as a rosary in a Baptist church. Gilly couldn't see car lights in front of her.

"Can you see anything?" Gilly asked. "Car lights? Flashers?"

Gavril, who was white-knuckling the steering wheel, shook his head. They were barely managing a five-mile-per-hour crawl. "We're going to have to pull off somewhere until this calms down," he said. "The last thing we need is to rear-end somebody or have someone rear-end us. The eighteen wheelers aren't helping either. They're producing so much spray that, even with mud flaps, it's like driving through twice the amount of rain."

Gilly agreed, putting a hand on the dashboard when a set of break lights suddenly appeared in front of them, less than a foot away. She resisted an instinct to put a protective hand out toward Gavril, like a loving mother would a child. He was definitely not a child, and she was no one's mother. But loving was what made her hand want to shoot out to protect him. That she felt to her core.

Gavril inched the Camaro along until they came up to a gravel road about two-hundred feet ahead. Lightning sizzled through the sky, and thunder boomed seemingly from every direction.

"What is that?" Gilly asked, pointing to a large, dull red building nearly five-hundred feet or so off the main road. It had no front door, just an open space in front of the building, wide enough to drive a tractor—or a car—through.

"Looks like a barn. See any houses near it?"

"Hell, I can barely see it," Gilly said. She scooted up to the edge of her seat to get a better look through the windshield and pressed her face against the passenger side window. "Don't see anything but the barn. No houses. No cars or trucks. Just that old building."

"Good," Gavril said, and before Gilly knew it, he squeezed the Camaro through the front opening of the building and drove until they reached a solid-wall cattle gate.

Rain pinged off the tin roof, but it was nothing compared to the sound of driving through gushing water.

Gilly got out of the car, closed the passenger door and stretched her arms and legs. "Man, oh, man, I don't remember the last time I've seen a gully washer like this one."

Gavril followed her out of the car. He did a quick survey of the place. Stables, but no horses or cows. Above them was a semi-circle second floor with bales of hay piled on top of one another.

"You were right about the hay," Gilly said, motioning overhead. "I wonder why there're no cattle here."

"Farmer might be grazing them in another pasture. Hopefully he's taken the hay he's needed for the day."

"But wouldn't he bring the animals in because of the rain?" Gilly asked.

"Cows and horses, unless you're talking high-bred stock, are used to the weather. It can be raining buckets, and they'll either be lying under a tree or still grazing grass. Wet doesn't seem to bother them much."

Gilly walked toward the open end of the barn, wanting to get closer to see if the rain appeared to be slacking. A bolt of lightning struck just outside, and thunder made the ground rumble beneath her feet. The rain had not only slacked, it had intensified, blowing sheets of rain drops the size of raisins.

She crossed her arms over her chest, lowered her head, and walked to the back wall of the building, thinking...thinking. Only there wasn't a damn thing to think about. She'd always known Moose to be a little slow in the brain department, but at least he had brains. She wasn't able to look past what Moose saw to get a handle on the location of these intense colors. The only thing that made sense was a carnival or circus, only she hadn't been able to see that to make it a fact.

Aside from attempting a come-hither call as she'd promised Gavril that she'd try with Evee, the only other option that came to mind was trying to contact Moose again to find out if one of the other dead Loups was with him—one that might be able to give them clearer directions.

Suddenly, Gilly sneezed. She was surprised to find herself shivering. It was too early in the fall for it to be cold, but the rain, together with the wind, made it feel like she'd been dunked in thirty-degree water.

Evidently, seeing her react to the cold, Gavril took off his shirt and wrapped it around her shoulders.

"But you'll freeze," Gilly protested. "You need to put it back on, or you'll wind up with a cold or pneumonia." Gilly felt slightly embarrassed because the entire time she addressed him, she hadn't been able to take her eyes off his chest, his ripped abs and his huge biceps.

Gilly took off his shirt and handed it back to him. "Please, for me. I'll be worried sick that you'll catch your death, and then what will we do without you?"

Gavril gave her a slow shake of his head and put his shirt back on. "I'll wear it," he said, "but we need to find a warmer place before I wind up having to take care of you in a hospital."

Gilly held her hands out. "Unless we sit in the car, we're kind of limited."

"Not at all," Gavril said, and held out his right hand. She took it without hesitation and followed him to a tall ladder that stretched from the bottom floor to the hayloft overhead.

"If we lay between the bales of hay, you'll warm up quickly," he assured her. As they made it up the ladder, Gavril said, "We're talking about a hayloft now, so don't expect the Ritz."

When they made it to the top of the hayloft, Gilly said, "You're right, it's not the Ritz. More like a Holiday Inn."

He smiled, and then started moving bales around.

"How are we going to know when the rain slacks off enough for us to drive out of here if we're stuck between bales of hay?" A crack of lightning, and then a roll of thunder, had Gavril raise both eyebrows.

"Whenever it will be, it certainly isn't right now." He motioned her between two rows of hay stacked three bales high. "And we've got that," Gavril said, and motioned to a small set of wooden doors at the north end of the loft.

"Funny place for doors, don't you think?" Gilly said.

"Not really. Instead of hoisting bales of hay down that ladder when needed, all the farmer has to do is toss however many bales he needs through the window. They land on the ground, and then he loads them into the back of his truck."

"And all we have to do is open those hay doors to check on the weather," Gilly said.

"You've got it."

Rain pummeled the metal roof of the barn, and thunder rolled continuously around them.

Gilly lay between the two rows of hay and immediately felt the difference in temperature. She wasn't shaking anymore. The problem was, she didn't know if it was the change of environment that had relieved her shivers, or if it was Gavril taking control of the situation and taking care of her, the way a man does for his woman.

Thinking of that made her nervous and excited at the same time. To stave off both feelings, she turned on her right side, put an arm under her head and said, "If I drift off, promise you'll wake me when the weather lets us?"

Gavril gave her a little salute. "Yes, ma'am. Immediately."

A few seconds of silence passed, and then Gilly said. "Gavril?"

"Yes?"

"Suppose the weather stays like this for hours? I don't want to be stuck here that long. We've got to find Viv."

"We'll find her, baby. I promise we'll find her." He squatted down, sat on his haunches and rubbed her pant leg gently.

Gilly gave him a soft smile and watched his eyes light up despite another hold up on their mission. She noticed how his attitude wasn't one of frustration and angst, but calm and certainty. He was sure of himself. Sure of how to care for her. For all of them.

Out of nowhere, Gilly suddenly sat up and leaned over so her face was right beside his. She held his face between her hands and said softly, "No matter how chaotic things have become, how we seem to conquer one thing and four more new ones pop up, I—I can't thank you enough for all you do. For all you and your cousins have done for the Triad, for our Originals. I know missing two entire groups of them was not in any Bender's plan, but despite how hopeless it makes everything seem, you never give up. You're always thinking of new ideas, ready to search longer, farther, regardless of how little sleep and food you've had. I didn't want you to think any of what you do goes unnoticed. I do notice and appreciate you more than I can express."

Seemingly left wordless, Gavril sat back, silent for a moment. "You give me far too much credit. You and your sisters have been right along with us on the fight. My cousins have worked and fought just as hard, so much so that it cost one his life. Thank you for the compliment, but don't forget we're all in this together. It isn't just me."

Suddenly Gavril's stomach grumbled, and a look of embarrassment crossed his face. "Well, that was a fine set of manners if I ever heard one," he said with a grin.

"You're hungry. I mean, geez, how long has it been since you've eaten?"

Gavril shrugged. "Not something I keep track of."

"We still have those burgers and Cokes in the

car. Would you like me to run over and get them for you?"

"No, thank you, but I can get them for you," he said.

Instead of answering, Gilly reached for Gavril's face with both hands and pulled him close. She kissed him lightly at first, just to taste his lips. "I am hungry," she whispered. "But not for burgers." She wrapped her hands around his neck and pulled him down to her and kept pulling until he lay right beside her.

"Gilly," he whispered, a worried look on his face. "What the Elders told you. All that's happening... I don't want you to feel—"

In response, Gilly lifted her body and kissed Gavril gently on the lips. As if it meant to orchestrate a romantic play, rain pinged heavier on the roof top, lightning cracked like an expert with a bullwhip and wind whistled through the cracks in the building.

When his lips left hers reluctantly, Gavril said, "I am starved, too, but not for food."

Feeling the same, and shoving all thoughts of chaos and heartaches to the farthest reaches of her mind, Gilly pulled Gavril down so his body rested upon hers. He put his hands on either side of her to lift some of his weight off her, and then leaned in to devour her mouth.

Gilly moaned reflexively. His lips were the softest, sexiest ones on the planet, and she couldn't get enough of them. Not only did it start a fire burning inside her, it caused something that felt like an electromagnetic field inside of her body that worked at pulling them closer, closer, so close that she wanted them to fuse together. His kisses were to die for, but if she didn't have the rest of him, she felt like she'd implode.

Gavril broke their kiss for a second and looked into her eyes. "Gilly, I—"

She wrapped her fingers in his hair and took his mouth as a ravenous woman would take a seven-course meal. She simply couldn't get enough of him. Not now. Not ever.

Silently, except for the rapid growth of his breathing, Gavril ran his mouth along the side of Gilly's throat, nipping at it, licking it, kissing her below the earlobe.

Unable to bear the heat of her own body anymore, and despite the itchy twigs of hay that had broken loose from its bale, Gilly reached down and pulled off her shirt. Unable to wait for him to reach other parts of her body, she stripped off her bra, moved him aside for only a moment, and in a flash, was out of her pants and underwear.

Gilly lay back down between the bales of hay, her arms stretched over her head, her legs crossed at the ankles. She saw Gavril's eyes travel hungrily over her and heard his sharp intact of breath. She could almost hear his thoughts… *I want all of her now! Where on earth do I start? Control, man. Control.*

And control he did. With Gilly's arms above her head, her breasts rode high, her nipples rigid, pointing upward, calling to him.

But Gavril accepted the challenge of control. He

leaned over Gilly and kissed the opposite side of her neck, sucking and nipping on it, his lips moving across her throat, just below her jaw, and then suddenly moving up and taking her mouth, his tongue plunging in to meet hers. She sucked on it as if she were sucking on the hardest part of his manhood right now, and he had to form an algebraic formula in his head to keep from exploding then and there.

He released his tongue from her grip and teased her mouth, shoving his tongue in and out...in...out, licking as he soon planned to do with the wettest part of her womanhood.

As his tongue and mouth teased her to a white-hot pitch, he cupped her breasts in his hands and smoothed his hands down from her breastbone to her nipples, where he finally caught them between a thumb and forefinger and squeezed. Gently at first, until he heard her groan. Once more, with his tongue still working her mouth, he slid his hands gently up and across her chest until he reached her nipples, which he then locked between a thumb and forefinger. He tugged at both, twisted slightly until she moaned, tugged and twisted more until she cried out his name with need.

Gilly tangled her fingers into his hair and pulled him down lower, lower, until she felt his breath on her right breast. She arched her back, wanting desperately for him to touch her, taste her.

Gavril's tongue flicked ever so gently over her right breast, and she moaned from a need so deep inside of her it sounded animalistic.

"More… More, Gavril, more."

The sound of his name seemed to throw Gavril into a feeding frenzy he had little control over. He licked her right breast while he fondled her left, suckled her nipples, moving from one to the other. Taking them between his teeth and nipping them gently, wanting, needing her to cry out his name, which she did again and again.

Gilly heard her breath go from rapid to almost nonexistent. Gavril had her so wrapped in need, she forgot to breathe.

Soon his lips and tongue moved lower, down to her stomach, his hands never leaving her breasts until he had reached the triangle of her thighs. Then his hands moved down, and he parted her thighs ever so slightly.

"Oh, Gilly…" The sound of her name from his lips sent her back into a high arch. There was no mistaking what she wanted or needed.

Even from where she lay, Gilly felt the heat from between her legs grow furnace hot. She felt warm, fresh juices run out of her slit that was so swollen and desperate for him, and she hadn't even had an orgasm yet.

Gavril spread her legs apart as far as the bales of hay would allow on either side of her, and then placed one finger gently against her wetness. He pressed slightly but didn't enter, causing Gilly to cry out his name.

"Gavril…"

He glanced up at her, his mouth swollen and full

from their kisses. "What, baby? Tell me what you want. Tell me what you need."

Gilly arched her back higher, threw her head back, all inhibition lost to this man. "I—I need to feel your tongue there. Your fingers…all of you." She knew how hard he was when he lay atop her. The length and girth of his cock made her all the more anxious to have him inside. She'd beg if she had to. Something she'd never thought she'd be capable of doing in her entire life.

"Tell me, baby," Gavril said. "You want to feel… this?" And he moved a finger slowly inside of her, only to the depth of one knuckle.

The sound that escaped Gilly was guttural.

"Or did you mean this…" And with those words, Gavril placed his mouth over the nodule that he knew would cause her to erupt, to drain every ounce of the sexual juices her body had been holding on to for so long. He licked and sucked and shoved his finger in deeper, widening her enough so a second would slide in easily.

With two fingers inside her, and his tongue over the mound that ruled her, Gavril sucked, licked and shoved his fingers in fast and deep. He pushed them into the farthest parts of her, where he knew that secret button would release more than Gilly had ever felt before.

So much was pent up inside Gilly that she opened her mouth to speak, but nothing would come out. She didn't want to lessen what was about to flood her with words. It boiled inside her like a pressure cooker that was set was on high and didn't a relief valve.

Gavril must have felt what was happening with her body because he took her clitoris between her legs, used the fingers of his free hand to spread the skin that hooded it as far back and away as it would go, and then he placed his mouth over it, working it back and forth, side to side with his tongue.

Gavril felt his fingers reach way inside of her and touch a place that had no words to describe the way it made her feel. Feeling or being sexual was one thing, but he touched what *was* the peak of her sexual drive. Relentlessly, he worked his fingers on that spot, holding his hand in place, stretching the top of his finger so that it reached it, touched it just so.

All Gilly felt was a tsunami swelling, swelling, ready to crash over her. She tried to tell him, to warn him, but before she could, come squirted from her into his mouth, all over his hand and his chest. It wasn't like Gilly was a prude. She'd had sex before, but nothing as intense as this. Nothing that made her insides feel like they'd just exploded all over him.

Gavril ever so slowly removed his mouth and fingers from her body. He lay beside her, smoothing her tousled hair that had landed across her eyes.

She looked at him, felt her body more at ease and peaceful than she'd known it to be in a long time. And her heart fuller than she'd ever thought possible.

Gavril kissed her on the forehead and was about to get to his feet when Gilly grabbed his hand. "But you…" she said.

"There'll be time for me, believe me," Gavril said. "But listen for a moment and tell me what you hear."

Gilly lay back, closed her eyes and listened carefully. Something occasionally falling on the tin roof...the meow of a cat who'd found its shelter in the same place they had. Suddenly, Gilly sat up. "The storm's passed," she said, becoming excited.

Gavril nodded. "It sure has." He held out a hand to help Gilly to her feet. "Come on, sweet thing. Let's go find your sister."

Chapter 8

When Gilly and Gavril returned to the François home, she found herself shocked into silence by what she saw. Sitting in the living room was Evee, Lucien, Taka, Arabella and Gunner Stern, one of the three true sorcerers who lived in New Orleans.

"What are you doing here?" Gilly asked Gunner.

"Gilly!" Evee said, reprimand in her voice. "There's no need to be so rude. Arabella and Taka asked him to meet us here, and he was kind enough to do so."

Infuriated that a sorcerer sat in her living room, Gilly glanced about. "Where's Vanessa?" she asked.

"Oh, she didn't want any part of this," Taka said. She took a ladyfinger cookie and napkin from a small silver tray that sat on a glass and mahogany coffee table. Beside that sat yet another tray, this one holding a small teapot and china teacups to match.

"Well, it seems like one of you made sense," Gilly said.

"Gilly, why don't you and Gavril have a seat, and we'll explain all we've been discussing," Arabella said.

"I don't have time for chit-chat," Gilly said. "I'm going to take a shower, and then go and look for Viv. The rest of you can eat cookies and drink tea until you choke on it. Whatever floats your boat."

Gavril lightly took Gilly by the arm and led her to the small couch that was across from the divan where Evee and Lucien sat. Near them, Taka and Arabella sat on the couch closest to the fireplace, while Gunner was in a wingback chair between the divan and one of the couches.

"Just listen to what they have to say," Gavril whispered in Gilly's ear.

She jerked her arm away from his grasp and dropped down with a plop in an overstuffed chair. "Okay, say what you've got to say, but I can't believe we're just spending all this time gabbing away while Viv's out there. Heaven only knows where she is, and in what kind of danger."

"I understand that," Arabella said. "Don't you think we're worried about her, as well? That's why I got Gunner involved. We've been working as hard as we can to try to get the Originals back and into their normal states. We've lost many of them along the way. I spoke with Gunner because I trust him, and I think he may be able to help, if not with finding the missing Originals, then helping us at least find Viv. She's the most important issue we have to concentrate on right now."

"I agree," Evee said.

Lucien nodded his head in agreement.

Gilly stared at Gunner. "You know what the issue between sorcerers and witches has been for generations, right?"

Gunner nodded and offered her the smallest of smiles. "I can understand why you feel the way that you feel. There's been animosity between witches and sorcerers for centuries."

"No, you don't understand," Gilly said. "I don't like Trey Cottle or his sidekick, Shandor Black. I guess they're in an occupation that suits their sleazy personalities, being attorneys and all. But attorneys or not, I don't trust them. I don't trust what they say. They're only out to help themselves. I've never seen them reach out to help anyone in this community, and I don't mean to sound crass, Mr. Stern, but you're with them an awful lot. Why should I trust you when all I see is you with Trey Cottle and his brownnoser?"

"That would probably be my sentiment exactly," Gunner said. "The truth of the matter is that the three of us are sorcerers. Sometimes we talk shop, but most of the time, believe it or not, I'm with Trey and Shandor just to keep an ear to the ground, so to speak. To hear and see what Shandor and Trey are up to. You're right. Most of what they do with spells or potions has to do with suiting themselves, benefiting themselves. How does that saying go? 'Keep your friends close, but your enemies closer.' I'm not saying that Cottle or Black are my enemies, but I don't exactly see them as tried-and-true Boy Scouts type. I don't agree with a lot of what they do."

Gilly scowled. "What does that matter if you allow them to gain over the community by their spells and their potions? A little potion here to get a city ordinance passed in their favor, a small spell there to get a judge to lean in their direction. Just stepping back doesn't do anything. Why don't you stop them?"

"Once they've issued a spell or used a potion," Gunner said, "I can't stop it. I can put a protection spell, which I've done many times, over the person or city council they're trying to take advantage of. Like you, I want these people's decisions to be their own and not something that's been generated by Cottle or Black."

Gilly blew out a frustrated breath. "If you can't reverse their spells, what makes you think you can help us find Viv? We're sitting here with what? You've got four witches and none of us are able to contact my own sister. What makes you think you can make a difference? You can't even go against your own. What makes you think you can conjure up something that'll allow us to find Viv?"

"I'm not saying that I can," Gunner said. "But I'm here to help in any way that I can."

"And what way is that?" Evee asked.

"I can offer a come-hither spell," Gunner said. "It may work, it may not—because she doesn't know my voice—but it's at least worth a try. You never know, because it's not a voice she recognizes, it may call to her, and she may appear. She may be able to untangle herself from whatever's deterring her so that she can come home."

"That makes sense," Taka said. "You know, if I heard a man's voice calling me, I'd come. But we've already tried that spell. It didn't work."

"Any man?" Gilly asked her. "Even if you don't know who he is? Especially with all that's been going on with the Cartesians and missing Originals?"

Taka took another bite of cookie, chewed for a second, and then said, "Yeah. 'Cause a Cartesian can't talk. They just make loud growling, grunting sounds from what you've told me. So, if it was a man's voice, and he could call to me like that, I'd at least go check it out. That doesn't mean I'd go running and bow at his feet, but I'd sure check him out. You never know, he could be good looking. Might be worth the chance."

"Oh, for the love of the universe, Taka," Arabella said. "We're not talking about a man for Viv. We're talking about Viv listening to a man's voice."

"I know," Taka said with a pout. "I'm not stupid. I understand exactly what you're saying."

"Just eat your cookies and have some tea, dear," Arabella said. "Let's finish this conversation so we can go about finding Viv."

"I'm scared, Gilly," Evee said. "Viv has never

been away like this. She would never just disappear and not tell us where she was going." Evee's lips started to tremble. "I'm afraid something's happened to her, and if it takes Gunner coming here to try and call so that she hears a new voice and comes to it, I'm all for it." A tear slid down Evee's cheek, and Lucien put an arm around her and patted her shoulder to comfort her. "I just want her back."

"I want her back, too," Gilly said. "I want her back in one piece." Gilly turned to Gunner. "Mr. Stern, do you have any idea what a Cartesian is?"

"Yes," Gunner said. "Unfortunately, I do."

"And how is it that you know of them?"

"We have known about Cartesians for many generations. For centuries. I've not seen one for myself or had to deal with any, but I know that they are monstrous creatures, and they are out for blood, for death. They want all who exist in the netherworld. To kill them and make their powers their own."

"That's right," Gilly said. "And what do you think they would if they captured a Triad?"

Gunner nodded again. "I know the Originals are in danger with the Cartesians, but so is the Triad. Believe me, I've had nightmares about it. That's why I have been so insistent about offering to help. Thankfully, Arabella allowed me to at least talk to you."

"And just what is it that you propose, Mr. Stern?" Evee asked.

"Please, call me Gunner."

"Fine," Gilly said.

"Have you tried a come-hither spell?" Gunner asked.

"I have," Taka said. "I did it the other day. The only thing that came, though, was a sparrow. It came and flew right into the window. Smashed its head and fell to the ground."

"We were just talking about this," Gavril said conspiratorially to Gilly.

Gilly shot him an "I know" look, and then turned back to Gunner. "Fine. So let's do it. Do you need potions, herbs, crystals?"

"No," Gunner said. "All I ask is that we join hands and form a circle. I'll stand in the middle of it and issue the command."

"Let's do it then," Gilly said impatiently.

Everyone got to their feet. Evee, Lucien, Taka, Arabella, Gilly and Gavril. They held hands as instructed by Gunner, breaking rank only to allow him into the middle of the circle.

Gunner closed his eyes, and Gilly could only assume he was visualizing Viv. He'd have no problem bringing her to mind, since he'd known the Triad for years. After a long moment, he held out his hands, palms up, and said,

Come hither, Triad.
One so true.
Although my voice be male and new.
Let not my command hinder thee.
But break all bonds.
And come to me.
I bind all bonds.

That hinder thee.
So come hither now.
To thine family.

After issuing the incantation, Gunner stood silently with his arms held out. Everyone listened intently, but heard nothing but the ticking of the grandfather clock at the end of the foyer.

"Well, so much for that," Gilly said. "Seems like you have the same effect that—"

Suddenly Gilly heard a loud bang at the front door.

Taka jumped and slapped a hand to her chest. "For the love of cheese and crackers, that almost gave me a heart attack! Who is that? Maybe it's Viv!"

Gilly released her grip on Gavril's and Evee's hands. She went over to the front door and peered through the security peephole. "I don't see anyone."

Taka marched up to the front door. "Probably some of those kids who live a few houses down from here. They bang on your door, then take off running. I'll catch those little boogers."

Taka yanked the door open, and Gavril yelled, "Shut the door, Taka. Now! Shut the door." Taka turned and looked at him, confusion on her face.

It was then Gilly caught the scent of cloves and sulfur. She shoved her Elder out of the way and slammed the door shut. When she looked through the peephole again, Gilly saw a Cartesian's long black talons. Had Taka stayed at the doorway a second longer, it would have gotten her.

"Goddamn," Gilly said to Gavril. "They know

where we are." She felt her hands start to shake as she pointed to the door. Soon her entire body began to tremble. "Th-they…they're out there. They know where we are!"

Gavril hurried to her side and put an arm around her. "It's okay," he said.

"It's not okay, Gavril. They found us. Where we live. How are we ever going to get out of here if they're out there waiting, watching? Gunner's come hither spell didn't work either. If they took Viv, they're waiting to get Evee and me and the Elders. First the Originals. Remember? You said that they wanted the Originals, the Triad and the Elders for our powers. How are we going to leave this place? How are we going to find Viv?"

"Oh, we'll leave," Gavril said. "Now listen carefully. When I give you the signal, I want you to swing the door open wide, then take off for your kitchen and go up the back stairs to the second floor and wait there. Taka, you and Arabella, Evee and Gunner do the same." He turned to Lucien "You've got your scabior on you, right?"

"Of course, cuz," Lucien said and patted the sheath attached to his belt.

"Good, because I think we've got a bit of a skirmish ahead of us."

"But you can't just leave us here," Arabella said. "We've got to fight together."

Gunner took Arabella's hand, and then grabbed hold of Taka's. "Let's just do what they've told us to. We have no experience fighting these Cartesians. But these men do. I'm going to lead you up the stairs, and I'll stay there with you until they call us back down. Don't argue over this one. These men know what they're doing. Let them do their job."

"I'm not going anywhere," Gilly said fiercely. "Gavril, if you're staying to fight, I'm here with you."

"Same with me and Lucien," Evee said.

"The two of you are going to go in the other room," Gavril said loudly. "Just like we said." He looked deeply into Gilly's eyes. "The last thing I want is to lose you."

Lucien took Evee by the shoulders and, in front of everyone, kissed her. "And I don't want to lose you. Please just go to the other room. We'll get you out of here. Don't worry."

Reluctantly, Gilly took hold of Evee's arm and they went into the foyer.

"On the count of three," Gilly told Evee. She held tight to her sister's arm, and then she yanked the door open and took off with Evee to the kitchen, across the foyer. "Go upstairs. I'll be there in a minute."

Evee scowled. "Promise?"

"Yeah."

"Gilly, please don't do anything stupid. We need you."

"Just get upstairs. Hurry. I'll be up in a few."

As Evee hurried up the stairs to the second floor, Gilly planted herself against the kitchen wall closest to the foyer. She wanted to, needed to hear if Gavril or Lucien called for help. Not that she'd know what to do in the help department, but at least she'd be there. Everything inside of her wouldn't allow her to desert Gavril, even at his command.

From where she stood, Gilly saw Gavril and Lucien rush outside, scabiors in hand. She took a chance and went to the window closest to the front door and looked out. She saw Lucien and Gavril aiming their scabiors up at the sky. From where she stood, Gilly saw rift after rift, large black slits overhead with Cartesians hanging from them, reaching for Lucien and Gavril. Long talons, slicing air, wanting to destroy, to kill.

Gavril and Lucien aimed and fired again and again, pushing the Cartesians farther into a different dimension. From his back pocket, Gilly saw Gavril pull out a second scabior, which she could only assume had been Ronan's.

Gavril activated the second scabior with his left hand and used it. He had perfect aim with his right hand, but his left was off center. He obviously had to concentrate on one Cartesian at a time in order to push it back.

Without thinking, Gilly ran to the door, wanting to, needing to, help Gavril. She heard Evee call to her, crying for her from the top of the stairs. "Gilly, stop. Don't, don't go out there. I can't lose you, too. Gilly, stop!"

Blocking her sister's cries from her mind, Gilly ran outside and grabbed the scabior that was already activated out of Gavril's left hand.

"What the—" Gavril said, shocked and motionless.

Ignoring him, Gilly pointed the scabior she'd taken from him at one of the rifts, and the Cartesian that hung from it, and aimed. She heard a loud pop, and the Cartesian flew back. She aimed again into a black hole, seeing the Cartesian's talons still trying to clutch and hang on to its present dimension. She shot again and again and yet again, pushing the Cartesian back as far as she could, until the rift closed up.

But then, three more rifts began to open up, just when they thought they had everything under control.

Gavril looked at Gilly and shook his head. They each took aim at a rift, and at the Cartesian hanging from it. Surprisingly, Gilly was the one that got her Cartesian sent back five dimensions, whereas Gavril and Lucien had managed only three. Regardless of the number, at least the rifts were closed and the Cartesians were gone.

Gilly turned to face Gavril and found both him and Lucien staring at her. She didn't know how long they'd been fighting the Cartesians but if she looked half as exhausted as they did, it had been a while.

Suddenly Gavril seemed to come to life again and wrenched the scabior out of Gilly's hand. "What on earth were you thinking coming out here like that? You've never operated a scabior before. For all you know, it could have blown up in your hand. It could have electrocuted you. We've never had anyone not trained use a scabior before."

"Well, obviously, I didn't blow up," Gilly said, "And you're more than welcome for the help." She spun about on her heels and marched back into the

Chapter 9

Once Gunner dropped the Elders off, he left in his silver Buick, heading to his own home to review his spell book.

Arabella could tell how disappointed he was that his come-hither spell had no effect whatsoever on bringing Viv home. She had been as disappointed, certain that, as powerful and stern as his voice had been, there would have been some kind of response from Viv.

Once they entered the house, Vanessa was full of questions. Arabella waved her off and said, "I'm going to take a quick shower. Taka will fill you in."

As Vanessa hammered Taka with questions, Taka took her time, made herself a cup of coffee and added

house. She stood by the grandfather clock at the end of the foyer and crossed her arms over her chest defiantly. She felt cheated from a win and angry at having been scolded.

Gavril and Lucien came back inside and put their scabiors back into their sheaths.

"We've got to get the Elders back to their homes," Lucien said. "And we've got to get you and Evee out of here now that the Cartesians know where you are. They're going to test their ground, hover over this place. They're going to stay near here now that they know where you are. There's no way we can stay in hiding and find Viv, much less the missing Originals."

"I have the Camaro," Gavril said. "We can use it to get everyone out of here."

"And I have my Buick," Gunner said. "I'll be more than happy to take the Elders home."

"Wait a minute," Evee said. "Talking about the Camaro, where is Nikoli?"

"He's still out looking for Viv," Lucien said.

"Where is he looking for her?" Gilly asked.

"I have no idea," Gavril said.

"Can't you take that watch thing you wear with the GPS on it and find him? Summon him?" Gilly asked. "Tell him it's an emergency or something so we can get his help here? You would think, with Viv missing, he'd be right in the middle of the conversation we had before the Cartesian attack."

"He's doing exactly what I'd expect him to do," Gavril said. "Hunt for Viv."

"Can you at least find out where he is? If he found her?"

Without answering, Gavril activated the watch he wore on his left wrist and signaled for Nikoli.

"We're going to take the Camaro and bring the Elders home, then we'll come back here for you," Gavril said. "Nikoli should be here by the time we get back."

After herding Taka, Arabella and Gunner into one place, Gavril went outside, double checked to make sure there were no longer any rifts around the house or anywhere close to it. Then he corralled the three of them into the Camaro and drove off.

"That was such a stupid thing you did, Gilly," Evee said. "You could have gotten yourself killed."

"That's true," Lucien said. "You shouldn't have gone out there." Then his eyes brightened. "But Evee, you should have seen her. She handled that scabior like she'd been born with it. She aimed and shot those Cartesians without a flinch. Even got the last one and pushed it back farther than Gavril and me put together. She's quite the shot."

"Don't make her head swell any more than it already has," Evee said. "Gilly had no business messing with the Cartesians."

"My head's far from swollen, thank you very much," Gilly said, knowing full well that there was a small bit of truth to it. She was just glad to have been acknowledged for her help with the Cartesians.

Evee turned to her sibling. "You have to promise me that you'll never do anything like that again.

We have to find Viv, and I need your help to do it. I don't want to lose you, too, so please, promise me you won't ever attempt something like that again."

Gilly gave her sister a weary look and sighed. "Yeah, yeah, okay, I promise I won't attempt anything like that again," she said...with her fingers crossed behind her back.

some Irish whiskey to it. Then she sat at the kitchen table, and Vanessa scurried to sit across from her.

"So what happened?" Vanessa said.

Taka took a sip of coffee-laced whiskey and sighed. "It was horrible. Those monsters are bigger than anything I've ever seen, even in horror movies. They had claws that were like talons of a hawk, only four inches long and black, and the tips curled inward. They were sweeping those talons out from a slit in the sky, trying to catch us. Anything they would've touched, they would've stabbed or skewered. We'd have been dead immediately."

"What did you do?" Vanessa asked, wide-eyed. "Wait, before you tell me, I want to get every detail." Vanessa got up from the table, hurried over to the stove, poured herself a cup of coffee and added a little more whiskey to hers than Taka had.

She hurried back to the table and sat across from Taka. "Okay, start from the beginning."

"Well," Taka said, "we got there, and Gunner did a come-hither spell."

"What happened with his spell? Did it work?"

"Do you see Viv here?"

"You don't have to be so snippy about it," Vanessa said. "Did anything happen?"

Taka took a sip of coffee and smacked her lips.

"Crickets," Arabella said, coming into the kitchen. She was dressed in blue linen pants and a white button-down blouse.

"Why are you so dressed up?" Vanessa asked.

"Because Gunner's coming back this way," Taka said. "She's gotta look good for her honey."

"Stop that nonsense, will you?" Arabella said.

"I was just asking Taka what happened," Vanessa said. "She told me those things were huge and monstrous. That they had long black talons."

"She wouldn't know," Arabella said. "She didn't even get a chance to see one."

Vanessa glared at Taka. "You mean you lied to me?"

"No, I didn't lie. I saw them through the window."

"How could you see them through the window?" Arabella asked. "You were hiding behind me the entire time the Benders were fighting."

"Yeah, but I could see through the window from where I stood behind you. I saw their talons come sweeping down. They were huge. They would've killed anything the moment they would've touched it. They were so sharp and pointed and curved."

Arabella shivered. She hadn't seen the talons. She'd only known to try to catch her breath to keep herself from having a heart attack when Gilly ran out to help Gavril and Lucien fight the Cartesians that had shown up over their home.

"Did all of that happen after Gunner did his come-hither spell?" Vanessa asked.

"Yes," Arabella said. "Unfortunately, his spell produced no results. Like I said…crickets."

"There weren't any crickets," Taka said. "I didn't hear one, and you know how it is when a cricket gets loose in a room and makes that aggravating noise.

It drives you crazy. If there'd been crickets, we'd have hunted them down, caught them and tossed them outside."

"I wasn't talking about real crickets, Taka," Arabella said with a sigh. "It's a figure of speech. It means nothing happened."

"Viv didn't show up. Not a word came from anywhere." Arabella swiped a loose strand of hair away from her forehead. "His spell didn't work. That's why he's going to look over his book now to see if there's not something stronger that he can use to beckon her to us."

"You trust him that much?" Vanessa asked. "Viv didn't show up but those Cartesians surely did. What about that? Maybe his spell had something to do with it."

"I heard every word of that spell," Arabella said. "It was a come hither specifically targeting Viv, and that's it."

"You're actually going to let a sorcerer use his spell book instead of the Triad using their Grimoires?" Vanessa asked. " By the way, have they even gone through them to see if there's something in there that might help bring their sister back?"

"Oh, yes, they've gone through their Grimoires many times, from what they told me," Arabella said. "But no matter what they've tried, nothing seems to work. The biggest problem we have now…not the only one, but the biggest one…is that the Cartesians now know where the Triad lives. We're going to have major issues with them even getting out of their own home and moving about to search for the missing Originals. Now that the Cartesians know where they are, they'll never give them a moment's peace."

"Talking about Originals," Vanessa said. "I don't know if either of you have heard yet, but we lost five more humans earlier in Slidell."

Arabella plopped down on a kitchen chair. "I hadn't heard."

"Yep," Vanessa said. "Word got to me pretty quickly from Trishmia, one of the sisters from the Circle who lives in Mississippi. Police are all over it. From what I understand, there was a Nosferatu and two Loup-Garous. How or why they didn't kill each other first, I've no idea. But they did get the humans."

"Damn," Taka said.

"Please mind the cursing," Arabella said.

"I didn't curse," Taka said. "'Damn' is just a word. A figure of speech. Anyway, so what do we do now? The Cartesians know where the Triad lives. The Originals are out killing humans. We tried Gunner's spell to bring back a missing Triad, and it didn't work. What now?"

Arabella put her elbows on the table and placed her head in her hands. After a moment or two, she rubbed her forehead and looked up. "I thought about calling everyone in the Circle of Sisters here for an emergency meeting. We may not have been able to get a spell to work since they are at such distances, but what if we got everyone together in one place and did the same spell, hands linked? You know—"

she looked at Taka "—the way we did when we did the come-hither spell with Gunner."

"It sounds like a great idea," Vanessa said. "I mean, we'll have to wait because some of them will be coming from other countries, but it might be worth a try. That would sure be a lot of power concentrated in one place."

Arabella let out a frustrated breath. "That's the problem. Concentrated in one place. If the Cartesians know where the Triad lives, and I call all of the Circle of Sisters to one place, we could be talking about the annihilation of an entire breed of witches. I just can't take that chance. They don't know what they'll be facing. We don't know if our spell will work. There's too much that I don't know that I fear to call and bring all of them here."

"Did Gunner say anything about getting Trey and Shandor involved in this?" Vanessa asked, her eyes growing dark.

"No," Arabella said. "He didn't mention either of them in regards to this."

"He didn't mention it to you," Taka said, "but he told me to stay away from Trey Cottle's apartment. Remember that time I went over to Trey's house, trying to find out where Gunner lived? Gunner told me over the phone to make sure to stay away from there. That's gotta be some kind of sign. And he did mention while we were at the Triad's that they weren't exactly the best of friends. Him, Cottle and Black, I mean. He likes to keep an eye on them, so he knows what they're up to. That's what he claimed, anyway."

"We already know that," Arabella said, "Trey Cottle is always up to something, and with Shandor, his brownnoser, always doing and saying whatever Cottle wants, it's no wonder Gunner always keeps an ear out for what they're up to. Maybe he's stopped more chaos from happening than we can even imagine."

"Maybe so, but if it was chaos he stopped, it had nothing to do with Cartesians, the missing Originals or the Triad. He's been useless," Vanessa said. "Why is he even bothering with looking for another spell? We have all of the spells ever known to the Circle of Sisters written down in three Grimoires. There isn't any reason why we can't get them from the Triad and go through them ourselves."

"Yes, there is," Arabella said. "They belong to the Triad, and it's their responsibility to find something that will work. You know how this works. I don't have to remind you. That's the way it's been designed since the 1500s. Working with the Grimoires is the sole responsibility of the Triad."

Just then they heard a knock on the front door. Arabella got up and looked through the peephole.

"It's Gunner."

"You sure it's not the cops?" Taka asked. "They could be hiding on either side of him, waiting for us to open the door so they can bust in. We've gotta hide. They're probably here because of those dead humans in Slidell!"

Arabella looked through the peephole again. "It's Gunner. And he's alone."

"Ah, your long-lost boyfriend," Vanessa said.

"Would you please stop saying that?" Arabella said in a stage whisper. She opened the door a couple of inches to verify that Gunner was alone, and then motioned him inside. Arabella couldn't help but notice how his blue eyes sparkled like the finest-cut sapphires when he caught sight of her.

He hurried inside, and Arabella closed the door and locked it behind him. "You have a lovely home," Gunner said, glancing around the foyer and into the kitchen. "Thank you for inviting me here."

"My pleasure," Arabella said. She lowered her eyes and felt her cheeks grow warm.

"Hey, we're over here," Taka said, waving a hand from the kitchen.

"Would you care for something to drink?" Arabella asked as she and Gunner headed for the kitchen. "Tea, maybe?"

"We're having coffee with a splash of Irish whiskey in it," Vanessa said. "How about some of that? That should get your guns moving."

Instead of taking offense to what she said, Gunner grinned and said, "I think I will join you in that drink. But just a half shot of whiskey, please."

Arabella motioned him to the last seat at the table, where they all sat.

"Have you any further news?" he asked, looking at Arabella.

"Vanessa told us when we got back that there've been more humans killed. This time in Slidell."

Gunner gawked at Vanessa. "How did they die?"

"A Nosferatu and two Loup-Garous, from what I was told. I didn't witness it, but the source is trustworthy," Vanessa said. When she said the word *trustworthy*, she gave him a small grimace as if not completely certain about her trustworthy source.

Gunner sighed. "You're in quite the predicament. Now that the Cartesians know where the Triad lives, it'll be all but impossible for them to go out and look for the missing Originals. They're going to have free rein over the humans around here. Many more are going to die."

"We know," Taka said. "We're not dummies."

Arabella scowled at Taka, silencing her with a look.

"What about you?" Arabella asked Gunner. "Did you find anything in your spell book?"

Gunner rubbed his chin and gave her a reluctant nod. "I did, but the spell is dangerous. It causes a person to move against his or her will. Not by following the sound of my voice because they want to, but because they have no choice."

"Well, then we should do that," Taka said. "No matter where Viv is. Just as long as we can get her back."

Gunner lowered his head for a moment, and then looked up at Taka. "I know how badly all of you want her back. The problem is, if Viv is hurt in any way, and I use this spell to force her to come here, she could die. It's dangerous."

"But we don't know if she's hurt," Vanessa said. "We don't know where she is."

"I have to think of the worst when using a spell like this," Gunner said. "It's the most responsible thing I can do. If she's hurt, and we force her here, she truly can die. She's not immortal. She's human, just as we all are. She can die."

"Then forget it," Arabella said. "I don't want to take that chance." Something in the pit of her stomach warned her to leave things alone, not to get involved in Gunner's spell, or they'd risk losing Viv forever.

"I don't understand why the come-hither spell didn't work," Gunner said.

"That's not all that didn't work," Arabella said. "I was told that Evee called on Moose, one of the dead Loup-Garous she was very familiar with, and one of Viv's Originals. Evee was able to connect with Moose, and at the same time, Gilly was to astral project to the sound of his voice so she'd be in the same location he was, seeing what he was seeing. But the message we got from Moose was so garbled, Gilly couldn't get a fix on his location."

"What did he say?" Gunner asked.

"Something about big heads, clowns and wheels," Arabella said. "Nothing that made sense. He just kept talking about the big clown heads and a devil head."

Gunner frowned. "That is perplexing. I can't think of any place around here that would have such things. No circus or carnival, nothing that he was referencing."

"We're left in the same predicament," Arabella said.

"Have the three of you, as the Elders of the Triad, tried a come-hither spell?" Gunner asked.

Arabella looked at Taka and Vanessa and wanted to slap her hand against her forehead. "No, we've not."

"That's the most brilliant idea we've heard yet," Taka said. "Why haven't we tried a come-hither spell on Viv? We know it. It's different than what you do, Gunner, but we're her Elders. Certainly she'd come to the sound of our voices if she can. And it wouldn't be forcing her to come if she was injured. It wouldn't be going against her will. She'd come because she could and wanted to."

"Then let's try it right now," Arabella said. "See if we can reach her."

"Can I help?" Gunner asked.

"You can help form the circle," Arabella said. "I'll do the call. Let's go into the sitting room, where we'll have more space."

Arabella led the way, followed by Taka, Vanessa and Gunner. When they stood in the middle of the sitting room, Taka, Vanessa and Gunner joined hands, forming a circle around Arabella.

"Now concentrate hard on Viv's face," Arabella said. "Concentrate on what she looked like the last time you saw her. Concentrate on her eyes, on all that she is."

Gunner, Taka and Vanessa closed their eyes, and soon they were swaying from side to side. Arabella held her arms up at her sides, hands open, palms up and said in a loud voice,

Come hither, Triad.
Your Elders call.
Let nothing cause you.
To stop or stall.
Come to us now.
One so tried and true.
Let not our voices hinder you.
Come hither, Triad.
Your Elders call.

No sooner than Arabella had finished the spell, a loud moan, like one from someone in severe pain, echoed through the house so loudly, it seemed to shake the walls and cause the floor to vibrate beneath their feet.

There was no question in Arabella's mind that they'd just heard Viv's voice. Everyone opened their eyes, and Arabella looked from one to the other. She felt her hands start to shake, her heart thudding painfully in her chest from fear.

"That was Viv," Arabella said. "She's injured. Somewhere. Seriously injured. And if we don't find her soon, she'll die."

"Then it's like we've been saying all along," Taka said. "Finding Viv has to be our top priority. I don't know how we're going to get past the Cartesians, but I'd rather die trying than not look for Viv at all."

"Agreed," Arabella said. She felt nauseous, having heard Viv's pain and knowing they'd have to tell Evee and Gilly.

"I'll help," Gunner said. "Just let me know what you need me to do."

"If you have a spell that can keep her alive," Arabella said, "use it. I'm afraid she doesn't have much time left."

Chapter 10

If he could've danced a jig without looking like a jackass in front of his army of Cartesians, he would have. He'd accomplished so much in such a short period of time. He managed to free the Nosferatu, all the while keeping his army from killing them. He wanted them alive so New Orleans would be filled with much chaos and death.

He'd done the same with the Loup-Garous. They certainly hadn't wasted any time attacking the humans. Such a sight to see. Large, wolf-like animals with claws and teeth made for shredding, tearing… and death. He loved watching each time an opportunity afforded itself.

He was aiming for the Chenilles next, when luck fell upon him, and he'd discovered where the Triad lived. Not only that, he'd actually captured one, it had been far easier than he'd expected. All he'd done was change the pitch of his voice to sound like one of the other Triad members, and Vivienne came running to her aide. One of his Cartesians simply scooped her up, as ordered, before she'd even had a chance to blink, much less yell for help or fight back.

It had taken every ounce of power he possessed to keep the Cartesian that had captured her from killing her. He wanted to use Vivienne François as bait. It would be too sweet to do away with the Triad as one unit, for all three of them together carried more power than just one alone. Vivienne had been a relatively easy catch. Why he hadn't thought of mimicking her sister's voice earlier was beyond him. It was something that he should have thought of from the very beginning. But his thoughts had been elsewhere— in growing his army to its present size. And his plan was to double it.

Unfortunately, in its enthusiasm, that Cartesian had injured her, as well. He could only hope she'd survive until he was able to get her two sisters, too. Then he would take them all and didn't care who died.

He had suspected that the sorcerer who was involved with them now would join their troupe. He was such a weak man, a sorcerer with few innate talents and little backbone. His spells were only as effective as the wind was in making leaves sway on trees.

He, on the other hand, had it all. The Loup-Garous

and Nosferatu he'd freed had already murdered five more humans from the last count, and there were more soon to follow. Feeding time was still hours away, but when that time came, and there was no Triad to manage them and corral them to the compound, they would find their own meal. That meant more human deaths, many more. They would be stacking the dead one atop the other in the morgues. They'd lose count of the number of deaths per day. All of it was exactly what he hoped for. What he wanted. What he needed.

Not only were the Nosferatu and the Loup-Garous feeding on humans, but he allowed a Cartesian to have one of the Originals and bring its power to him. He'd felt such a surge of power when he took the Original from his minion that he grew heady and drunk with its power.

And now that he had one of the Triad in his possession, hidden away, waiting for her sisters to find her, which would only be a matter of time, the strength growing inside him felt like he could take Mount Everest and toss it to one side with a hand slap.

His mental capacity felt just as strong. He felt as though he could call upon the water that filled the oceans and have it evaporate into the sky, killing every form of ocean life. As though he could cause, just with a thought, volcanoes to erupt and earthquakes to split entire states in half. Fire to consume large cities, where the blazes would be so intense, all the firefighters in the area would fail to extinguish it. And he wanted more. If one Original could make him feel this way, he could only imagine what it would be like to take all the Originals and the Triad. He'd be invincible. He'd finally get payback for all the many, many years he'd suffered. Having such great power would make it all worth while, and his eternity would finally be directed by his own hand.

But feeling one way about a task and having the ability to do it were two separate things. And he knew he needed the rest of Triad in order to accomplish all that he longed for.

Whenever he felt his power begin to wane, he gave his Cartesians the permission to kill one of the Nosferatu, a Loup-Garou or a wayward Chenille. There was a Chenille that had stood too close to the gates of St. Louis I Cemetery, far enough away from the Benders' stupid electronic canopy that it was no longer under its protection. That was a rare catch. So he kept his mind focused on simpler tasks.

It didn't make sense to fight for something that was so elusive, like confined Chenilles. He needed to keep it simple. What would the Chenilles do once he had all the Triad? When that happened, they'd be on their own, anyway, without a leader to protect them, feed them. In time, the electric dome that protected them would collapse, and they would free themselves, knocking through the gates of the cemetery and running through the city, looking for marrow to eat. They would be his for the taking.

He couldn't have been happier. His plan to capture Vivienne had gone better than he'd hoped. It had been so easy to mimic Evee's voice because she sounded, to his ear, like a little child calling, "Viv, I need your help. Please, I need your help!" And just as he'd suspected, Vivienne had taken off without a second thought to help her sister, and that's when he had one of his minions capture her.

The Benders were proving to be as useless as the sorcerer they'd added to their troupe. Yes, he had lost some of his Cartesians due to their stupid little toy wands. He was more than a little surprised during the last encounter he'd had with the Benders that one of the Triad had used a wand as effectively as any of the Benders since they'd arrived in the city.

But the toy didn't belong to her. Yet he still had to count on there being four, not three left to attack his army. But he didn't fear four any more than he did three. They could only push the Cartesians back into other dimensions for so long. If he allowed rift upon rift upon rift to open up into the sky, his Cartesians would annihilate anything and everything in their path. Which was not something he was ready to do just yet. He wanted to make his plan work. He had much left to do.

First, he needed the remaining Triad members, and not by a happenstance death either. He wanted them all fearful, he wanted them together, he wanted them as one, joining together, so that he would have their ultimate power. Even when the Triad members were children, their combined power was greater than any one witch, even the oldest in the Circle of Sisters. He knew this because he'd been there, watching, always watching them. That's the kind of power he wanted flowing through him.

The Originals that the Triad ancestors had created had many powers of their own, but that Triad would give him charge over the universe. Every element they were linked to, he'd possess: fire, water, earth... And with that power he'd be able to control air on his own and so many things on this earth that humans would fear him. They'd bow down to him.

With that kind of power, he could eliminate human interference. The president of the United States. The Vice President. Even in this small city, he'd take on the mayor, the city council, whatever it took to get them out of the way. In order to get down to the common man so there'd be no power left greater than his. No laws to fear but his own. No one left to bow to but him. Oh, how they'd fear his superiority.

That's what he was after. First this place, and then the world, and all on it would bow at his feet. Eventually, his army of Cartesians would be so large, he'd be able to manipulate the very universe itself. The placement of the stars and planets. The shadowing of the moon and sun. And he could make it all happen with nothing but a thought. All he needed was that supreme power. Oh, and he'd get it. Yes, indeed, he'd get it.

In the meantime, as his plan began to unfold, he allowed his Cartesians to pick from the netherworld. A fae here, a leprechaun there, a vampire, a werewolf, anything with an ounce of supernatural power.

He allowed them to take those, for they were nothing but baubles attached to a string of invaluable pearls. Baubles, yes, but each bauble added a dash of power here, a pinch there—small, but there nonetheless. They still added to his greatness, and he needed all of the strength he could get.

For, to master the universe, one needed to be the most powerful being alive. One needed to be a god.

Chapter 11

"We're going to have to figure out a way to split up," Gilly said. "I know we only have the Camaro, but I want to go and check the north compound. If Nikoli knows anything about Viv, that's where he'll be looking for her. One man covering five-hundred acres is a lot. If that's where he is, he's definitely going to need some help."

"We should know soon," Gavril said. "Nikoli should be here any moment. He's been summoned, which means, unless he's in dire straits, that he must show up."

"How long do we wait?" Gilly asked.

"If he's at the north compound as you think, I'd give him twenty minutes to a half hour to get here," Gavril said.

"That's a long time," Gilly said.

"Well, it's not like he can fly here," Evee said. "Give the man a break."

"Fine. Good. We'll give the man a break," Gilly said a hint of sarcasm in her voice. "Sorry, didn't mean to come across like a bitch. I just hate being trapped in here. Hate that the Cartesians know where we live. Our Originals have become secondary now. Viv is our priority, and above all else, we have to find her. And here we are stuck like geese in an oven."

"Would you mind going over to St. Louis I Cemetery with Lucien and check on my Chenilles, while I go to the compound and hunt for Viv? Make sure Nikoli's okay, too," Gilly asked Evee. "I know they're my responsibility, but I don't want to put you out in the open at the compound. You and Lucien can take the Camaro and check the cemetery. At least the car will offer some type of protection."

"Sure," Evee said. "But how are you and Gavril going to get to the compound? You can't do it on foot. That'll leave both of you too exposed."

"Hell, we could be too exposed by simply walking out the door," Gilly said. "But we've got to do something. I'm going stir crazy here. I can't just sit in here and do nothing."

"I agree," Evee said.

"We'll wait here for Nikoli," Gavril said. "Then wait for you to get back with the Camaro. Once you return it, we'll take the car to the dock and put it on the ferry. That should minimize our exposure.

We'll figure out the rest once we've made it to the compound."

"There's nothing to figure out," Gilly said. "It's easy. Viv keeps an old blue pickup truck hidden in a grove of oak trees and willows. It's almost impossible to see unless you know where to look for it. If Nikoli or Viv haven't taken it, we can use the truck to get to the compound. Viv always kept a spare truck key under the driver's side visor."

"I guess that's the part we'll have to figure out," Gavril said. "Whether the truck's there or not."

"I'm hoping it is, then hoping it's not," Gilly said. "The truck, I mean. If it's not there, then that means Viv's taken it, which means she's got to be somewhere on the compound. Oh, and remember, Viv's got ranch hands out on the southern end of the compound. They take care of the cattle that go through the feeding shoot, so make sure when we go out there, we don't get them involved in any way. We stay in the north compound. That's five-hundred acres. A lot of land to look for Viv. The other part of it is if the truck is there, Viv either decided to investigate the compound on foot, or…she's not there."

"Maybe Nikoli will have some good news for us," Gavril said. "We can only keep our fingers crossed."

"It all sounds like a decent plan," Lucien said. "If it works out in that order. You know how often we've been surprised by the Cartesians, so watch your back when you're at the compound, cuz."

"Always," Gavril said with a short nod.

Lucien turned to Evee. "I'll get the Camaro and

pull it up to the front door. Evee, you keep an eye out for me at the side windows by the door. When you see me pull up, unless I signal you otherwise, just come running out and jump into the car. I'll have the passenger door open and waiting for you. We'll hurry over to the cemetery, check on the Chenilles, then get back here, so Gavril and Gilly can use the car to get to the ferry."

"I'm with you," Evee said.

When Evee and Lucien took off for the cemetery, Gilly went to the fridge and made a couple of ham sandwiches. She handed one to Gavril. "It's not much, but I have no idea when we'll get another chance to eat."

"Thanks," he said, and then he wolfed down the sandwich in four bites.

"Want another?"

"If you don't mind," Gavril said. "I don't mean to sound like a pig, but I didn't have breakfast or lunch today. Didn't realize how hungry I was until I all but swallowed that ham sandwich whole."

"No problem," Gilly said.

She was in the middle of making Gavril two more sandwiches, when she heard a knock on the front door.

Gilly and Gavril exchanged glances, and then Gilly went to the front door with him in tow. She looked through the security peephole and was surprised to see Trey Cottle and Shandor Black standing on the other side of the door.

"What the hell do they want?"

"Who is it?" Gavril asked.

"Cottle and Black. The other two sorcerers who live in New Orleans. They own a law firm off of Canal. I don't trust either of them, though. Neither do my sisters or the Elders."

"Then don't let them in."

Gilly chewed on a fingernail for a few seconds. "I have to. I don't know how, but they might have news about the Originals."

Having said that, Gilly yanked the door open. "May I help you?" she asked, her voice hard and not the least bit welcoming.

Trey smiled, and Shandor nodded his head like a manipulated marionette.

"Come in," Gilly said, not out of kindness but because she didn't want to leave the door open and take the chance that a Cartesian might see her and attack.

Trey and Shandor walked into the house. Gilly left them standing in the foyer, not offering them a seat in the kitchen or sitting room.

"How may I help you gentlemen?" she asked.

"We're looking for Gunner," Trey said. "Word has it that he was over here helping you with a spell or something. We thought we might be able to help."

"What word?" Gilly asked. "Who told you he was here?"

"Oh, just word," Trey said. "We were supposed to meet with him for a game of poker, then dinner, but he never showed. We went over to his apartment, and he wasn't there."

"So what? Some homeless guy off the street sent you this way?"

Trey laughed, a phlegm-filled, gurgling sound. "Of course not. If I'm not mistaken, it may have been one of his neighbors or someone in the Quarter. I can't recall at the moment."

"Yeah, right," Gilly said.

"As I said," Trey said, looking a bit hurt and forlorn, all of it an act, that Gilly knew for sure,

"We've come all this way to offer our help. I'm not completely sure what the problem is, but you have our help if needed."

"There is nothing that we need from you, Trey or Shandor," Gilly said.

"So Gunner was here?" Trey said.

"What if he was? What business is that of yours?"

"I was only asking. You know, with everything that's been going on in the city. I don't know if you've heard or not, but there was a group of people in a bar down on Bourbon. Some of the Originals got to them. The Loup-Garous killed ten to twelve people. The police are all over the place. I thought if Gunner was out here trying to give you a hand, you might need some backup. It's ugly out there now, but it's going to get a hell of a lot worse. If that many people were killed right on Bourbon, can you imagine how many more might be killed in the surrounding suburbs, where there's not so much action and noise?"

"What a minute. What's this about the cops? How would they tie us to the Originals?" Gilly asked. "We've never let it out to the public that we were

Triad, nor that we were responsible for the Originals, nor that the Originals even existed. We've kept that very hush-hush for generations."

"Oh, well," Trey said, shrugging his shoulders slightly, "word does get around."

"Hold on," Gilly said, fury boiling in her veins. "Did you tell them we took care of the Originals?"

Trey sighed. "Well, you know, when the police asked me, I couldn't exactly lie. That would have implicated me in the situation."

"Why, you son of a bitch! You put me in danger, along with my sisters and the Elders. We have enough problems to deal with. And now we have to worry about the police coming and banging on our door, asking about the humans that were taken by the Nosferatu or the Loup-Garous, or whichever one of the Originals killed those people? We don't even know where the Originals are. What kind of sick asshole are you?"

"We could tell you," Shandor said. "We can tell you. We could tell you because we saw them at the bar. We saw the carnage at the bar. There was blood everywhere. They ripped those people up. The bodies were ripped to shreds. It was really bad, wasn't it, Trey?"

"Shut up," Trey said to Shandor, "until you can talk like you've got some sense."

"Do you mind if we have a seat?" Trey asked Gilly.

"Yes, I do mind," Gilly said. She had to work hard to stay focused, her mind wandering and heart hurting over the humans who'd been killed. "I'd prefer that you not be here at all. If your mouth is big enough to tell the police that we're caretakers for the Originals, especially the ones who murdered those people in the bar, I don't want to have anything to do with you. I've always known you were not to be trusted. And Shandor, my feelings for you are exactly the same. You keep your nose stuck so far up Trey's ass, I don't know how you breathe."

Shandor looked down at the floor, his pale cheeks turning dark pink.

Trey balled his hands into fists and held them at his side.

It was then that Gavril appeared alongside Gilly. "Gentlemen, the lady's asked you to leave. She's been quite clear that she doesn't need or want your help. I would take her advice and leave immediately."

"What do you have to do with any of this?" Trey asked. "You're not a sorcerer or a witch. This is between us and the people who live in this city. I'm concerned about them. I don't know what Gunner did to try to help, but evidently it didn't work, which makes sense because Gunner, in and of himself, is relatively useless. He's too weak."

"And you think you can make things better?" Gavril said with a sneer. "From the looks of things, the only thing you make better is trouble. You and Shandor think you can simply walk in here and make the whole ugliness of this disappear."

"Oh, I know I can," Trey said. "I'm quite confident of it."

"Well, I don't care what you're confident in," Gilly said. "I don't want anything to do with you. The farther you are away from us, the better. I don't want you at this house ever again."

"I'll be glad to come and be a spokesperson for Trey if you'd like," Shandor said.

"I said shut up, Shandor," Trey demanded. "I'm the one with the power here. If you need to call the Originals back, then you need me. If you need to find your sister, you need me. Shandor alone, much less Gunner, is useless."

Gilly held up a hand and felt her heart start beating triple time. "Wait a damn minute. How did you know one of my sisters was missing?"

Trey lifted a brow. "Word gets around, little girl. I told you that once before. There's not much that gets by me. Ever. I always keep my ear to the ground. There's a lot that goes on in this city, and it's my responsibility to stay on top of it. I have to know what's going on at all times so that we're always protected."

Gilly glared at him. "Since you know one of my sisters is missing, do you know where she is?"

Trey shrugged. "Maybe. Maybe not."

"What are you talking about? What's with this maybe, maybe not bull. You either do or you don't."

Gavril suddenly grabbed Trey by the lapels of his jacket. "You need to listen up, little man. If you know where Vivienne François is and don't tell us right this minute, I'll send you flying across the lawn so fast, you won't know what hit you. I'll make sure your head hits concrete so it splatters like a water balloon."

"If you're smart, you'll take your hands off of me," Trey said to Gavril. "You forget. I'm a sorcerer. You're just a commoner." And with that, Trey waved a hand, and Gavril's hands suddenly released Trey's lapel, and his arms fell limp at his side.

Gavril looked over at Gilly, dumbstruck.

"You think you've come over here to save the day," Trey said to Gavril, "but all you've done is stir up more trouble."

"That's right," Shandor said. "That's right. More trouble. All trouble. Look at all the humans that are dead and all of the Originals that are missing. You caused the trouble. You are the trouble."

"Shut up, Shandor," Trey said, his voice harsh. "You're just talking to hear yourself talk."

Shandor lowered his head.

Trey gave Gilly a stern look. "Now you either want my help or you don't."

Gilly stepped closer to Trey, until she was almost nose to nose with him. "I asked you a question. I don't want an ambiguous answer. Do you know where my sister is?"

"And my answer, once again, is the same. Maybe, maybe not," Trey said.

"I don't understand what you mean by that," Gilly said.

"If I issue a spell to find her, we will find her," Trey said. "But you have to be willing to accept my help."

"Mine, too," Shandor said. "Because I'm with Trey, so mine, too. I can do spells, too. I can do a lot of spells."

Trey gave Shandor a hard look that made the sorcerer quickly shut his mouth.

"I don't know what you and the elders have been trying but it's obviously been useless. Things have gotten far worse. Because I am always alert, always aware of what goes on around me, I have the spells that are needed to bring back the Originals and find your sister. I can make all this ugliness disappear."

Something in Gilly's gut began to churn and made her nauseous. "You're lying, Trey. I wouldn't believe you if you were standing right next to Buddha and introduced him for who he was. You're conniving. You're a liar, and you always do things in your own best interest."

"So you're going to stand there and tell me that you're just going to deny our help? You're going to leave your sister alone to die?" Trey asked.

Goose bumps spread up Gilly's arms. "What do you mean, to die? You said you may or may not know where she is. Is she ill? Has she been hurt?"

"Maybe, maybe not," Trey said again.

Gilly let out a small growl. "I want you out of here. I can't take this anymore. You're driving me insane. I don't want to get caught in your trap, owing you for anything. You're nothing but a snake. So take yourself, Mr. Snake, and get the hell out of this house. You're not needed or wanted. If you know where Viv is, then get her and bring her home. And do it simply from the kindness of your heart, Trey. If you have a heart, which I seriously doubt, because if you'd really cared about my sister and knew where she was, that's what you would've done in the first place, brought her home. As for Gunner, you already know where he is. There's nothing here that you've questioned me about that you didn't already know the answer to. That's why I don't trust a thing you say, and I have nothing more to say to you. Now either step back and step out or we'll see whose spell works better. Yours or mine, when I turn your face into a goat's."

Gilly opened the door and ushered them out quickly. "I don't ever want to see the two of you back here again. Understand? No matter what information you think you have, the things you don't have are integrity, truth or hope. So get your asses back to the snake pits they came from."

And with that, Gilly slammed the door in their faces.

Then she turned to Gavril and laid her head on his chest, exhausted.

After a moment, she lifted her head and said to him, "I'm scared. Suppose Cottle was right. Suppose Viv is in serious danger, near death even."

"I'm with you on not trusting that dude," Gavril said, holding her close. "I think ninety percent of him is bullshit."

"But what if—"

"Shhh, baby, no worries. I promise you that we'll find Viv if it's the last thing I do on this earth."

Chapter 12

As they sat in the kitchen waiting for Lucien and Evee to return with the car, Gavril said, "Remind me next time never to piss you off." He gave her a half-hearted grin. "You handled those bastards, Cottle and Black, just right. I was thoroughly impressed."

"You were, huh?"

"Heck, yeah. You blasted them with words, which was the way to go. Me? I'd have knocked Cottle's front teeth out. No worries about Black. That form of dentistry would have sent him running home to mama or daddy."

"You've got that pegged right. Black is Cottle's yes man, no man, anything-you-want man. You saw the two of them in action. At any time, did you see

Cottle allow Black to take charge of the conversation?"

Gavril chuckled. "Take charge? Black could barely get a cohesive sentence out."

"Exactly. I've heard Black talk before in a different venue, and he's articulate enough, but when Cottle's got him shaking in his boots, his brain seems to revert back to a nine-year-old's."

"Have they always been that way?"

Gilly nodded. "As long as I've known them, which, unfortunately, has been most of my life. For the most part, we've stayed out of one another's business. Everyone in town, witch or human, knows that Cottle is a slimebucket. How he keeps clients is beyond me. Well, no, rephrase. He uses spells to generate clients. Definitely not his Humpty-Dumpty looks or charming personality. Pretty pathetic when the only clients you can get are the ones you conjure up, forcing them to you."

"To overcome looks and lack of charm, he must have to go through the entire day spouting spells."

"Wouldn't surprise me," Gilly said. "I just hate that those sons of bitches even had the nerve to come over here, acting like they wanted to help. Cottle does that 'I'm innocent' look so well, and, of course, Shandor follows suite. A leader like Cottle always has a follower. It makes their balls grow."

"Not to question what you did, but are you sure that they really can't offer you some kind of help?" Gavril asked. "I mean, I trust you implicitly. I don't know these men at all."

"You can trust that there is something in this that they're after, and they're going to do whatever it takes to get it. I don't have the slightest idea what it is. But whenever Cottle is after something, it usually has money or power tied to it. They're not out to help us. They could care less about saving anyone but themselves."

"How could anyone stand doing business with a guy like that, human or otherwise?"

"Like I said," Gilly said. "The only thing he could use to have anyone tolerate him are spells. Desire spells, hope spells, desperation spells. You name it, I'm sure he's got a bag full of them."

"Then why doesn't he use them on you?" Gavril asked. "Make you want him to help?"

"Because we're witches. The spell would wind up bouncing back on him."

"Does he hide the fact that he's a sorcerer to humans the way you do about being a witch?"

"As far as I know, yes."

"Then why in the hell would he talk to the cops about you? Wouldn't that lead them right to him, being a sorcerer and all?"

"Because, in truth, he's a greedy, manipulative dumbass who oftentimes doesn't think past his nose. Believe me, I'm not going to be surprised if the police suddenly show up here looking for us because Trey pointed them in our direction. I can't believe he told the cops where we lived, all the while knowing that could implicate him, as well."

"Then we need to get out of here and not give the police the chance to find you."

"But how do we get out of here?" Gilly asked. "Evee and Lucien still have the car. The only other way for us to make it to the docks is on foot."

"I don't want to take that chance with you," Gavril said.

"We'd be safe enough, I think," Gilly said. "You've seen me use a scabior before. You wouldn't be taking a chance with me, because I can fight Cartesians right alongside you. I'm pretty good at it, if I say so myself. Not as good as you, Lucien or Nikoli, but good enough." Gavril's eyes suddenly went wide.

"What's wrong?" Gilly asked.

"You just reminded me about Nikoli. He should have been here by now."

They stood up simultaneously, both fidgeting nervously.

"Why do you think he isn't here yet?" Gilly asked. "Do you think… Could he be in trouble?" She grabbed Gavril by the arms, barely able to put her hands around his huge biceps. She squeezed his arms. "Could he be where Viv is? Could he be trapped? In trouble?"

"I don't have the slightest idea, because I don't know where Viv is." Gavril swiped a hand through his hair. "This is getting weirder by the minute."

"Doesn't Nikoli have a watch like you? You know, the one with the GPS thing on it that lets him locate you?"

"Not if he's been stripped of it. Then he'd have

no idea we're trying to contact him, and he'd have no way to let us know where he is."

Gilly swiped a hand over her face. "Gavril, we've got to find them. We can't leave anything to chance. Someone somewhere knows where they are. But who?"

"I have no idea. And, yeah, I know about Nikoli. For him not to show up is a pretty serious matter. It's a code of honor thing with Benders. A code of ethics. When a Bender, especially two of us, me and Lucien, contacted Nikoli, he should have dropped what he was doing and come to us right away. The only reason he wouldn't is if he was in danger himself, and that's what I'm afraid of."

"So how in the hell do we get to the docks?" Gilly asked. "That's the most logical place for us to start looking for him and Viv."

"Unfortunately, I think you're right. I don't know what's taking Lucien and Evee so long, but we can't wait here any longer," Gavril said. "Especially with Nikoli not responding. And now we have the police to worry about."

"I'll be right there with you," Gilly said. "And I think, if we run headlong into some Cartesians, all you have to do is charge Ronan's scabior, and I'll use it and fight with you side-by-side. Cartesians or not, we'll get to the ferry and cross over. That's the only logical place that they could be. It's a lot of land, a lot to cover. We can't take a vehicle into the feeding area, anyway, because it's thick with trees and brush. No vehicle has ever gone past the front gate.

Viv used her truck just to check the perimeter of the acreage, make sure the fencing was secure. At least the tree coverage in the feeding area, if that's where they are, will give them some kind of protection."

"I don't want you using the scabior again," Gavril said. "I still can't believe you yanked the second one out of my hand."

"But I got the Cartesian, right?"

Gavril's brow knitted together.

"Come on, you've got to at least give me that. I got the Cartesian without your or Lucien's help, right?"

"Yeah, okay, I'll give you that. But that doesn't mean it'll happen again."

"Just give me a chance," Gilly pleaded. "I've done it once. I can easily do it again. I've got a great aim. Look, I can't just sit in this house. Not with Trey having alerted the police. I'll either have to face the police or a Cartesian. I'd rather it be a Cartesian. At least I can do something about one. If the police catch me, they can hold me for questioning for hours."

"True," Gavril said, worry etched on his face.

"All we have to do is get through the Garden District, grab the trolley, take it to the Riverwalk, then we'll only be a couple hundred feet from the ferry."

"I don't want to take that chance with you," Gavril said, suddenly pulling her close. He held the back of her head, pressed a hand at the small of her back. "Don't you understand?" he whispered. "I don't want to be without you. I can't lose you and can't take the chance that something might happen to you. I can't chance that a Cartesian might get you, even a trainee with a scabior. And now we have Cottle and Shandor on our ass, and the police. God, what do we do if we see the police while trying to make the ferry? If they see us while we're out there running to the ferry like we've got something to hide—because we do have something to hide—"

"For universal sake," Gilly said, "for all we know, they could have wanted posters out for me by now." She wanted to say much more, to let him know she couldn't live without him either. But she held her tongue, fearing the Triad curse would bring those words to naught.

"You're right about the questioning part," Gavril said. "Only you'd probably be manhandled and put under arrest if for nothing but questioning. They'd probably put you in a holding cell until they were good and ready to interrogate you. You know how the cops are around here. Act now, question later. We simply have to figure out a different way."

Gilly pushed away from him. "Then the only other choice we have is using the Camaro as soon as Evee and Lucien get back. Can you at least try contacting Lucien with your GPS, find out if they're okay, if they're on their way back? They were just going to do a head count and make sure those Chenilles were still protected."

Gavril did as she asked, pressing buttons and knobs on his watch. Then they waited, holding their breath, listening for the slightest sound.

Gilly's ferret, Elvis, came into the room and slithered between and around her legs. She shooed him away. "I want you upstairs. I don't want you to be in the middle of this. You can't follow me."

"But you mustn't go," Elvis said. "It's dangerous in more ways than one. You're an idiot for even considering half of what you're thinking of doing."

Although Gilly knew that Gavril couldn't understand what Elvis' squawks and squeaks really meant, she had to talk to her familiar and convince him to stay, even if it meant Gavril thought her to be crazier than a loon.

"I'm going to be fine," Gilly said to Elvis. "Remain here with the other familiars, and that's an order. I'll be safe. I promise I'll come back to you."

"You can promise all you want," Elvis said. "But you can't control everything. Suppose whatever has Viv in danger gets a hold of you. Then what? You still going to fulfill your promise to return?"

"Now you're just being a smartass."

"At least it's better than being a dumbass," Elvis said. He looked at Gavril, and his beady eyes grew darker. Then he slowly turned about and took off for the stairs, squeaking and chittering the entire way up.

"That was your familiar, wasn't it?" Gavril asked.

"Yes."

"And you talk to him that way? I mean, in English, and he understands what you're saying?"

"Of course."

"Those funny noises he makes, I take it you understand what he's saying to you?"

"Yes. To me, those sounds are as easy to understand as English. The only ones who can understand the familiars are their mistresses and the Elders."

"What does he think about all of this?" Gavril asked.

"He doesn't want me to go, of course. He thinks I'm stupid for attempting it and wants me to stay here and out of danger."

Just then Gilly heard the sound of squealing tires coming from the front of the house. Gavril must have heard it, too, because they both took off for the front door at the same time.

Before they reached it, Evee burst through the front door, her face white and eyes large. Lucien was right behind her.

"What's wrong? Are you okay?" Evee asked Gilly.

"I'm fine. But you look anything but. What's wrong?" Gilly asked.

"When Lucien's beeper thingy went off, I thought you were in danger…and that was after we discovered that all of the Chenilles are gone."

"What?" Gilly said, taking a step back. "What do you mean, they're gone? Did you check the old tombstones? The open grave slots?"

Evee nodded. "We checked everywhere. Not one Chenille in sight. The electronic dome that had been set up in the cemetery to protect them was dead. Nothing. No power."

Gilly began to pace, feeling like she might lose her balance at any moment. Panic and fear were inching their way up to her heart by way of her spine.

"I don't know what we're going to do," Evee said.

"We can't find them all, Gilly. We have no more Nosferatu, no more Loup-Garous and, now, no more Chenilles. They're all gone, and only the universe knows where they are. When it comes to feeding time, every human on the street will be in danger unless we do something."

Gilly took a deep breath, holding back tears. "The most important thing we have to do first and foremost is find Viv. I hate to say it, but the humans in the city and the suburbs surrounding it are going to have to fend for themselves. Viv is our priority. She's part of us, Evee. Like a kidney, heart and lungs make a body function. As a Triad and sisters, without Viv, we're only two-thirds of a whole."

Evee stood silent, tears streaming down her face.

To stop her tears, Gilly decided to give her news that she knew would piss her off. "By the way, Trey Cottle and Shandor Black came here while y'all were gone."

Evee wiped the tears from her cheeks, and her eyes grew fierce. "What the hell were Trey and Shandor doing here?"

Gilly gave her sister and Lucien the rundown of their confrontation with Cottle and Black. "The police could show up here at any time. We have to stay away from them, as well, or we'll get locked up for hours under questioning. Right now, Gavril and I will take the Camaro over to the docks so we can head to the north compound."

"We can come with you," Evee said. "We can help you look."

"What I want you to do," Gilly said, "is to go into the workshop behind the house where all of our crystals and herbs are. See if you can put something together with the herbs and crystals that might help. Whether or not you find something, the two of you hunker down there. If you hear anyone knocking on the door, don't answer it. The workshop isn't in view from the front or sides of the house, so no one will know to look for it. Stay there until we get back."

"But—" Evee said, her face drawn.

"It's like you told me earlier," Gilly said to her. "I don't want to lose you either, Evee. Gavril and I will take care of the north compound. I will come back for you, whether I have Viv or not. If I don't, we'll figure out what to do from there."

Evee nodded reluctantly. "I'm sorry about your Chenilles. I know what it feels like to lose your entire brood."

Gilly closed her eyes for a second, envisioning her Chenilles, and felt the hole in her heart from their loss grow wider. She shook her head to clear her thoughts. "Viv first, okay?"

Evee nodded. "Viv first."

"Nikoli, too," Gavril said.

"What do you mean?" Lucien asked.

"We signaled for him, but he never showed."

"He never showed?" Gavril said. "That can only mean one thing."

Lucien's expression grew hard. "He's in danger. I wonder if he's with Viv. Maybe they're in the same place."

"Evee, take Lucien to the workshop. Check your Grimoire. See if there's anything in there we might have missed. We've been focused on spells, but maybe there's an herb-crystal combination that might be effective. Gavril and I will head to the docks. We'll find them. Viv and Nikoli. We'll find them. I'll get back to you as quickly as I can."

"Promise?" Evee said.

"I promise, sister, with all of my heart. I will get back to you. And somehow, someway, the three of us will be together again. You, me and Viv. It's the way it's supposed to be. I still feel her life force, which is a positive thing. And I promise you'll always feel mine."

Chapter 13

The ferry seemed to move slower than ever before. Gilly grew so frustrated, she told Gavril she had to keep herself from jumping into the river and swimming to the other side. She felt she would have gotten there faster.

When they finally made it across the river to Algiers, Gavril parked the Camaro behind some brush and went hunting for Viv's blue truck. Gilly was right behind him.

"It's here," Gilly said, her voice low and trembling. She pointed to a grove of oak and willow trees about two-hundred feet away. The look she gave Gavril tore a hole in his heart.

"If her truck is here," Gilly said, "chances are she isn't. Nikoli either. She would have taken it to the compound. If it's still there, that means there's a good chance she never made it here. She'd not stupid. Viv would have never tried going out that far on foot."

"Nikoli either. I'm not ready to jump to conclusions, though," Gavril said. "Both could have left the truck to keep from drawing attention to themselves and simply dodged in and around trees to get to the feeding area. Nikoli would have chosen that way for sure."

Gavril jumped into the blue truck, and Gilly scrambled onto the bench seat beside him.

"Keys?" Gavril asked.

"Check the visor," Gilly said. "She usually kept an extra set there."

Gavril pulled down the driver's side visor and a set of keys dropped into his lap. "Good call."

With that, he shoved the key into the ignition, revved up the engine and drove as quickly as he could down a dirt path that sat beneath a huge canopy of large oak trees.

When they reached a fork in the road, Gilly pointed right. "That way."

Gavril had to slow the truck down due to an overgrowth of trees. Their thick, long branches scraped, scratched and screeched against the roof of the truck. Dusk was setting in, and with the heavy foliage, which darkened things even more, he had a hard time staying in the center, on the dirt road.

He didn't want to turn the truck lights on for fear of being noticed. Gilly had mentioned the ranch hands that lived on the south side of the compound and how she didn't want to get them involved. If they noticed headlights bouncing around back here, one or more of them might be tempted to come out this way and make sure it wasn't someone who shouldn't be there.

They finally reached a clearing.

"Stop the truck here," Gilly said. "The inside of the compound is worse than what we just drove through."

"Crap."

"There is no vehicle access in the compound. Viv used the truck only around the perimeter to maintain the fencing. If we're going to go into those five-hundred acres, we're going to have to walk it."

"And leave you exposed to the Cartesians? No way," Gavril said. "You know how I feel about that. Scabior or not."

"Well, I guess you'd better charge the other scabior and let me hang on to it, because it'll be the only chance I have if we run into any of those ugly bastards," Gilly said. "Especially if they show up in bulk."

Gavril shook his head. He was about to say something, but Gilly beat him to the punch.

"You know that I'm right," she said. "You've seen me use it. I'm good with it, almost as good as you."

Gavril sat in silence for a moment. He then finally blew out a breath and got out of the truck. Gilly followed him.

He took the second scabior out from behind his back, where he'd tucked it into his jeans. With one last look at Gilly, he flicked his wrist, then twirled the scabior between his fingers lightning fast, which charged it. He handed the scabior to her. "You know, you've got to be one of the most hardheaded women I've ever known."

"And that's why you love me the way you do, isn't it?"

Gavril looked at her, felt his expression soften, his heart wanting. He opened his mouth to affirm her statement, but then thought better of it. He didn't want to share his whole heart with her now. Not when they were in the middle of hunting for Nikoli and Viv. It felt like the wrong time and the wrong place to bring up such matters.

"Keep your eyes on the sky and be careful with the scabior," Gavril said. "We're going to have to call out for Viv and Nikoli, which means nothing is going to be quiet about this. Call Viv as loud as you can. I'll call for Nikoli, but we're going to stick together through this."

"But we can cover more ground if we separate," Gilly said.

"We're not separating," Gavril said sternly. "Period. We'll start at the west side and work our way east until we get back to the truck. If they're not here, we head back to the ferry. We can't afford to keep running in circles, staying out in the open this way. We're taking a big chance as it is, tree coverage or not."

"Agreed," Gilly said. She opened the large gates

as she'd seen Viv do a hundred times, and they stepped inside the compound.

Gilly held out the scabior, kept an eye on the skies and started calling for her sister. "Vivienne! Viv! Answer me!"

At the same time, Gavril shouted for Nikoli. "Answer me, Nikoli. Where are you?" Every couple hundred feet they walked, Gilly would call out for her sister, and Gavril for his cousin.

The only response either of them received was the sound of leaves rustling in the trees. The whine of insects. The croak of frogs. No howling from any Loup Garou, no human answer to be had.

They walked for what seemed like hours before they finally made it to the back of the compound and started heading east.

Suddenly, Gilly said, "Up there, look!" She pointed to a rift opening up in the sky and a second one below it. A third one suddenly appeared on top of the first.

"You aim for the one at the bottom," Gavril said. "I'll get the one in the middle and the one at the top."

The second the Cartesian laid a claw outside of the bottom rift, the maw not yet having opened wide enough for it to stick out its grotesque head, Gilly aimed her scabior at the third rift and shot. It pushed the Cartesian back, but didn't close the rift.

All the while, Gavril aimed his scabior for the middle Cartesian, and then the one above it.

Miraculously, they closed all three rifts in less than ten minutes.

"That was too quick," Gavril said. "Not one of them put up a fight or tried to push out of the rift."

"What do you mean?" Gilly asked.

"I don't know. Something just doesn't feel right. It's like they gave up too easily. Usually they struggle to get out, head, talons, leaning over the rift at the waist. Those three barely had their talons out and disappeared too quickly."

"But isn't that a good thing?" Gilly asked.

"Yes and no. It feels too much like a setup. They could be setting up for a takeover."

"A takeover? Of what? Who? Is it us? Are they trying to take us over? Is that their plan?"

"I think so. Like letting out ten to twenty Cartesians at once. We need to get out of here before we get slammed. Just in case."

Gavril took Gilly by the hand, and they took off at a run, still calling for Viv and Nikoli.

"Viv, where are you?" Gilly shouted. "We need you! Where are you?"

"Nikoli, answer me," Gavril yelled.

By the time they made it back to Viv's pickup truck, there were no other rifts that had opened up in the sky as Gavril had suspected.

Out of breath, Gavril opened the passenger door for Gilly, and once she was safely settled inside, he hurried to the driver's side and jumped behind the wheel of the truck.

Gilly handed Gavril the scabior she'd been using, and he disarmed it, as he did his own, and sheathed his and stuck the second in the back of his jeans.

Gavril started the engine, peeled out of the compound and headed down the dirt road again toward the dock.

Once they tucked the truck back under its haven of overgrown oaks and willows, Gilly leaned her head back against the seat, trying to catch her breath.

Gavril did the same. "I thought for sure the Cartesians were going to push back a second time," he said. "It just doesn't make sense. It's not like them to give up so easily."

"I'm just glad they did," Gilly said.

Gavril sat upright. "You know, I wonder if it may have had something to do with you."

"Me? Yeah, like I'm a big, bad Bender. How do you figure?"

"They're used to Benders fighting them, but never a Triad. Maybe that confused them."

"Well, if they're confused about me using a scabior, that's pretty dumb," Gilly said. "I might weigh a hundred fifteen pounds soaking wet, and they have to know that I don't have the experience with a scabior the way you do. So, you're right. It is weird that they didn't come back and try to attack us again."

"They are pretty dumb creatures. They follow the orders of a leader."

"Who's this leader? Have you ever tried to capture him? Kill him?"

"In all our travels, we've yet to figure that out. It doesn't show itself. Only allows its minions to do its dirty work. As for the Cartesians, sometimes it seems they get this leader's orders right, and other his back, scratched him, pulled him toward her and held him tight.

Gilly pulled his hair, pushed his head back, kissed his mouth, his chin and rode him even faster until he could stand it no more.

She lowered her head and bit into his shoulder hard once more, and then he heard her cry out, felt her contracting over her him again and again, and her orgasm spilling out of her, soaking him.

Gavril felt himself unable to control his body any longer, and he exploded inside of her, throbbing as if there were such a well of come inside him that could never be completely emptied.

As he felt his hardness continue to throb inside her, she sat up on him, and contracted around him, sucking him with her body, milking him dry.

Gavril knew this was exactly what Gilly wanted. The control. Wanted to own him for that moment. Wanted to own him every time she touched him. He knew this was her way of giving herself emotionally, fully to him during a time when most women would have been huddled in a heap in a corner, refusing to face the danger and problems muddying their lives.

The problem was she not only owned him now, she owned him for the rest of his life.

She just didn't know it yet.

times, it seems like they're simply winging it and screw up."

Gilly yawned. "Like I said...dumbasses."

Gavril grinned, watching Gilly's eyes slowly close.

"I don't think I've ever yelled so much or run so fast in my entire life," Gilly said, her voice growing hoarser the more she spoke.

Gavril locked the truck doors. "Come here," he said. He pulled her close to him, put her head on his shoulder and smoothed her short black hair with a hand, comforting her. He did this until he felt her breathing grow slower, easier, and then he leaned over and kissed the top of her head.

Then he kissed her again.

Suddenly, as if waking from a deep sleep, Gilly grabbed hold of Gavril's shirt, pulled him close and kissed him back on the lips with the same fervor she did everything. All or nothing. Fierce, hungry and determined.

Gavril couldn't help but react to her kiss, to her desire. They were here to hunt for Viv and Nikoli. Had Cartesians appear, and then suddenly disappear. How could his mind be on anything else?

Making love to Gilly was an experience he'd never known with any other woman. There was no mandatory cuddling. Tender moments were short. A touch on the cheek, a kiss on the lips, but even those wound up becoming hungry and fierce. She emptied his mind of everything but her, which only served to fill his heart all the more.

As if to prove the point he was thinking, Gilly put her mouth on his neck and bit down, tasting the essence of him. He did the same to her, nipping at her neck softly, and then harder, until she groaned with desire.

Then, just as fast as they'd run the last half of the compound, they began to rip off clothing. He couldn't get to her skin fast enough.

In a matter of seconds, he had her breasts in his hands, her nipples in his mouth, sucking, rolling his tongue over them, so hungry for them. She had her hands wrapped in his hair, pulling him closer. He kissed her, sucked on her, flicked her nipples with his tongue until she moaned and cried out.

"More, goddammit, more!"

Suddenly, without any indication from him, Gilly quickly unbuttoned, and then unzipped her trousers and slid them off along with her bikini panties. Then she turned to undo his pants, his belt and zipper.

Gavril took hold of her hand, moved it away from his pants and unfastened them himself.

He was hard, had been hard since the first time they'd kissed.

"Gavril…" Gilly uttered his name hoarsely, and before Gavril knew it, Gilly maneuvered herself from the passenger seat and straddled him. She lowered herself onto him until the tip of his hardness touched her wet opening.

So much heat emanated from her, it felt like a furnace. That alone had Gavril biting the inside of his cheek to keep from coming right then and there.

Gilly lowered herself slowly, slowly. An i[nch] and half an inch more, teasing him. The ex[pression] on her face was one of determination and [de]sire. Her eyes never left his.

Then, without warning, Gilly slammed h[erself] down the length of him. She took his fac[e in her] hands and kissed him with all the ferocity [she] had as she rode him up and down…up…do[wn.]

Because of their position, and closenes[s to the] steering wheel, as much as Gavril wanted t[o match] her move for move, he had a hard time doin[g so.]

Somehow, though, he knew that was exact[ly what] Gilly wanted. He knew her well enough to kn[ow that] if she'd needed it any other way, she would h[ave po]sitioned it so. But she rode him hard, wantin[g more,] and before long, Gilly bit into Gavril's shoul[der,] then threw her head back and howled as he[r body] shuddered with a powerful orgasm. She con[tracted] against him over and over, and he could feel h[er wet]ness leaking down the length of him.

The power of her orgasm had been so stro[ng,] Gavril thought it had satiated her. He couldn['t have] been more wrong.

Gilly continued to ride him like she was a [starv]ing woman without enough to eat. He allowed [her to] pummel him, and he tried matching her move[ments,] albeit slightly because of his position.

He wanted to turn his leg sideways so t[hat he] could penetrate deeper, but when he attempted [to do] so, she bit into his neck, stuck her fingernail[s]

Chapter 14

"Did you find anything?" Gilly asked Evee when she and Gavril returned home.

"Nothing that even came close to a come-hither spell," Evee said. "I've been through the Grimoire twice, felt through the crystals and herbs. Nothing."

Gilly leaned against Gavril, not concerned about letting her attention to him show in front of Evee or Lucien. She already knew those two were a couple. Despite the warnings the Triad had been given by the Elders to stay away from the Benders in order to stay safe, Gilly didn't feel one ounce of guilt for having been with Gavril. She'd been close to him body and mind, and the soul part was growing closer every day.

As they sat around the dining room table, Gilly

gave Evee and Lucien the run down on what had occurred— except for the sex—while they hunted the compound.

"The place is so deserted, it's creepy," Gilly said. "I've never seen it that way before. I mean, I've never been inside the compound because of the Loup-Garous, but inside or out, you barely heard bugs chittering. It was as if the universe had simply deserted the place as part of the planet. Like it no longer existed. Just dirt and trees."

"That's how I felt while going over the Grimoire, crystals and herbs," Evee said. "It felt like something was blocking me from seeing something that should have been right in my face."

"Is there anything else we can try?" Gavril said.

"It doesn't make sense for us to go out hunting for the Originals right now," Lucien said. "Viv and Nikoli trump the Originals by far."

Gilly nodded.

"What if I try connecting with another dead Original, someone other than Moose?" Evee said. "Then, if we get a decent connection, you can astral project and see things from their eyes."

"I'm open to anything," Gilly said, "but who do we summon this time? Who can you picture well enough in your mind's eye to summon them, attempt to communicate with them?"

"Maybe Chank," Evee said. "You know, the Nosferatu that Pierre had to put down. I remember what he looked like because of his red hair when he was human."

Gilly frowned. "I don't know. Chank was a bit like Moose—a bit wobbly in the brain. How about if we try to connect with Pierre? He was sharp, responsible."

"Yes, but if he's not dead, there's no way I can connect with him," Evee said.

"Let's try him, anyway. If he doesn't come through, we'll work on Chank," Gilly said.

Evee nodded. "I'll channel anyone to get Viv back."

"Great," Gilly said and got up from the table. "Let's go into the sitting room, where we'll have more room to form a circle."

Evee, Lucien and Gavril followed Gilly, and when they reached the center of the sitting room, they held hands as they had done before, leaving Evee in the middle to call upon the Nosferatu.

"Instead of just focusing on them and repeating what you see or hear, try a spell to go along with it," Gilly said. "Maybe that'll throw more power at it."

Evee sighed, closed her eyes and spread her arms out wide, while the three remaining encircled her.

Come hither, mine Nosferatu.
Your mistress calls.
Pierre, tune thine ear.
To mine voice; that is all.
If death has claimed thee.
Rise above its chains.
Open thine eyes and speak to me.

Everyone held their breath, waiting and watching Evee as she stood stock still, her arms still outstretched. After a moment or two, she opened her eyes. "Pierre must still be alive. I hear and see nothing from him."

"Try Moose again with a spell. That might help him speak more clearly," Gilly said.

Evee pursed her lips, looking unsure. Then she closed her eyes and lifted her head slightly.

Come hither, Moose.
With clear head and mind.
Tell me, show me.
What I seek to find.
Let thine words be strong.
And they direction true.
Show me now that I may follow you.

With her eyes still closed, Evee cocked her head to one side as if to listen more closely. Blindly, she held out a hand in Gilly's direction, and her sister immediately broke the circle and held Evee's hand.

"A lot of water all around," Evee said. "Tall building. Giant heads with bright colors. Clowns, devils, animals. The heads don't move. The heads don't talk. They're simply there."

Holding tightly to Evee's hand, Gilly closed her eyes and followed the sound of her sister's voice with her mind's eye. She felt her body lighten as if it was filled with air instead of blood and bone. Soon she found herself standing near the shore of the Mississippi River, overlooking it. Nothing in sight but water and faraway bridges.

The sound of Evee's voice made her want to turn around and face the opposite direction, but for some odd reason, she wasn't able to move. Gilly knew in her heart of hearts that if she could only turn around, they'd have the answer to where Viv was. But her feet felt sealed in concrete, her body stiffened by rods of steel, her head like that of a concrete statue. She felt molded, held, imprisoned in place. She strained to hear sound, anything that might give some indication as to what lay behind her. All she heard, however, was the lapping of water as it hit the shore. Seagulls cawing.

Then, from somewhere far away, she heard a tapping sound, like someone knocking on a door. It came from behind her, though, and no matter how hard she struggled, she couldn't turn around to investigate what might have been making the sound.

Frustrated, she let go of Evee's hand and opened her eyes.

Evee's eyes were already open.

"I saw water," Gilly said. "It was the Mississippi River—I know that for sure. But all I heard were seagulls, the lapping of water and a tapping sound like someone knocking on a door."

"Could you make out where the tapping was coming from?" Gavril asked.

"No. I was frigging stuck in place. Really stuck. I couldn't twist my body around, not even my head."

"I didn't get much more than the first time," Evee said. "He kept talking about big heads with a lot of color. Clown heads, devil heads, animal heads. He did mention the water, though, which is what you picked up on, I guess. I don't know why you couldn't see the rest of what he was talking about."

Gilly started pacing the sitting room, thought about Trey Cottle and Shandor Black. "Because some son of a bitch doesn't want you to get too clear a picture by words and doesn't want me to see it at all."

"You're talking about Cottle and Black, aren't you?" Lucien said.

"Damn right I am," Gilly said. "We pissed them off by denying their help, so they're going to make it as hard as they can for us to do this on our own. They *want* us to call them for help." Gilly kicked the leg of a chair. "I'll lay eggs before that happens!"

"Can they actually stop you from seeing when you astral project? Or keep Evee from hearing clearly when she contacts Moose?" Gavril said.

"With the right spell, and Cottle knows plenty, they can do just about anything. I'd bet anything that they're involved in this."

"Can't you do a protective spell or some kind of binding spell to keep them from affecting you?" Gavril asked.

"Of course we can," Gilly said. "But it would be like children shooting at each other with water guns. We do a binding spell or protection spell, they'll come up with something stronger to make our lives and our efforts more difficult."

"Even if they don't know you're putting a spell on them to stop their antics?" Lucien asked.

"That's right," Gilly said. She saw the question still in Lucien's eyes. "Look, I'll show you."

I bind thee now.
Enemy of mine.
Powerless unto your kind.
Powerless unto mine.
So—

Gilly felt her lips still moving but heard no words coming from her mouth.

"Why didn't you finish it?" Gavril asked.

"Because they shut me down before I could finish," Gilly said, satisfied that she'd proven her point.

"Holy crap," Lucien said.

"Can they hear everything you say?" Gavril asked.

"Only spells directed at them. Then again, where Cottle is concerned, it's hard to tell. He may have a spell that allows him to eavesdrop on us from anywhere."

Evee shook her head, rubbing her temples with the tips of her fingers. "We need help, Gilly. Big-time. I just don't know where to get it."

"Since we're dealing with the sorcerers, I think we need to get the Elders involved again," Gilly said. "Arabella was the one so set on getting Gunner involved in this mess. Maybe he let something slip to Cottle or Black. Maybe that's what led them here. I mean, I seriously doubt they pulled it out of their ass. Visiting us, I mean."

"Didn't they claim they heard word on the street about all those humans dying on Bourbon, and that's what sent them here?" Evee said.

"Yeah, but when have you ever known Cottle to tell the truth?"

Evee shrugged. "Problem is, I don't deal with him enough to know when he's lying either. We confirmed the deaths, so that's a given. It's the part about him and Black coming here that's the question. It makes more sense to me that those two would have been celebrating all the chaos we're dealing with instead of offering to help."

"My point exactly."

Gilly looked at Gavril for confirmation.

Gavril frowned. "All I know is what I saw when he was here. In that brief visit, I wouldn't trust the guy with his own mother. But I could be wrong. This witch-sorcerer animosity has gone on for generations, from what you told me. If that's the case, then the cards do seem stacked against them."

"I think getting the Elders here is a good idea," Lucien said. "Maybe they can help with your mediumship, Evee, and Gilly with your astral projection. I don't think the sorcerers would think the Elders would get involved at this point, unless Gunner told them different, so having them here helping might just take them by surprise."

"It might be easier for us to go to them," Evee said. "You know how long it takes the Elders to get dressed just to go to the supermarket."

"Yeah, but if we go to them, we could very well be leading the Cartesians to them, as well," Gilly said. "At least we can bring them here in the Camaro, then get them back. The entire time the Cartesians will know we're here. They wouldn't have a reason to track the Elders. Not now, anyway. I'm sure once we're out of the way, they'll be the next target, but until then, we should try to keep them as safe as possible."

"I don't know," Evee said. "The Cartesians have sprung more than one surprise on us. I'd hate to see any of the Elders taken. Even if we bring them here, what's to keep the Cartesians from following the Camaro back to their house and seeing where they live?"

"Because the Cartesians are single-minded," Gavril said. "If their leader wants them to get the Triad, that's where their focus is going to be twenty-four-seven, especially now that they know where you live."

"That's why we bring the Elders here," Lucien said. "If we all piled into the car and headed to the Elders, the Cartesians might follow simply because you're in the car."

Gilly let out a long, frustrated breath.

"What keeps them from breaking into our home?" Evee asked. "If they know we're in here, why don't they just crash the place and take us?"

"Remember, they only come out of their rifts up to the waist," Gavril said. "I'm not sure what would happen if one fell out and wound up on the ground in full sight. Rumor has it, and those rumors come from other Benders, that they'd lose some of their strength because their legs can't hold the bulk of their bodies and heads."

"Well, that's pretty friggin' stupid," Gilly said. "Whoever created those creatures sure didn't think past his ass if he or she created the Cartesians to be limited to the waist."

Lucien shrugged. "Stupid, sure, but it's in our favor. Can you imagine what would happen if they were able to fully drop out of those rifts and start chasing whatever or whomever they were after?"

"True," Gilly said.

"Who exactly created the Cartesians?" Evee asked.

"From what we've been told," Gavril said, "one man was turned into a Cartesian for having defiled a witch's secret meeting. Once it turned, from what I understand, anyway, it figured out that killing anything from the netherworld gave it more power and allowed it to create more Cartesians."

"How?" Gilly asked.

Gavril shrugged. "Stories vary too much on that account. I really don't know. I haven't seen it happen. Something about the power a Cartesian brings to its leader strengthens the leader, and it is able to birth another Cartesian due to that additional power."

"You mean birth, as in a baby?" Evee asked.

"Birth as in waving a hand and another Cartesian appears—at least, that's the best I can put together from the stories I've heard," Gavril said. "No Bender has actually seen it happen, so we're all working on hearsay."

Gilly frowned. "So are Cartesians kind of like the

Originals, only they have to eat from the netherworld in order to survive?"

"Yes," Lucien said. "But before they can consume it, they must bring the essence of that netherworld creature to the leader so it can drain it of its power. Then the Cartesian is allowed to feed on the rest of it."

Gilly started pacing the sitting room again. "In order to destroy the Cartesians and be done with them, we have to get to the leader."

"You're absolutely right," Gavril said. "The only problem is, no Bender has been able to detect where it hides. Its minions do the work. The leader only oversees their work, but from where, we don't have a clue."

Gilly suddenly stopped dead in her tracks and looked at Evee. "We've wasted a few Cartesians since the Benders have been here. I don't know what happens to them when they're pushed back to other dimensions, but what if you try to communicate with one, and I'll astral project to where its voice is coming from?"

"Absolutely not!" Gavril said. "I don't know what happens to the Cartesians that are pushed back to far dimensions, but I do know, if you attempt to astral project to whatever one you wind up communicating with, you'll get stuck in that dimension, as well. And we wouldn't have a clue as to how to get you back or if we could ever get you back. Out of the question."

"What about if I just try to communicate with

one," Evee said, "and Gilly doesn't astral project? Would that be safe enough?"

Lucien chewed his lower lip and threw a glance Gavril's way. "I honestly don't know. I would think communicating with them wouldn't put you in harm's way, but the problem is, no one has ever tried it. Suppose you do wind up communicating with one, and someone, while you're talking with it, winds up pulling you into the dimension it's stuck in."

"Since you're not a hundred-percent sure," Evee said, "I'd take the chance. Especially if it can identify the Cartesians' leader."

"That's going to be the key," Gavril said. "*If* it identifies the leader. For all we know, all Cartesians could have sworn some kind of destructive oath never to reveal who their leader is."

"Another thing," Gilly said. "I've never heard a Cartesian talk. They only make growling, grunting, howling sounds. How would you understand what any one of them would be saying, Evee?"

"Just a feeling," Evee said. "Their grunting and growling is their language. I might be able to interpret it. I might not. But don't you think it's at least worth a try?"

"Not if it puts you in danger," Gilly said. "If you start communicating with one and you suddenly start disappearing piece by piece into some other dimension, what am I supposed to do? Tackle you?"

Evee rubbed a hand across her forehead, and then suddenly looked up. "Hey, what if I try to communicate with one and use an illusion spell? That way, they'll see multiple images of me and not know which one to go after."

Gilly stared at her, contemplating. She had to admit, her sister could be right. "That might work, but we need a fallback position if it doesn't and they wind up with the real you."

"Oh, that's easy," Evee said. "I can have all the images of me speaking at the same time, while the real me is hiding away somewhere. Either upstairs or in a closet. They'd be expecting me to be one of my illusions that's standing out in the open."

Lucien glanced at Gavril, who looked at Evee and then Gilly.

"Could that really work?" Lucien asked. "Would that help keep Evee out of danger?"

Gilly squinted her eyes, thinking the plan through. Finally she nodded. "I think it has some potential. We have a lot to gain by finding out who the leader is, but I have more to lose if something happens to my sister. So all I ask is that Lucien and Gavril be on standby with their scabiors. Since we're only going to be dealing with a voice and not a body, I'd say, aim an ear for their voice if one happens to come upon the real Evee."

"No problem," Gavril said.

"You've got it," Lucien agreed.

"Wait," Gilly said suddenly. "Before we attempt this, I think we need to get the Elders here. If we're going to do this, find their leader, I mean, then we should gather all the power we can to make it happen."

"Good idea," Evee said.

"I'll contact them," Gilly said. "Lucien, would you mind going to the Elders, picking them up, bring them here?"

"Not at all, if you think it will help."

"I'm not sure of anything," Gilly said. "Only that, the more power we can throw at this, the better."

Chapter 15

A couple of hours later, when Lucien arrived with the Elders, they seemed harried and nervous as he all but shoved them through the front door.

"What's going on?" Arabella said. "Lucien came rushing over and said you needed us right away."

"We do," Gilly said.

"Yeah, Lucien came pounding on our door," Taka said. "We thought it was the cops at first. Arabella checked the peephole, saw it was Lucien and let him in. He all but grabbed us and shoved us into the car like we were convicts or something. Then, when we got here, he did the same thing."

"Sorry," Lucien said. "We've had some major issues with the Cartesians, and I didn't want any of you endangered in any way."

"Cartesians?" Vanessa asked. "Where?"

"Had I not rushed you into the Triad house as quickly as I did, you would have seen them overhead. They've figured out that the Triad lives here, and I think they're bound and determined to wait them out so they can catch them. Kill them."

Taka slapped a hand to her heart. "Why would they want to kill them?"

"Because they're Triad, and the Cartesians' leader wants their power, just like he wants the power from every Original. And I fear, once they've accomplished that, they'll come after the three of you, as well."

"Not if I've got anything to say about it," Taka said, hefting her purse so it hung in the crook of her arm. "How do we help?"

"We want to try something," Evee said. "I want to channel one of the Cartesians and see if we can find out who their leader is. It stays well hidden. No one, not even a Bender, has seen it. Maybe if I can connect with one of the Cartesians, I can get him to talk."

"That's dangerous territory," Arabella said. "You have no idea what kind of power they possess. Suppose you summon one and it suddenly drags you into the dimension where it's stuck?"

"We've thought of that," Evee said. "That's why we wanted you here. I'd like you to do a protection spell over us. Then we'll do an illusion spell. The Cartesian will hear me, but twenty or thirty of me, and won't know which is real. In the meantime, I'll be hiding in the closet beneath the stairs."

Taka blew out a breath. "I don't know. You're talking about some dangerous crap here. We can't afford to lose you, too."

"Talking about being lost, have the three of you tried to contact one of the Originals to see if they have any idea where Viv might be?" Arabella asked.

Evee nodded. "Twice. The first was Moose, one of Viv's Loup-Garous, and the second was Chank, one of my Nosferatu."

"And?"

"They're communicating back with me, but what they're saying makes no sense."

"Like what?" Vanessa said.

Everyone had been standing in the sitting room as if on high alert. Evee motioned for them to have a seat.

Once everyone was settled, Evee stayed standing and said, "Moose keeps talking about big heads, clown heads, devil heads and bright colors. Chank keeps talking about water and big heads."

Arabella frowned. "Instead of going for a Chenille first, let's circle and see if we can get Moose or Chank again. Maybe one of us can make sense out of what they're saying."

Evee shrugged. "I'm game for anything where Viv's concerned."

Everyone stood back up and held hands, forming a circle around Evee.

Evee held out her arms as before; only this time, Arabella did the incantation.

Come hither, Moose.

With clear head and mind.
Tell me, show me.
What I seek to find.
Let thine words be strong.
Thy direction clear.
Show me now if Viv's far or near.

As Evee kept her arms stretched out, her eyes rolled up in her head and a male voice came from her mouth.

"She is far, but not too far. She is where the big heads live. The clowns, the devils, the animals. So many colors, it hurts your eyes."

"What else do you see?" Arabella demanded.

"Large, huge boxes with wheels. And blood. I see lots of blood."

"That's the clearest he's been," Gilly whispered. "Keep him talking. I'm going to astral project to him, to where he's seeing all of this."

Arabella nodded but didn't take her eyes off Evee. "What else, Moose? What else is there?"

"Things that make music, but the music isn't playing. The music is dead."

"Is Viv dead?" Arabella asked, her voice trembling.

"Not yet, but not long now. They got her. The bad man got her."

"What bad man?"

"The one with the black fur. The big head with the black fur. Bad, evil eyes, bigger than saucers. He caught her. Hid her."

"Where did he hide her, Moose?" Arabella asked.

"With the big heads."

"Where are the big heads?"

"I don't know. Never been there. Never saw this place before."

Gilly had her eyes closed, concentrating on every word Moose spoke. Images started flashing in her mind's eye. Row after row after row of large papier-mâché heads. Clowns, demons, jesters, princesses, dragons, trailers with ten-foot walls on each side.

"Mardi Gras!" Gilly suddenly shouted.

Evee's eyes rolled back into place, and she lowered her arms.

Everyone turned to look at Gilly.

"Moose is talking about Mardi Gras. I saw the scenes, just like they were in a parade," Gilly said excitedly.

"But Mardi Gras is months away," Taka said. "That can't be it. Maybe it's a circus. I don't know of any going on in town, but maybe nearby. We could check. Look it up online."

"Computer's down," Gilly said. "But it sounds like he was talking about something bigger than a circus. It sounded like Mardi Gras. Where do they store the floats when it's off-season?" Gilly asked.

Evee, Arabella, Taka and Vanessa looked at each other, and then all four of them shrugged.

"We've no idea," Arabella said.

"Who would know?" Gilly asked.

"Someone on the city council, probably," Arabella said.

"Fine." Gilly headed for a house phone, and then

turned on her heels. "Sorry, ladies. I just remembered, it's past five. The City Council building closes at four."

"What about the police department?" Taka said.

"Well, that's a bird in a bush if I ever heard of one," Arabella said.

"Huh?"

"We could call the police to find out where they keep the Mardi Gras floats stored, but they've been beating our door down, trying to get to us," Arabella said. "Bad call."

"Then who?" Taka asked. "How about the Office of Tourism? I bet they'd know. Or we could Goggle it."

"Google," Vanessa said.

"Can't," Evee said. "Computer crashed two months ago. Tourism sounds like a good idea, though."

Arabella suddenly lifted a brow. "I bet Gunner would know."

"Whoa," Evee and Gilly said simultaneously. "No sorcerers."

Arabella looked deflated. "What now? He's helped us in the past."

"That may be," Gilly said, "but it could have been a setup."

"What are you talking about?" Arabella asked.

Gilly filled her in on Trey and Shandor's visit to their home and how secretive they'd been about who told them where they lived.

"The only one I can think of who knew and would have told them is Gunner."

"No way he would have done that," Arabella said adamantly. "He knows Cottle and Black are snakes in the grass. There's no way he would have given out that information."

"Then who did?" Gilly asked.

"For heaven's sake, child, remember who they are," Arabella said. "Cottle and Black are sorcerers. It would have been easy for them to get a handle on your location."

Everyone stood silent for a moment.

"Fine," Gilly suddenly said angrily. "Call your boyfriend, Gunner. If that's the only option we have to find out where this Mardi Gras warehouse is, we'll just have to take our chances."

"He's not my boyfriend," Arabella insisted.

"Yeah, okay, whatever," Gilly said. "The house phone's in the kitchen. You can call him from there."

As Arabella hurried off to make her call, Evee shook her head and began to pace. "I think getting Gunner involved is a big mistake. He did help us before, sure, but it's like you said, Gilly—it could have been to use us for info." Her voice shook with worry.

"The two of you need to breathe for a moment," Gavril said. "If anything goes south with this Gunner dude, Lucien and me will take care of him."

"But he's a sorcerer," Evee said to Lucien. "You're not."

"He might be a sorcerer," Lucien said, "but he's twice my age and moves slower. Before he gets any mumbo jumbo curse out of his mouth, I'll have smashed his teeth in. End of story."

"To hell with 'end of story,'" Gavril said. "Not until I knock his balls up into his belly button."

Gilly grinned at Evee. There was enough testosterone flying around the room to rebuild a third man. She felt something warm growing in her stomach, over her heart, as she watched Gavril—his protectiveness, his strength and determination. As hard as she'd tried to keep herself for the sake of the disasters she and her sisters faced, just looking at Gavril always managed to soften her insides and quiet her mind.

Arabella came into the sitting room.

"Any luck?"

"Yes," Arabella said, eyes shining. "I told you Gunner was a good guy and just wanted to help us. The Mardi Gras warehouse is a giant metal building just off the New Orleans pier."

Gavril whistled through his teeth. "Good distance away."

"Doesn't matter if it's in Nebraska. We've gotta go find her," Gilly said.

"What about the leader?" Gavril asked. "Remember the reason you wanted the Elders here in the first place?"

"But Viv's our priority," Gilly said. "We can deal with the leader crap later."

"But what if he sends his entire troupe to follow you to the warehouse? At least if we know what we're looking for, we can take him out and kill two birds with one stone."

"Fine, fine," Gilly said impatiently. She turned to

Arabella. "We're trying to reach one of the Cartesians. I can't astral project because I don't know if it'll have the power to pull me into another dimension. So to protect Evee while she channels one, we wanted your help with a protection spell, then an illusion spell. Like she said earlier. She'll be hiding in the crawl space beneath the stairs."

"Then let's get to it," Arabella said. "Join hands—everyone except Evee. You're in the middle of the circle, like before."

As everyone stood and held hands, encircling Evee, Arabella said,

Oh, enemy mine.
Keep thy anger at bay.
And leave us here.
Among thine fray.
Thy shall not touch.
A person here.
But shall run instead.
In voluminous fear.

Arabella nodded, and Evee began her chant.

Come hither now,
Enemy of mine.
Tell me words.
That have kept me blind.

A booming male voice suddenly came from Evee's mouth.

"What do you want from me, you slimy bitch?"

"In what dimension do you reside?" Evee asked.

"None of your business."

"I demand that you tell me by the will and power

of all the elementals on this earth. In what dimension do you reside?"

"S-sixth. Happy now, bitch witch? If you want to talk to me, keep your childish spells to yourself."

"I will do as I please, for it is I who commands you now," Evee said.

A loud, bellowing laugh filled the room.

"You control no one," the voice said. "You can't even control your own. You're a weakling, and you're attempting to play games with one who will be master of the universe."

Evee frowned but kept her eyes closed. "And would that be you? The one who will master the universe?"

"No, you imbecile. The master will soon have enough power to take over this planet you call earth and the entire universe that surrounds it."

"And just who is this master of yours."

"None of your damn business."

Evee pursed her lips for a moment. "If it's none of my business, then why are you making it my business? Why are you after my sisters and me?"

"Are you that dense, witch? Because my master desires your powers. All three of you. Why do you think we've been wasting so much time on the Originals, on the lower echelon, like vampires, elves and such? It's all for the master, and it all leads up to taking the three…well, actually, the six of you down."

"What do you mean six?"

"Well, we certainly can't leave your Elders out

of the mix," the voice said. "Wouldn't want them to feel neglected."

"You know, I'm tired of you blowing smoke up my ass," Evee said. "I already know who your master is."

Another boisterous, booming laugh. "And whom do you think it is, Miss Pollyanna?"

Evee held silent for a couple of seconds, letting her mind disconnect from the Cartesian. Then she blurted out, "Your leader is a sorcerer."

Silence filled the room. No booming laugh, no sarcastic remarks. Silence. This set every nerve in Gilly's body on edge.

After a moment or two, the voice said, "You think I'm that stupid that you can trick me by throwing out the first thing that comes to your mind?"

"Oh, it wasn't just something that first came to mind. I know it to be a fact," Evee said.

Gilly knew Evee's proclamation was a ruse but she kept silent.

A roar that sounded like the jet engine of a plane sounded throughout the house, shook the walls.

"Who is the one who told you?" the voice demanded.

"None of your damn business. All that matters is that I know."

Another moment of silence.

"And has your source identified which sorcerer?"

"Of course." Evee tilted her head, taunting it.

"Well, speak, woman!" the voice shouted. "Who is your source?"

"The man himself."

"What man?"

"Your master, ass-wipe."

Another thunder blast shook the walls of the house.

"You want to play games, little bitch witch, then let's play." At that, a crash sounded in the foyer, and long black talons reached through the broken window. Seconds later, another shattered, this one in the sitting room.

"Now," Arabella said.

Evee took off for the crawl space beneath the staircase, while Arabella shouted an illusion spell.

Double, thrice, by tens shall ye see.
No longer one to be seen by thee.
Thine eyes shall fully confuse thine mind.
Making all evil intentions blind.
Blunder thee blunder now.
I call upon thee Poseidon, Tiamat and Apsu.
To bring strength to my command.
So it is said.
So shall it be.

Gilly gritted her teeth as for more than a half hour, windows throughout the house shattered, and talons reached for an Evee they only perceived existed. Arabella's spell had copied Evee's likeness so it appeared that twenty Evees ran through the house, purposely moving from window to window.

When nearly every pane in the house had been destroyed, Arabella called back Evee's lookalikes, and almost immediately, the crashing, banging, howling and screeching stopped.

Gilly went to the storage cabinet beneath the stairs and found Evee inside, sitting with her legs drawn up to her chin and trembling.

"It looks like they've gone," Gilly said. She reached out and took Evee's hand, helping her out of the storage area. Seeing her visibly shaken, Gilly wrapped an arm around Evee and held her close. "We'll get through this, sis," Gilly whispered in Evee's ear. "I promise."

Everyone looked around at all of the broken glass strewn about the house.

"I'll have that taken care of right away," Lucien said. "I'll contact a repair company and throw them a little extra for emergency, after-hours service. Either way, you won't be without windows tonight."

"Th-Thank you," Evee said, her voice shaky.

"Well, the house might look like crap right now, but at least we found out something," Taka said. "Something to work with, anyway. The master of those hideous creatures is one of the sorcerers here in the city."

Arabella nodded. "You made a good choice twisting your words around, Evee. It finally got him to admit that the master was a sorcerer."

Gilly ran her hands through her hair, staring at all the broken glass in the sitting room, the foyer. "Yeah…but which sorcerer is it?"

Chapter 16

Taka yawned expansively. It seemed contagious, as Arabella immediately hid a small yawn behind her hand. Gilly understood their exhaustion. Everyone had been carrying a boatload of worry and running around the city looking for or protecting the Originals and fighting Cartesians.

"Lucien, would you mind bringing us home?" Arabella asked.

"But aren't you going to come and help us look for Viv?" Gilly asked.

"Of course we are, dear," Arabella said. "But we can't all fit into that Camaro."

"So how do we all get there?" Gilly asked.

"No worries," Arabella said. "I'll get us a ride, and we'll follow each other."

Gilly's eyes narrowed. "Where do you plan on getting this ride?"

"I'm going to call Gunner. He's got quite a fine vehicle. A Buick, I believe. Plenty of room. That way, if we do find Viv, and she is in dire straits, we can take her straight to the hospital."

"What do you mean, take her to a hospital?" Evee said. "We can heal her right then and there."

"That's right," Gilly said. "And you heard the whole thing that Evee was talking about when she connected with that Cartesian. One of the sorcerers is their leader. How do you know it's not Gunner?"

Arabella shrugged. "I don't know what else to tell you except that I just know. You're going to have to trust me on this one. I just know."

Lucien looked from Gilly to Evee, and then back to the Elders. "Of course I'll give you a ride home. But when you do get that ride, we'll follow each other closely so we can keep an eye on you. It's either that, or you stay here."

"Oh, we'll follow. Not to worry," Arabella said. "I have no idea how to get to the warehouse, anyway. I'm hoping that GPS thing you're wearing on your wrist will get us to the location as quickly as possible."

Lucien nodded. "You know the one thing we didn't ask about was Nikoli and where he might be."

"I have a feeling," Gilly said, "that wherever Viv is, Nikoli's with her." She prayed that was the case. The thought of her sister being alone and injured, seriously injured, made her nauseous. She'd give her life for either of her sisters.

"So, for all intents and purposes, they could both be hurt and in danger," Lucien said. "Suppose Nikoli is already dead? Why don't we try to contact him? Evee, can you do that?"

"Instead of wasting our time in attempting another connection that may or may not work, I say that we go to the warehouse and start searching," Arabella said. "We'll find out soon enough whether Nikoli is there and what condition he's in. First thing's first."

Arabella gave Taka and Vanessa a short nod, and then turned to Lucien. "If you don't mind, we should be leaving now."

Taka picked up her purse and held it close to her chest. "I'm ready."

"So am I," Vanessa said.

"I'm going with Lucien," Evee said.

"No," Lucien said. "You need to stay here, where it's safe."

"What's safe?" Evee said. "They've busted damn near every window in the house. If we can fit everybody in the Camaro, I'd want to take Gilly and Gavril with us, too. If I go with you, at least I can help keep an eye on the Elders, especially if they're going to contact Gunner. I can help with some kind of spell if need be."

"Let her come along," Arabella said. "I'll make sure no harm comes to her. She won't be in any danger."

Shaking his head, Lucien went to the front door, peered out to confirm that there were no rifts awaiting them. Evidently seeing that all was clear, he ran out to the Camaro that was parked in front of the house and opened all four doors. He then signaled for the Elders and Evee to hurry to the car.

When everybody was loaded into the car, Lucien slammed the doors shut, jumped into the driver's seat, turned the engine over and took off.

Lucien was headed for the Elders' home when Arabella said, "If you don't mind, Lucien, I need you to make a stop first before we go home."

Lucien looked at Arabella through his rearview mirror. She was sitting in the middle of the back seat. "And where would that stop be?" he asked.

"Trey Cottle's office."

Evee, who was riding shotgun in the front, swung around in her seat to face Arabella. "Are you freaking crazy? The Cartesian told us that their leader was a sorcerer. It's early enough in the evening that all three of them could be together."

"We don't know that for sure," Arabella said. "But I need to find out some information from Trey and find it out now if we're going to help Viv."

"And Nikoli," Lucien added. "This is against everything I believe in, every rule I've ever followed."

"What is?" Arabella asked.

"Sticking your head into the mouth of a lion before you have a surefire way of locking its jaws open."

"Trey doesn't have a lion," Taka said. "I know because I've been in his apartment. I'd have seen a lion if he would have had one. They're too big to hide."

Vanessa tsked. "That's not what he meant, Taka. He's not talking about a real lion."

"Then what is he talking about?"

"If you'd stop yammering about stupid stuff, you'd find out," Vanessa said, and then pursed her lips.

With a loud exhale, Lucien took a left on Iberville and headed toward Trey Cottle's office.

"I know this isn't something you'd do, Lucien," Arabella said. "You're just going to have to trust that we know what we're doing. Remember that we're witches. There are certain things we can see, know and do that you can't."

"It's not that I don't trust you," Lucien said. "I just don't want any harm to come to any of you, especially Evee. She's not going to get involved in this in any way."

"You're talking for me now?" Evee asked Lucien with a raised eyebrow.

"No, he's not," Arabella said. "He's talking for us. We wouldn't want you to be involved in this in any way. This is a job for me, Taka and Vanessa. It will be over quickly, but there's something that I need to confirm." When they arrived at Cottle's office, the office lights downstairs were off, but the apartment upstairs, were Cottle lived, as Taka pointed out, had the lights on.

After much shuffling of purses and squeezing through the opening of the car, Vanessa, Arabella and Taka got out of the Camaro. They looked up at the lighted windows. The alleyway gate leading to the stairs that reached Cottle's apartment was locked. Standing at the far side of the gate, Arabella caught sight of the three sorcerers sitting at a table near one of the lighted windows. It looked like they were playing some sort of card game.

"They're all together," Arabella said to Taka and Vanessa. She pointed to the window.

"So what do we do?" Taka asked.

"Get this over with," Arabella said firmly.

"But what do you plan to do or say?" Vanessa asked.

"I plan on finding out which one is the leader of the Cartesians," Arabella said.

"Have you lost your mind?" Vanessa said. "We have no more powers than they do. If one of them really is the leader of the Cartesians, what powers do we have to stop him from turning into one of those monstrosities and destroying all three of us? We'll be toast!"

Arabella looked from Taka to Vanessa solemnly. "I know this is dangerous. I'm well aware of that. But if we don't find out who the leader is, the whole world—the very universe—becomes his. I'm determined to figure out a way to stop him. For now, if one of them comes after us, no old-lady business. Get your running shoes on. If you're wearing heels, take them off and run barefoot. That's it. Be prepared to run if it comes down to it."

"I can barely walk up a flight of stairs without

limping," Vanessa whined. "How do you expect me to run away from something like that?"

"I just expect you to," Arabella said. "Now put your big-girl panties on, because we're going, and we're going in for blood, if it comes down to it."

By the light of a nearby street lamp, Arabella searched for a service bell or knocker that would notify Cottle he had company. She found nothing.

"If you're looking for a bell," Taka said, "he doesn't have one. The only way to get attention is like I did last time."

With that, Taka scooped up a handful of pebbles from the side of the street. She threw one at the window where they'd seen the three sorcerers. Instead of breaking the glass, Taka managed to get the pebble to simply ping against the glass.

The sound obviously caught Trey's attention, because within seconds, he was peering out of the window. He looked from side to side, spotted them, smiled, said something to the other two sorcerers, and then disappeared from the window.

Before long, his apartment door opened, and he headed down the stairs and over to the gate.

"How lovely to see you, ladies. Shandor, Gunner and I were just in the middle of a poker game. Would you care to join us?"

"We'll pass on the poker," Arabella said, "but we would like to speak to the three of you, if you don't mind."

"Of course," Trey said. "Please, do come in." He unlocked the gate, and then led them down the alley, up the stairs and into his apartment, where he motioned them to a small sitting room.

The room had a card table near the window, a shelf against one wall that was crammed with books of every genre imaginable and a fireplace against the opposite wall with ladder-back chairs flanking it. From the looks of the hearth and cleanliness of the bricks, Arabella had to assume it had never been used.

When Gunner and Shandor saw the three women enter the room, Gunner stood up.

"What a surprise," Gunner said, his eyes on Arabella. "How wonderful to see the three of you."

Shandor stayed seated, and Arabella caught him giving Trey a look that said, *What the hell are they doing here?* His face was pinched as always, his expression one of anger or confusion. Both emotions looked the same on his narrow face.

"We have a couple of questions to ask you gentlemen," Arabella said. "Please—" she motioned to Trey and Gunner "—have a seat. We won't be here long, and I'm sorry we interrupted your game."

"No, not at all. Please, you have a seat," Trey said. "Would you care for tea or coffee?"

"Nothing for me," Arabella said.

"I'll have some water, if you don't mind," Taka said.

Arabella elbowed Taka who quickly said, "Never mind about the water. I'm not really that thirsty. I just thought I was."

"I'm fine," Vanessa said. "Thank you."

Settling back at the card table, Trey asked, "How may we help you?"

Arabella cleared her throat. "We have it on good information that one of the sorcerers in New Orleans is the leader of the Cartesians."

Taka's and Vanessa's mouths fell open, as did Gunner's; all of them were obviously shocked by her abrupt revelation.

Shandor eyes shifted from Cottle to Gunner, and then back to the card table. He shoved his glasses farther up his nose.

As if they were talking about nothing more serious than the weather, Arabella continued in a calm voice. "Since the three of you are the only true sorcerers in the city, we'd like to know which of you happens to be their leader."

Trey let out a hearty, bellowing laugh. "I don't know who your sources are, but they're very, very wrong."

"I don't know," Arabella said. "Our source seemed extremely confident when relaying the information. Anyway, I just wanted to let you know, in case one of the three of you happens to be the Cartesians' leader, that you've already lost the fight. You're not going to control this world or this universe. It belongs to the humans and other beings who have purposely been placed here. You're not going to affect the weather or any of the elementals. In fact, you'll no longer get a taste of any more of the Originals."

Cottle fidgeted in his seat. Shandor kept his eyes on the playing table. Gunner looked up at Arabella.

"I have no idea what you're talking about," Gunner said.

"I know you know what the Cartesians are," Arabella said.

"Of course I do. We all do."

"Well, again, we have a source that has directed us to you. 'You' being one of the three of you, the leader of the Cartesians. The one who's murdered all of the humans by releasing the Originals. The one responsible for killing one of the Benders' cousins, the one responsible for causing our Triad to live in terror. I just want you to know that no matter which one of you it is, that it will be no more. The three of us are involved now."

"The three of you are old hags who don't know a spell big enough to get yourselves out of a paper bag," Trey said, his voice low and angry, his eyes suddenly ablaze with fury.

"You'd be surprised what we know. We're not like you. We don't throw our spells around just for any reason. They always have a purpose, and that purpose is always to help someone. When you utter spells for your own gain, Cottle, the universe has a way of throwing them back in your face, and not in a good way. So if any of you were planning to take over this world, forget it. We've got that covered."

"You don't have anything covered," Trey said. "You don't have the slightest idea what you're talking about. This source that you claimed gave you information was probably drunk or on drugs, and you were stupid enough to believe them."

"Oh, I don't think they were on drugs or drunk," Arabella said calmly.

"And what makes you so sure of that?" Trey asked.

Arabella cleared her throat again. "Because the source who gave us the information was a Cartesian."

Suddenly Trey jumped to his feet and held his hands out at his sides and balled them into fists. "That's not possible! It's not possible that a Cartesian would point a finger at its master. They are trained to serve, not to give out information. They are to receive it and comply. But never, ever to defile the name of its master."

"Really," Arabella said. "Then I think you'd better have a refresher course, Trey."

"Why are you directing that derogatory statement at me?" Trey demanded.

"Because I have a very strong feeling that the Cartesians' leader is you. There are three of us and one of you. You may have thousands of Cartesians at your beck and call, but all it will take to bring all of them down is chopping off the head of the dog. The rest of the body will die without it. As you know, we're from the Circle of Sisters. Within our group are thousands, which we'll call upon and have here to help our cause. To call the leader of the Cartesians out so it can be confronted and destroyed. We will capture your Cartesians. We will torture them, pummel them with questions, until they'll be begging to give us information."

Trey's body began to shake, slowly at first, and then harder, faster, as if he were having a seizure. He shook so hard, his glasses fell off his face, and his jowls jiggled like so much Jell-O.

With a look of shock on his face, Gunner got up from the card table and backed away from it. In that moment, Trey's head became five times the size of a normal man's, and it was instantly covered with black fur. His arms began to swell, until they were at least five to six times the circumference of a normal man's, and his fingers suddenly turned into talons, just like the Cartesians'.

"You will not interfere with any of my plans," the creature who once was Trey Cottle said. It's voice held a low, menacing growl. "You'll die here tonight, and no one will know any different. You are nothing. You are and have never been nothing. It's you and your own from generations ago that caused this to happen. That turned me into what I am. I will have my due. You turned me into this creature. I will take it back. I will use it to take back what should have been mine in the first place!"

The Trey-creature swiped a hand with its talons backward, seemingly ready to swing at Arabella. Instead it caught Shandor, who had scrambled out of his seat when he saw the transformation happening to Cottle and was standing beside him. Cottle's talons dug deep into Shandor's gut.

With a roar, the creature shook Shandor about like a ragdoll, evidently trying to free itself from the man's entrails. There was no question that Shandor was already dead.

"Run!" Gunner shouted at the Elders. "Run!"

The creature continued to roar, shaking, pushing, trying to free itself from Shandor. Its talons seemed to be cemented into the dead sorcerer.

The creature reached out for Arabella with his other hand, but the Elders were already ten steps ahead of him, followed closely by Gunner.

They flew out of Trey's apartment, ran down the back steps and through the alleyway.

"My car's parked around the corner," Gunner said.

By this time, Lucien was standing outside of the Camaro. "What the hell is going on?"

"Get to the warehouse," Arabella yelled toward him. "Hurry!"

The Elders followed Gunner to his Buick. He hit a key fob that unlocked all four doors, and the Elders jumped inside. Gunner hurried over to the driver's side, scrambled behind the wheel and keyed the engine to life.

As Gunner slammed his foot on the accelerator, Lucien revved up the Camaro and followed him until they got to a side street, where he could take the lead.

After taking a hard left on Bienville, Lucien floored the Camaro, and the Buick followed bumper close, both racing off at breakneck speeds.

Chapter 17

Gilly paced the floor from the kitchen, through the foyer, into the sitting room and back so many times that her feet hurt.

"This waiting is driving me crazy," she said to Gavril. "When are they going to be back?"

"They'll be back soon, I'm sure," Gavril said.

"Can you contact Lucien and find out if they're at least okay?"

"Of course." Gavril hit two buttons on the sides of his watch, and within a matter of seconds, there came a beeping noise.

"That indicates that he's fine," Gavril said. "I don't know how far away they are or where, but at least we know they're all right."

Gilly nodded, stared at the floor, still pacing.

"You know, if Viv and Nikoli are really hurt, we need to come up with something more than just a normal healing spell."

"Wouldn't taking them to a hospital be the best course of action?"

"I don't trust doctors and hospitals. We've always healed our own. I'm going to check my Grimoire to see if there's anything in there we can use that's more powerful than the standard healing spell."

"Don't you know that book cover to cover by now?" Gavril asked. "I remember you telling me that the three of you read yours every day."

"Reading it every day doesn't mean I can't re-check it," Gilly said. "Especially if I'm looking for one specific spell. It's a lot easier to go through it focused on finding one than it is reading each one, knowing that you're reading just to read. Make sense?"

"Totally."

Gilly took off for the stairs, and Gavril followed her. She turned when she got to the fourth step and looked back at him.

"Where are you going?" Gilly asked.

"Oh, I'm following you. I'm not leaving you alone in this house. Look at all the windows that are broken. Do you really think I would leave you in any room with Cartesians hanging around outside, just waiting to break through another window and snatch you at any moment? It's not going to happen."

"But no average human has ever seen our Grimoires," Gilly said. "It's not allowed."

"There are a lot of things that aren't allowed that I think we have allowed," Gavril said. "Besides, is that all I am to you? An average human?"

Gilly bit her lower lip and continued up the stairs, knowing that Gavril was right behind her. When she reached her bedroom, she went to her dresser and pulled open the bottom drawer. After moving aside shirts and lingerie, she pulled out a thick wood-covered book with an odd symbol on the front.

"What is that?" Gavril asked.

"It's an *absolutus infinitus*," Gilly said. "The symbol for eternity."

"Ah, I see now," he said as she held the cover up to him.

She nodded. "Triads have carried the symbol on their bodies since the 1500s. Mine's on my ankle." She twisted her foot to show Gavril and noticed that hers had turned from black to gray, just as Viv's and Evee's had after they'd been intimate with Nikoli and Lucien. Right now, she didn't care what color it was. She opened the book and gave the mirror inside the cover only the slightest glance. She didn't care that it still revealed only gray swirls.

Gilly sat on the edge of the bed and started flipping through the pages, and Gavril sat beside her, looking as she turned them. She went farther toward the back of the book, running a finger across faded words written in a language he didn't understand. The words had been written with what appeared to be a quill pen. Some of the letters were fading and had been retouched with a standard pen. Which made sense. If these books had been transferred from one generation to another, without a touch-up here and there, the words would have quickly become illegible.

"This is something that might work," Gilly said, tapping her finger on one page. She nodded, and then closed the Grimoire and laid it on her nightstand. "It just might work."

"What is it?"

"A different healing spell. One that I've never used before. Neither has Evee or Gilly to my knowledge. But there are a lot of spells in these books we've never used before. The one I just found for healing is different... I hope."

Gavril took her by the hand and pulled her up and close so that she stood between his legs. "I'll take care of you through this. You're not alone, Gilly. Neither are your sisters. Lucien and I are going to be right beside you. We'll find Viv and Nikoli, as well. If you can heal Viv, I trust that you can heal Nikoli."

Gilly looked down at him solemnly. "Unless he's dead. I can't bring back the dead."

"That's a given," Gavril said, "but I don't believe he is. I still feel him, the essence of him, if that makes any sense. If he was dead, I'd know it, just like I knew Ronan was gone when the Cartesian first slashed him. There's an empty spot that I carry in my heart because he's gone for good, but I don't have that same sensation when it comes to Nikoli." Gavril pulled Gilly closer, reached up and put a hand behind her head and kissed her. "We'll hope for the best, right? I don't want to do dead family again. Ronan was enough for a lifetime."

"For the best," she said. Then Gilly leaned into him, their mouths parted and their tongues touched ever so gently. Before she knew it, Gilly had pushed Gavril back onto the bed. She straddled him, kissing him as she always did with the ferocity of an animal that hadn't eaten in days. Starving for food, craving, always craving. She kissed him, and then lowered her lips to his throat, licked him, the essence of him—the scent of musk and male and fresh spring soap. As her lips moved over to his Adam's apple, she began to unbutton his shirt and lowered her mouth even farther. She pulled the shirt from the confines of his pants and pushed it away from his chest. She licked his nipples. First the left, which she teased and toyed with using her tongue; she scraped it with her teeth, and then slid her tongue across his chest to his right nipple and did the same. Only this time, she bit down a little harder.

She continued to lower her mouth down the ripples of his stomach muscles, and as she licked there, flicking her tongue and sucked on his skin, her hands began to work on his belt and the zipper of his pants. When both were undone, she tucked her hand inside of his pants and freed his hardness from its confines. Once she had him, she stroked him once, twice, three times. After the time it took for her mouth to travel south, she was able to take him into her mouth. The taste of him was exquisite. It was like tasting the essence of him, times a thousand. She wanted to consume him right then and there.

Gilly lowered her mouth, for even as big as he was, she wanted the entire length of him as far back in her throat as she could get it. She was only able to manage a little over half before her gag reflex kicked in. She tried to relax and take more of him. When she reached the deepest point, her mouth and throat would allow, Gilly raised her head, licking the head of his penis. Then, lowering her mouth again, she sucked on him. She used her right thumb and forefinger to circle the bottom of his cock that her mouth couldn't reach and stroked him.

While she licked, and then sucked on him hard, she heard Gavril groan and moan her name. "Gilly… Oh, Gilly…"

She didn't want to hear what he had to say, only wanted to feel him in her mouth. She wanted him to come inside her there so she tasted all of him, all of who he was and more. She kept her lips moving up and down, lower and higher, and then moved one of her hands up and across his stomach to his nipples, teasing first one, and then the other. She used a thumb and forefinger to pull them, flick them, rub them.

Then Gilly took the hand that had been stroking him and moved it lower until it covered his balls. She squeezed them gently, and then released. Squeezed. Released. Just as she felt them tighten in her hand, heard his breathing grow fast and shallow, Gavril suddenly grabbed Gilly by the shoulders and pulled her up.

Gilly had only a second to feel confusion when Gavril quickly flipped her over on the bed so she was beneath him. Gilly fought like a cat, wanting to be back in the same position he'd pulled her from. But he had her on the back, and he was too strong for her to flip over. "No... Gavril..."

Gavril held Gilly's hands over her head, pulled off her blouse and bra, so that her breasts were exposed, and this time he was the teaser. He ran his tongue over her left nipple. He bit down on it and pulled until she cried out, and then he did the same with the other. He encircled them with his lips, suckled on them, scraped them between his teeth. Then he lowered his lips down to her stomach, as low as he could manage to go and still hold her hands over her head.

He put her right nipple into his mouth and sucked and licked, all the while working her pants with one hand, pushing them down, along with her panties, until they were at her knees. From there, she worked her clothes off her body with her feet, until she lay naked from the waist down.

Gavril stopped for a moment and looked into her eyes. "If you move your hands away from where they are right now, I'll stop and walk out of this room. Got it?"

"Don't threaten me, big man."

"Oh, it's no threat, my sweet." Gavril grinned. "It's a promise."

Gilly whimpered and nodded, and Gavril lowered his mouth down the length of her body, down to the sweet part of her that was already soaked with her juices. He teased her, nipped her, and then set his mouth and tongue over her mound with its swollen nub, until she screamed his name.

Gilly felt herself tense. She had to move her hands. Had to touch him. Grip him. Gavril must have sensed the same from her, despite the order he'd given her, because he reached up and grabbed her hands once more, holding them over her head. This time he lay atop her, holding his weight up with one hand so her body wouldn't have to bear it. Then he pushed himself inside of her, his hardness deep into her hot, wet slit.

Gilly immediately bucked up against him, matching him thrust for thrust. She wanted it hard. She wanted it fast. She always wanted it that way. But Gavril took his time, driving into her slow and deep, until she thought she'd go insane. She moved with him. Slow and deep. Deeper, slightly faster. Over and over and over, until she exploded around him.

"More," Gavril said. "I want it all. All of you." Then he shoved himself inside of her again, touching a spot she didn't even know existed. It felt like fireworks suddenly went off in her body, and it threatened to take her head with it…into orbit…into Wonderland. And in that second, her body erupted into an even stronger orgasm than her first. This one soaked him, soaked the sheets beneath her, leaked down her thighs. Only then did he allow himself to release inside of her.

Gavril's orgasm had him calling out her name. He held on to her tight.

When Gavril let go of her hands, Gilly wrapped her arms around him, and he laid there, his head nuzzled in the crook of her neck. She shivered, waiting for the throbbing in her body to slow. He shifted his body ever so slightly so he lay beside her and pulled her close. She curled her body against his, and he smoothed her hair with a hand, stroking slowly, softly, over and over. Her eyes closed, and her breathing grew steady and easy.

With her eyes closed, Gilly had never felt so relaxed in all her life. She had to fight sleep. They had to get up and get dressed. Lucien would be back soon. They had to get up…

Just not this second.

Chapter 18

Gilly lay face up and naked, in a huge vat of whipped cream. She didn't care that it covered her hair or got into her ears. It felt luxurious as it lapped over her body, like a thousand silk ribbons caressing her body. It made her feel relaxed, and she didn't want to leave it. Something in the back of her mind kept niggling at her, though, reminding her that it would be someone else's turn soon, and she'd have to relinquish her little piece of heaven. She pushed the thought away and just allowed herself to float, moving her arms and legs ever so slightly, so that the cream covered her breasts, rolled over her thighs and between her legs. It felt sensual. Glorious. She couldn't remember how she'd gotten into the vat of whipped cream to begin with and really didn't care. All that mattered was she was here.

"They're here." Gilly felt her body suddenly tense when a strange voice seemingly came out of nowhere.

"They're here. You need to get up."

With a start, Gilly realized she'd fallen asleep and had been having one of the best dreams of her life. A place where she floated without trouble, concern or worry. Her eyes blinked open, and she saw Gavril looking down at her.

"I hear them downstairs," he said. "The Elders, Evee and Lucien. They're back. We need to get downstairs and meet them before they come up here looking for us."

Gilly's brain jolted to full consciousness, as did the realization that she'd just had sex with Gavril. She sprang out of bed, straightened her clothes, put on whatever clothes she was missing, and then hurried to her dresser mirror to make sure she looked as normal as possible.

As she panted and fluttered, Gavril buttoned his shirt and tucked it into his pants. He combed his hair with his fingers.

Gilly grabbed a brush from the top of her dresser and ran it through her short crop of hair, which was sticking up and disheveled.

When she was done, she eyed Gavril, gave him a nod, indicating that he looked about as guilty as she did, but they'd done the best they could.

"I'll go down first," Gilly said. "You follow later. If they ask what we were doing, I'll tell the truth.

That we were looking through the Grimoire. Evee will give me hell about having you there while I went through the Grimoire, but I'll deal with her about that later."

As Gilly hurried down the stairs, she caught a loud tumble of voices coming from the sitting room. Amid the mayhem, she heard Arabella, Taka, Vanessa, Evee and Lucien talking over one another.

When Gilly made it to the sitting room, she found them all standing near the fireplace, all gibbering at the same time.

"You should have never—"

"—could have gotten killed!"

"I should have let—"

"—you had no choice."

"I can't believe—"

"We were that close."

"We had no business—"

"It was our business, can't—"

"I should have figured right from the—"

"—and you had no way of knowing."

"Well, we know now."

"—that was a stupid move."

"What an ass he was."

Gilly let out a shrill whistle, which stopped their conversation dead, and everyone turned to look at her.

"Oh, Gilly," Evee said. "You're not going to believe this!"

"Where's Gavril?" Lucien asked.

Gilly looked over her shoulder. "Must be in the restroom. I'm sure he'll be here any second."

As if by command, Gavril suddenly appeared at the sitting room doorway. "What's all the hubbub in here?" he asked. "All of you are talking over one another like a gaggle of squawking geese."

"You're not going to believe this," Lucien said to him. "We know who the leader of the Cartesians is."

"What?" Gavril and Gilly said in unison.

"It's Trey Cottle," Lucien said.

"Get out," Gilly said.

"I should have known," Arabella said. "Right from the beginning. There were signs. The way they stayed cloistered, always up each other's behinds. Their evasiveness, then sudden attentiveness. Their eagerness to help when things really started to turn sore."

"What kind of signs?" Taka asked. "Other than him being a jerk like always?"

"You can't blame yourself," Vanessa said to Arabella.

"Wait a sec," Gilly said, holding her hands up. "How did you find out he was the leader?"

Arabella took the lead and told Gilly and Gavril how they'd convinced Lucien to stop at Trey's apartment.

"And you listened to them?" Gavril said to Lucien.

Lucien shrugged. "I know, I know. I've been beating myself up about it since it started."

"Are the three of you out of your minds?" Gilly asked the Elders.

"Do you want to hear the rest of the story, or are the two of you going to bitch and complain the entire time Arabella's trying to tell it?" Taka said.

"No, I'm sorry," Gilly said. "Please continue. But I think I'd better sit down for this one." And she plopped down onto a couch.

When Arabella got to the part of the story where Trey began to mutate into a Cartesian, everyone, including those who'd been with her, seemed to be holding their breath.

"What did Shandor do while all this was going down?" Gilly asked.

"Die," Arabella said.

"Huh?" Gavril said.

"Trey had those long black talons, and he swung back to strike at me," Arabella said, "but when he swung back, Shandor was standing in the wrong place, at the right time. Trey's talons wound up in Shandor's gut. He kept trying to shake him loose, but those hook-like things on the ends must have gotten caught on Shandor's entrails, because every time Cottle tried to shake him loose, Shandor just jiggled around like a ragdoll. No way Shandor survived that."

Gilly swiped a hand through her hair. "Sweet mother earth. Then what?"

Arabella sighed heavily as if saying anything more would lead her into a coma stemming from exhaustion. "Gunner got us out of there. We took off from Cottle's and jumped into Gunner's Buick. There was more room in there, anyway. We told Lucien and Evee to follow us here. The thing is, we've got to get out of here. Go and find Viv and Nikoli, of course, but we have to leave."

"Yeah," Taka said. "'Cause the first place he's going to come looking for us is our house, then here."

"Where's Gunner now?" Gavril asked.

"After he dropped us off here," Vanessa said, "I heard him say something about going to his house to get tools. He plans on helping us find Nikoli and Viv and figures we might need something to either get into the warehouse or help them out of wherever they're trapped. Things like bolt cutters, screwdrivers, a hammer and heaven only knows what else. He said he'd be back here to pick us up so we can all go to the pier."

"Y'all aren't going to the warehouse," Gilly said. "There's no way. I just have this sick feeling in the pit of my stomach that Viv and Nikoli are at the warehouse, but Cottle, if he is the Cartesians' leader, put them there as bait. He's waiting for us all to go out there and look for them so he can take us out in one fell swoop."

"If you think you're leaving me behind," Taka said, "you're crazy. We're the ones who found out who Cottle really was. We deserve to be there and help."

"We want to find Viv and Nikoli," Vanessa said. "Viv is one of our own. We have every right to be there to look for her. Besides, we'll have you, Gilly, Lucien, Gunner and Gavril there to help protect us.

If these creatures come out of rifts from the sky, they can't reach us in the building."

"That may be true," Gavril said, "but you have to get from the car into the building, then back out again. We have no idea what kind of shape Viv or Nikoli will be in, so it may take us some time to get them loaded into the car. It's putting too many people at risk if we all go. It leaves no one here."

"That's our point," Arabella said. "What good would just one of us being left behind do if the rest of us get destroyed by Cottle? His intention may be to collect us all in one place, but that doesn't mean he's going to win. We just have to keep our wits about us, find Viv and Nikoli and do what we have to do to get out of that place as quickly as possible."

"He's got hundreds, if not thousands, of Cartesians at his command," Gavril said. "If he calls them all to one place, we might as well kiss our asses goodbye. It won't matter how many of you are left. I don't know how we'll get past his army."

"Pretty down-and-out talking for a Bender," Gilly said.

"I'm only being realistic," Gavril said. "You've fought them with us. You know how long it takes to close a rift. Imagine a thousand opened at one time."

"But can all of the Cartesians get to our dimension all at the same time?" Gilly asked.

"For all we know, Cottle could have them waiting in the very next dimension, which would take nothing for them to rip into ours," Lucien said. "All Cottle would have to do is issue the command."

"Well, we'll drive right into that damn warehouse if we have to," Arabella said. "We wouldn't even have to get out of the car. We'd just slam right into the building."

"Uh, you said the D-word," Taka said.

"Oh, get real," Arabella said. "I've got a few more choice words to give this whole issue."

"Hopefully, it won't come to that," Gavril said. "We have no idea how many steel struts hold up that place. We might wind up slamming headlong into one, killing all of us before Cottle gets a chance to. Maybe Gunner's bolt cutters will help us get the job done."

"Wait," Gilly said. "Since Gunner is a sorcerer, Cottle wouldn't harm him, would he?"

"Yeah, I think he'd slice him wide open," Lucien said. "Especially now that he's with us. To Cottle, that means betrayal, and certain death if he gets his hands on him."

"We just need to take one thing at a time," Gilly said. "First we've got to find the frigging warehouse, then—"

"I know where it is," Taka said. "I visited it a few years ago with a group of tourists."

"What do you mean, you know where it is?" Vanessa said. "Why didn't you say something when Evee was channeling Moose and Chank? Did nothing they say ring a bell? I'm ashamed that it took us as long as it did to figure it out, but you'd already seen the place. Couldn't you put two and two together?"

Taka gave her a "pfft."

"None of that matters now," Arabella said. "What's done is done." She turned to Gavril and Lucien. "The biggest worry we're going to have, despite the hundreds or thousands of Cartesians, is Cottle being there. I just know that he'll want to be there for what he'll consider to be the *coup de grâce*. I doubt he's ever been in the middle of any of the other Cartesian attacks before. That would have been beneath him. But this, having the entire Triad and their Elders wiped out in one shot, he'd think himself to be king of the world."

"That's what he's wanting, anyway," Vanessa said. "Remember what he said at the apartment when he started to morph into that horrid creature?"

Arabella nodded. "Oh, yes. This will be a big deal for him. No doubt. And he set it up perfectly, releasing all the Originals without killing them so they'd wreak havoc on the humans in the city. Enough chaos to keep us running from one direction to another, all the while he's planning this coup."

"We have to focus on him," Gavril said. "The other Cartesians are important, ridding ourselves of them, I mean, but Cottle is the one we have to kill. It's just like we've always said—if you cut off the head of the dog, the rest of it will die. The same logic applies here."

"So, the game plan is to have Gilly, Evee and the Elders look for Nikoli and Viv, while we fight Cartesians and find that bastard Cottle?" Lucien said.

"Sounds about right," Gavril said.

"But Gunner will be there," Gilly said. "He can

take my place hunting for Viv and Nikoli, and I can help the two of you fight Cartesians. You know I can do it. I already have. Twice."

"No," Gavril said. "If you find Viv and Nikoli, they're going to need all the healing spells the Triad has to offer."

"I get that," Gilly said, "but the two of you alone can't take on hundreds of Cartesians." She balled her hands into fists, released them. Balled them up again. A hundred Benders wouldn't be able to kill hundreds and hundreds of Cartesians. She felt angry that the situation felt so humongous and hopeless.

"Neither can three," Gavril said. "We'll come up with our own strategy to get as many of them out of the way as possible and keep our eyes peeled for Cottle. For all we know, he may show up in human form so he can gloat. Either way, he's going to want to take a lead role."

"That will be his last mistake," Arabella said.

"Most definitely," Gilly said.

At that moment, a knock sounded on the front door. Gavril went to look through the peephole, while everyone else stood stock still, seemingly holding their breath.

"It's Gunner," Gavril said, and then opened the door.

"Sorry it took me a while," Gunner said, a little out of breath. "I had trouble finding my bolt cutters. Thought we might need them if there was a locked gate we had to get through. I brought other tools, too, in case Viv and Nikoli are trapped in some place too difficult for us to access. I have a hammer, a crow-bar, a screwdriver, chisel and a flashlight. They're all in the trunk of my car."

"Did you notice anything coming up here?" Gavril asked. "Any rifts in the sky?"

"Not that I could tell. But to be honest, I wasn't looking for any. I was in too big a hurry to get the tools and get back over here. We've got to go and get Viv and Nikoli before it's too late. Before we do, though, I want to apologize to all of you." Sorrow filled his deep blue eyes.

"For what?" Gilly asked.

"Cottle, Shandor. Especially Cottle. Just the fact that I've spent so much time with both of them over the years and had no clue about any of this."

"It's not your fault," Arabella said. "When you don't harbor evil in your own heart, sometimes it's difficult to see it in someone you're close to."

"Back on track for now, guys," Gavril said. "We think Cottle's set up a trap."

"Captured those two just to get all of us over there. Have us all in one place."

Gunner nodded. "You can probably count on it being a trap."

"Have you heard any word on Shandor?" Evee asked. "Is he involved in this? Is he a Cartesian?"

Gunner shook his head. "The last time I saw Shandor was when the Elders came over to Cottle's apartment. From the looks of Cottle's talons jammed in Shandor's gut, I don't think he survived. I know this is going to probably sound pretty cold, but at least we won't have him to worry about. Because I assure you, if he was alive, he'd be on Cottle's side, fighting to make certain all of you were dead."

"All right," Gavril said. "So how do we split up?"

"You should be able to hold four in the Camaro comfortably," Gunner said. "And I can roll five in my Buick, no problem. We'll make room somehow when we get our hands on Viv and Nikoli."

"Evee and I will take the Camaro," Lucien said. "Gilly and Gavril can ride with us. That'll leave the Elders with you, Gunner. We'll have to follow you there, because the only person here who seems to know where this place is happens to be Taka and Gunner. She'll tell you how to get there. We'll be right behind."

"In case we get separated," Gunner said, "just stay east on River Road. Follow it until the end near the peninsula. You can't miss it."

"Got it," Gavril said. "Now, first things first," "I want to make sure there are no rifts outside this house with Cartesians waiting for us. I'll check out the area. When you hear me give the all clear, hurry to the vehicle you're assigned to and jump in as quickly as you can."

Gilly felt her stomach twist up in a knot. Every nerve ending in her body on alert. She couldn't wait to get to Viv and wasn't looking forward to the battle sure to come once they found her.

Everyone nodded and followed Gavril to the front door.

Gavril opened the door, stepped outside and called

for Lucien. Within a matter of seconds, his cousin was at his side.

"There are two rifts—east side. I don't see any Cartesians hanging out of them, though. Still, I think we should close them before we attempt to get to the cars. It wouldn't surprise me if they're just out of sight, waiting for us to come out. Let's blast them. See if we can make anything happen."

"I'm with you, cuz," Lucien said.

Both of them pulled their scabiors from their sheaths, snapped their wrists, twirled the wands between the fingers of their right hands lightning fast, and then aimed them at the rifts.

Although there were no Cartesians in sight, they still heard loud popping sounds—the same sound that occurred whenever a Cartesian was pushed back a dimension. That confirmed that two Cartesians had indeed been hiding within the rifts, waiting for them to come out of the house.

"Keep shooting until the rifts close," Gavril said.

Together, Lucien and Gavril kept their scabiors aimed at the rifts until finally, after what seemed like a lifetime, the gaps finally zipped closed.

"Now!" Gavril shouted to everyone waiting behind him in the house. "Evee and Gilly in the Camaro. Gunner and the Elders in the Buick. Now! Now!"

As Taka, Vanessa and Arabella scurried outside, looking nervously overhead, Gunner opened the doors to the Buick, jumped into the driver's seat and set the engine to roar. He hit the horn on the steering wheel, indicating to the Elders to get a move on. Within seconds, Taka and Vanessa were sitting in the back seat of the Buick, and Arabella rode shotgun next to Gunner.

Gilly, Gavril, Evee and Lucien scrambled into the Camaro. When Lucien turned the engine over, he lowered his window and signaled for Gunner to go.

Gilly felt they were driving the race of a lifetime. As engines roared and tire rubber squealed on the road beneath them, Gilly wanted, needed them, to go faster. She heard her heartbeat thudding loudly in her ear, over the voice in her head that kept crying out, "Please be alive!"

Chapter 19

Trey Cottle did not know what to do with all the blood. After Gunner and the Elders had run out of his apartment, it had taken him quite some time to calm down enough to morph back into a human. Only then did the hooks on the talons release, enabling him to slide his hand out of Shandor's stomach.

Unfortunately, the poor fool had been in the wrong place, at the wrong time. Shandor had been a decent friend, and it certainly hadn't been Cottle's intent to kill him, but he'd gotten in the way, as he so often did. Cottle had meant to get rid of Arabella, that bigmouthed bitch witch who refused to shut the hell up. She'd taunted him, coerced him, angered him until he had no choice but to allow his true nature to emerge. He'd meant to swing back a taloned hand

and swipe not only the smirk from Arabella's face, but her head, if possible, from her shoulders. But Shandor had messed up his plans. Evidently frightened by Cottle's transformation, Shandor had gotten up from the card table and stood behind Cottle's right side. Wrong move.

Cottle had intended to swipe his right arm forward and do away with Arabella. But when he swung his arm back, talons extended, Shandor had been standing too close to Cottle's backswing and wound up stabbed in the gut by Cottle's talons.

Cottle had done everything he could to shake Shandor loose, which only exasperated the problem. If one could exasperate death.

His remorse for Shandor's death lasted all of two minutes. He grew angrier by the second, unable to disconnect from Shandor, all the while watching Arabella escape.

For years, he'd tolerated Shandor Black. The man had always followed him around like a starving puppy, eager for any bone Cottle might throw his way. He was worth the time and effort, though, because no matter what Cottle asked Shandor, he was more than glad to oblige. He could've asked him to piss in a glass and drink it, and the idiot would have done it without question. It saddened him to see such loyalty lost. But now he had much bigger plans.

His true being, his true self had been revealed; the Elders and Gunner, whom he'd planned to destroy, had found out his secret.

Gunner had broken the sorcerers' rule of silence.

How dare he side with those witches instead of standing by Cottle's side and helping to take care of Shandor? Cottle had been slightly shocked when Gunner had taken off at a full-out run, like a little girl, leading the Elders out of his apartment. Gunner was a sorcerer. He should have stuck with his own.

Although Cottle had not quite planned to bring things to a head today, sometimes circumstances presented themselves that removed all choices. He presumed that today was one of those days.

Oh, yes, he had captured Vivienne and one of those ridiculous Benders. He'd hurt them badly, and then stashed them away, using them as bait, knowing full well that somehow the rest of the Triad and Elders would find them. It would only be a matter of time, and that time consisted of the remaining Triad members and Benders finding them before they died from their wounds.

Cottle counted on the former more than the latter. Although he'd injured Vivienne and the Bender, he'd made sure the wounds were serious but wouldn't cause instantaneous death. The only thing that had concerned him was the possibility that both might bleed out before being found.

As a Cartesian, he didn't exactly have full control of the talons that he used to catch and kill his prey. Sometimes they seemed to have a mind of their own, just reaching out, digging deep, ripping, tearing, stabbing. It had taken quite the effort to keep the witch's and Bender's injuries to what he considered to be a minimum. They had been walking and talking among each other when he caught them by surprise from behind. From the sound of their conversation, the Bender had been out looking for Vivienne, wanting to protect her, then found her and planned to return her to safety.

Too late. Luckily, there'd been no witnesses around when he'd sliced Vivienne's stomach open and cut deep into the Bender's head.

So now the better part of the show was about to begin. He knew that the Elders, the rest of the Triad and the Benders had been looking for Vivienne and Nikoli. He also knew that the remaining two of the Triad had the ability to connect with the dead. One by direct communication, the other by astral projection. Knowing this, he'd stashed the injured Triad and Bender in a place that would cause confusion, if in fact, the Triad member with the ability to communicate with the dead latched on to someone, especially an Original, who might have seen where he'd hidden them. Either way, he really didn't give a damn. He just knew that they would eventually find Vivienne and Nikoli alive or dead. And the condition they found them in didn't matter to him either. They were only bait. To that end, he knew the other two Triad members and the Elders would move heaven and earth to find them, even forsaking the hunt for their Originals for a time.

This was going to be his day of glory.

Cottle went into the kitchen and washed Shandor's blood from his hands. He watched the red turn to pink and get swallowed up by the drain.

He contemplated over what to do with Shandor's body. It was not like he could very well go behind the house and bury him in an unmarked grave. The neighbors were too close, too many and too nosy.

To expedite the situation, Cottle decided to take the easy way out. He morphed back into a Cartesian, the largest of them all, the smartest of them all, and began to dismember Shandor with his talons. He sliced and diced the man into small enough pieces so he'd easily fit in a trash bag and the can outside, the one scheduled to be picked up and dumped in the wee hours of morning by a sanitation company.

When he finished, he allowed himself to turn into a human again. He triple-bagged the body and placed it next to the kitchen door. Then he started scrubbing the floor and carpet. So much blood had soaked into the carpet, he didn't know if he could get all the stains removed.

Nothing a little spell couldn't handle, however. Even though he didn't feel up to doing that at the moment, sometimes crap had to be handled pronto. Should someone come looking for Shandor, which he seriously doubted would happen, he had to do something with the evidence of blood all over the floor. It had to be handled before he could continue the quest he'd set for the day.

Cottle gave the command, a short spell that caused the blood that had soaked into his carpet to disappear as if it had never been there before. He checked every room for red specks. The sitting room where they'd been playing cards, the hallway, the kitchen, the bathroom. Even his bedroom, although Shandor had never gone into it.

With that task completed, he wiped down every doorknob and piece of furniture that might be carrying Shandor's fingerprints. Only then did he leave his house. He brought the trash bag with Shandor's remains along with him and carried it down three blocks, where he found a large garbage container. It would have been easier, and he could have gone farther, if he'd owned a vehicle, but he'd never had the need for one until now. All of the business he tended to was done in his office downstairs or somewhere within walking distance of the Quarter. He'd never considered that he might need a car for this.

With the evidence in the large garbage bin, all he'd have to do was wait until trash service made its rounds around four thirty in the morning. Their vehicles would hook up to the Dumpster and simply toss its contents inside the garbage truck.

No one was the wiser. Everyone used trash bags. And he had triple-bagged Shandor's remains to make certain no blood leaked out. It was almost as if Shandor Black had never existed. That's how he viewed it, anyway.

Now, with Shandor out of the way, Cottle was free. He had a long way to go to get to the warehouse where he knew the Elders, the Benders and the two remaining Triad members were waiting. Waiting to see if they could rescue Viv and Nikoli. Walking there would take too long, and he didn't want to alert a cab driver by having him drive him to the location that in and of itself could signal trouble.

Left with few choices, Cottle took a trolley as far east as it would take him, and then hiked the rest of the way on foot, determined to meet his fate.

No more waiting. Too many people knew who he was now, what he was. If the city thought it had a catastrophe on its hands when they were confronted with Originals, they had no idea as to what was about to hit them right between the eyes.

The leader, the master, the god of the Cartesians, was ready to reveal himself in all his glory and begin his fight for power. The waiting was over, and it had been worth it. He would've rather that it would have been on his own schedule, and he blamed the Elders for causing him to have to rush about as he had to now. He wanted to be in a Zen state of mind when it came time to destroy the Triad and the Elders, even the Benders. He wanted to make sure that he would absorb every ounce of power they possessed.

His mind was still on Shandor and on the fact that Arabella, simply by her words, had caused him to become so upset that he'd morphed. Cottle wanted to kick himself for that. For now, they would be on the watch, and his surprise attack as he had planned wouldn't go as neatly or as sweetly as he'd hoped. They'd be on the lookout for him, knowing that he was out and about and probably heading to take charge.

Yes, the world would be his. As would the universe. But for now, he would take the city by storm.

And with the Triad and Elders out of the way, no one in the city would have anyone to protect them. It would be death upon death upon death, which is exactly what he'd hoped for, what he'd planned for, what he meant to have happen.

With great power came great responsibility, and he was ready to take on any and all responsibilities thrown his way. Humans would bow at his feet. Those remaining from the netherworld, like vampires and werewolves, would fear him with great trepidation.

Neither human nor remaining netherwordly creature would ever know what to expect from him at any time. With his power, he could easily wipe out every human.

The thought of so much power and control made him feel heady and anxious.

He'd dreamed so many times of all he would do as he moved on to take over the world, and then the universe. With a flick of a finger, he'd be able to create great tsunamis, huge hurricanes, rains of biblical proportions, earthquakes that would destroy whatever territory he chose.

Oh, yes, that much power was heady. And he was impatient.

The Triad had to go.

Chapter 20

The Mardi Gras warehouse was a much bigger building than Gilly expected. It was a large gray metal structure with six huge bay doors. The landscape behind the building was the banks of the Mississippi River. To the right of the warehouse was a small peninsula.

To the left of the massive warehouse were storage units. In comparison, the Mardi Gras warehouse was square and looked to be the size of one and a half football fields.

Gunner pulled up to the warehouse, and Lucien, who'd been driving the Camaro, backed up, and then went forward so that they were facing driver to driver.

"Okay," Gunner said. "There are locks on the bay

doors, but nothing my bolt cutters can't handle. I'll just have to get my cutters out of the trunk. I'll open the bay door closest to the peninsula. I think that'll leave us a little less exposed. What do you think?"

"Decent plan," Lucien said. He stuck his head out of the window and already saw the rifts forming in the sky. "The rifts are already opening, which means you've probably got one minute after you get the bolt cutters in your hand to get the bay door open. Think you can swing that? I know that Cartesians are nearby. They're already waiting. Do you think you're strong enough to cut through that bolt?"

"All I can do is try," Gunner said.

"Tell you what," Lucien said. "Pop your trunk. I'll get the cutters and give the bolt a try."

"No," Evee said. "If something comes out of those rifts, we're going to need you and your scabior to get rid of them."

"It won't take me long," Lucien promised. "One snip from the cutters, and I'll have that door open in seconds. Then we'll be able to get inside."

He looked at Evee and gave her a half smile. "It'll be all right. Cross my heart. Now I want you to climb over the seat so that you're near Gilly. And let Gavril sit in the front. He's going to be my wingman. I'll cut the lock open, and if any Cartesian tries anything, Gavril will fry his ass."

"But what if all of them decide to come out of those rifts at the same time?" Evee said. "There's no way Gavril can handle all of them alone."

Lucien gave her a somber look. "If that happens, we'll have to abort."

Turning to Gunner, Lucien said, "Pop it."

Gunner reached for a lever on his dash, pressed it and the trunk of his Buick swung open. Lucien jumped out of the Camaro with Evee yelling in the background, "No!"

Gilly tugged on her sister's arm. "Do as Lucien said. We've got to make this easier, not harder. Come back here with me so Gavril can sit up front. At least he'll have a chance to fight off some of the Cartesians long enough for Lucien to get the bay door open."

No sooner had Gilly said that than she saw in the rearview mirror that Lucien already had the bolt cutters in his hand and was working on the lock. The handles looked at least four feet long; the jaws could have fit around the neck of her familiar.

"Get it now, cuz!" Gavril said, aiming his scabior at one of the rifts.

With a loud grunt, Lucien squeezed the handles of the cutters together and sliced through the lock. No sooner did the lock hit the ground than he slid the bay door up and open.

"In the warehouse! Everybody, now!" Lucien shouted.

Everyone sitting in both vehicles began scrambling like mice. The Elders and Gunner out of the Buick, Gilly, Evee and Gavril out of the Camaro. All of them raced for the open door of the warehouse.

Fortunately, Gunner had the forethought to bring a flashlight, because they couldn't find a light switch anywhere near the opening, and it was darker than pitch inside. Not that turning on the lights in the warehouse would have been a smart idea. Might have drawn unwanted attention.

Gunner aimed the flashlight toward the back of the warehouse, and as far back as Gilly could see, there were big heads, most of them as tall as five feet, all made from either papier-mâché or Styrofoam. There were clown heads, devils, voodoo priestesses, snakes, giant bubbles, princesses, kings, animals and cartoon characters. Every theme was so typical for a Mardi Gras celebration in New Orleans. Colors beyond imagination glittered everywhere: red, gold, purple, green, silver, white and blue. The heads sat atop what looked like flatbed trailers with ten- to twelve-foot sidewalls, where, during the parades, riders stood dressed in costumes, tossing beads and trinkets to onlookers.

The walls of the floats were too high to look inside from either end. Behind each, however, were two doors, which Gilly assumed was the only way the riders had access into or out of the float. She opened one set of back doors and saw a retractable set of steps.

For them to go through every one of these floats, door by door, step by step, to find Viv and Nikoli, would take them nearly a month.

"Viv!" Gilly shouted.

"Nikoli!" Gavril yelled.

Their voices echoed throughout the building.

No voices returned, save for their own.

Gilly heard a skittering sound nearby and caught a mouse running by in her peripheral vision. It was obviously running to safety.

"Great," Gilly said. "Just what we need. Mice."

Although the inside of the building was quiet, the tin structure caught the sounds of traffic two streets away. The rumble of tires, the screech of brakes, the blast of horns.

"There's no way we're going to find them," Gilly said to Lucien. "Not unless we climb into each and every frigging float in this place."

Gilly walked farther inside the warehouse and saw pieces of Styrofoam strewn about the floor near places where mice had chewed off a decorative nose or ear.

"Viv!" Gilly yelled again. She cupped her hands around her mouth to form a haphazard megaphone. "Viv, are you in here?"

Still no response. As hard as Gilly worked at holding back tears, they came anyway, stinging her eyes.

Viv couldn't be dead. She refused to believe it. She still felt her sister deep inside her heart and mind, which told Gilly she was still alive. But the feeling was beginning to wane, flashing on and off like a flashlight with dying batteries.

Gilly knew they didn't have much time to find Viv or Nikoli. Her own steps were growing slower, her voice weaker, all signs reflective of Viv's condition.

"Nikoli!" Lucien shouted from behind Gilly.

Everybody stood quietly, listening for a few seconds.

"I'm not hearing anything," Taka said. "And we

can't just stand here and keep complaining that we'll never find them in all this mess."

"She's right," Arabella said. "Vanessa and Taka, you two come with me. We'll start on the other end of the building and work our way to the middle. Lucien, Evee, Gavril and Gilly can work it from this end until we meet up."

"I'll come with you," Gunner said to Arabella. "It's darker back there. You'll need this flashlight. I'll also be able to get the back doors of the floats open and the stairs down for you."

"Sounds like a plan," Gilly said. "But keep calling Viv and Nikoli. They might hear us, or more importantly, we might hear something from them."

As the crew divided, Gilly jumped toward the first float in her line of sight. It had a princess head, and the trailer it was attached to had been shaped like a pumpkin with many windows. She unlatched the back doors, pulled down the retractable stairs and scrambled up the stairs onto the float. "Viv! Are you here?"

Dusk was pressing in on the sky and pressing into the open bay door. Although Gilly was working the floats near the door, it was getting harder and harder to see anything.

"We've got to find some lights in here," Gavril said. "No matter what attention it may draw. If we don't, we could lose Viv and Nikoli forever. The two of you, keep searching floats. I'm going to look for some kind of light switch."

Somehow, amid the chaos, Gilly found her rhythm.

She unlatched the back doors of floats one handed, pulled down retractable stairs, ran up the stairs and throughout the float, calling Viv and Nikoli's name. She didn't bother righting the stairs or closing the back doors of one while she ran off to the next.

"Viv! Nikoli!" Gilly yelled until her throat hurt. She heard the Elders calling the same names from the opposite end of the warehouse.

Gilly saw the flashlight bouncing from one wall to the next and assumed that Gavril had managed to confiscate the light from Gunner, at least until he found the warehouse's light switch.

"Hey, wait, I think I found something!" Gavril yelled. By the beam of the flash, Gilly saw a long metal box with a large lever connected to it, and all of it was attached to a steel pole.

"This is either going to set off an alarm or turn on the lights," Gavril said. "So hold on to your drawers."

"Push it!" Gilly shouted. "Push it up! If it's an alarm, we'll get the hell out. If it's lights, we'll go to church."

Gavril nodded and threw the switch up.

Suddenly, the inside of the warehouse lit up like a football field at game time. It made the colors of all the decorations nearly blinding to the eye.

Gilly saw a devil's head and remembered how, when Evee had connected with him, Moose kept talking about one. She understood now why all he could talk about was big heads, lots of colors.

Gut instinct sent Gilly running to the float with the devil's head. "Viv! Where are you?"

Then suddenly, from somewhere, about a quarter of the way where the Elders were, Gilly heard the softest of moans.

"I heard something!" Gilly shouted. "Arabella, it's not far from you. A moan. I heard someone moan."

"We're going through them as fast as we can," Arabella shouted back. "We're even taking them two at a time."

"Please hurry!" Gilly took off running to the area where she thought she'd heard the moan come from. She remembered how Moose had kept talking about a devil's head. Although there was more than one float with a devil's head, she took off for the biggest one. The one with the red horns, the evil grin set in perpetuity by black glitter.

When Gilly reached the float, she unlatched the back doors, and before the stairs had a chance to unfold all the way to the ground, she scrambled inside.

There, from around the center aisle that gave the float a second tier, she spotted a foot. It took only two more steps for Gilly to confirm it was her Viv. Her pulse quickened and tears immediately stung her eyes.

"She's here! She's here! I found her!"

Within seconds, Lucien jumped onto the float beside Gilly and scanned the inside. He spotted Nikoli at the head of the float.

"Nikoli's here!" Lucien shouted. "He's here!"

"Look at the blood," Gilly cried. She pressed two

fingers against Viv's jugular. "She's breathing, but it's shallow. She barely has a pulse."

"Same with Nikoli," Lucien said. "Cuts on his face. His stomach."

In a matter of seconds, the rest of the crew was inside the float, everybody wanting a firsthand view of Viv and Nikoli.

"Oh, mercy," Taka cried. "They're dead. They're both dead."

"Stop your yammering," Vanessa snapped, and then looked over at Gilly. "Is she dead?" She glanced over at Lucien. "Is he dead?"

"Both have lost a lot of blood. Pulses, but barely. Shallow breathing."

"Mercy, mercy, so much blood," Taka said.

"Nikoli," Lucien said. "You can't waste out on me now, man, you hear? You come back to me. Come back to us. Wake up. Wake up!" Lucien lay his hands, one over the other, and placed them over Nikoli's heart; he pressed five times, and then pinched Nikoli's nose closed and blew air into his mouth. He did that over and over.

Viv's pulse was fading fast.

"They're here," Gilly yelled. But where was here? "They needed help in the worst way. I need your help, please. Their injuries are bad. I don't know if we can save them. We may already be too late."

"Can't you use your spells?" Gavril asked.

"I don't know," Gilly cried. "Look at them. Look at them. We can't bring back the dead. No spell can." If there had been a spell to bring back the dead and it called for the sacrifice of her own life, Gilly would have gladly given up hers for Viv's. Her heart ached that it wasn't that simple.

Chapter 21

As Gavril held Nikoli's head in his lap, and Gilly held Viv's, Arabella, Vanessa and Taka paced the back end of the float.

"Oh, my goodness. Oh, my goodness," Taka said. "What are we going to do? They're dying, and there's nothing we can do."

"We're going to heal them. That's what we're going to do," Gilly said.

Gilly motioned to Evee to come over to her and said, "I want you to put your hands on her, over her wound. Concentrate on healing her."

In that moment, howling and growling echoed through the building. There was scratching and scraping overhead on the tin roof that sounded like nails on a chalkboard. The howling grew louder, and the scratching and scraping stronger. All of it was so loud, Gilly couldn't hear herself think. Not that she wanted to. She'd have preferred this to be a nightmare she could wake from.

"They're trying to get inside," Vanessa cried. "The Cartesians are trying to get in."

Gilly saw Lucien's face grow beet red with anger. "Gavril, you hold on to Nikoli. I'm going to see what's going on out there."

"Don't go out there by yourself, cuz," Gavril said.

"I have to at least assess what's happening."

"Then I'll check it out," Gavril said.

Gunner stepped forward and said to Gavril, "You stay with them. I'll go out there and see what's going on."

Arabella cried out. "Gunner, no! You have no way to battle those creatures. There're too many of them."

As if to confirm what she said, the howling and growling amplified tenfold. The scratching, ripping, scraping against the tin roof grew louder, as well, adding to the cacophony of horror.

Gilly had never seen a Cartesian, save from the waist up. But Arabella, Taka and Vanessa had when they'd witnessed Cottle's transformation. They'd know what to look for.

"Stay here with Viv," Arabella said to Gilly. "I'm going."

"No, you're not going by yourself," Gilly said. She laid Viv's head gently back on the floor of the float, and then got to her feet.

With everyone on the float yelling for her to stay

put, Gilly climbed down the ladder at the back of the float. She was about to hurry for the open bay door at the far end of the warehouse, when she felt a strong pair of arms grab her beneath her arms and pull her back onto the float. It was Gavril.

"You're not going anywhere," he said. "You stay here. I said I was going, and I am."

Before Gilly could protest, Gavril scrambled down the stairs, folded them back onto the float, and then closed the back door and locked it so she couldn't follow.

"Stay put," Gavril said to Gilly from the other side of the door. "I'm serious. Stay put."

"Open the damn door!" Gilly shouted.

The screeching and scratching that had been deafening on the roof suddenly changed direction. The same sound was now coming from the sides of the warehouse. Gilly wanted to put her hands over her ears for the sounds were so tinny, the scratch-scratch so disturbing, it made her teeth hurt.

When Gavril made it to the bay door, he heard Gilly shout, "What do you see?"

For a second, he didn't answer. The only word that came to his brain was *hell*.

"What do you see?" Gilly repeated.

"Hell," Gavril yelled back. "There are more rifts in the sky than I've ever seen before. Hundreds of them. Thousands of them. It looks like somebody took a giant razor blade to the sky and sliced it a thousand times over."

Gavril hurried back to the float, unlocked the back door and dropped the stairs.

"Well?" Taka asked.

"We're in deep," Gavril said. "There are thousands of rifts out there. So many, I couldn't see them all. Not one Cartesian hanging out of any, though."

Taka pointed with a shaking finger to the back of the warehouse, where the bay door was open. "If there are that many out there, how are we going to get back to the cars? We won't be able to? We're trapped."

"I can help fight them with the extra scabior," Gilly said, and before Gavril had a chance to protest, she turned to Evee. "Did you say your healing spell over Viv?"

"Yes, twice," Evee said. "But it's not working. I need your help."

"Quit being such a wuss," Gilly said angrily. "You've got to concentrate."

"I did!" Evee cried.

"Try again."

Gilly looked from Lucien to Gavril. "We've got to get the rifts that are closest to the opening of the warehouse closed. Give me the extra scabior so I can help."

As Gavril started to object, Gilly reached around him and yanked the extra scabior he kept tucked in the back of his pants.

"Now, you either come with me and charge this damn thing, or I'll go alone and figure it out by myself," Gilly said. "Either way, we've got to get the rifts closest to the warehouse opening closed. There may be hundreds, even thousands, up there, but not all of them can reach this far. They're held at the waist. Not all of them will be able to reach us. I know we can fight the ones closest to us so we can at least get out of here."

A piece of tin overhead ripped open, and they saw a black talon from a Cartesian punch through the roof.

"Are we having fun yet?" a voice called from the back of the warehouse. "Tell me you're having fun. That would make me so very happy."

Gavril and Gilly froze, as did everybody else.

The sound came from the back of the building, low and muted but distinct. It was the voice of Trey Cottle.

Chapter 22

Gilly's heart was torn in two. She didn't want to leave Gavril and Lucien alone, fighting all of the Cartesians that obviously were preparing to drop from the sky. But her Evee needed her help with Viv, and she couldn't just turn her back on them.

She suddenly thought of a plan. A spell.

Above the howling, growling and scratching sounds echoing through the building at a deafening rate, she yelled at Evee, "Use the elemental spell."

"I can't," Evee said. "Not by myself. You know that. It takes all of us to do that."

Gilly felt like an ass. She did know that.

With a growl of her own, she ran back to the float where Viv and Nikoli lay, seemingly lifeless. Evee was leaning over Viv, her hands on her wounds and covered in blood.

Viv's eyes were closed, her breathing too shallow, her pulse barely there. Gilly had no other choice. Lucien and Gavril would have to do the best they could with what they had. Her sister had to be her priority right now.

Above the howling and growling, she moved Viv's hands over to her wounds, and then laid hers on top of Viv's, and Evee rested her hands on top of Gilly's.

The Elders stood to one side, whispering to themselves what Gilly could only imagine was a healing spell of their own.

"All right, you start," Gilly said to Evee.

Evee closed her eyes and issued her incantation:

Oh, king and minions of water be.
Ever mindful of my voice to thee.
Loose thy healing powers from depths below.
So that health through this woman shall flow.

Gilly quickly followed with her portion of the elemental spell:

Oh, warriors of fire.
Hear my plea.
I invoke thy healing powers unto me.
That they shall bring healing for all to see.

Since Viv was unable to complete the incantation, Gilly and Evee said it for her:

Giant earth thy orbit bound.
Release their power from underground.
From which fire, water and earth abound.
And instant healing shall now be found.

Ingus, Hosomus, Faroot—So let it be!

Gilly opened her eyes and saw that Viv's eyes were still closed, and blood still trickled from her abdominal wounds.

"Again, Evee. We say it again, as loud as you can. Scream it if you have to!"

Evee nodded and yelled:

Oh, king and minions of water be.
Ever mindful of my voice to thee.
Loose thy healing powers from depths below.
So that health through this woman shall flow!

Gilly shouted d her part until her throat hurt.

Oh, warriors of fire.
Hear my plea.
I invoke they healing powers unto me.
That they shall bring healing for all to see!

Gilly nodded at Evee and both bellowed Viv's part at the top of their lungs.

Giant earth thy orbit bound.
Release thy power from underground.
From which fire, water and earth abound.
And instant healing shall now be found.
INGUS, HOSOMUS, FAROOT—SO LET IT BE!

In that moment, Viv's eyes fluttered open.

Gilly removed her hands, as did Evee, and both saw, right before their eyes, the wounds on Viv's stomach close up as if they were being sutured from the inside out. No more blood. Relief tumbled over Gilly's heart in huge waves. Exhaustion weighed down her shoulders.

Viv looked up at them, confusion on her face. "What are you two doing here? Where am I?"

"It's a long story, sweetie," Gilly said. "But for now, we're going to need your help. How are you feeling?"

"Strong as an ox. Feels like I just woke up from a long nap," Viv said. "What happened?"

"You were hurt pretty bad. We just finished an elemental healing spell on you," Evee said.

Viv sat up as if nothing had ever happened to her. She got to her feet, wobbled for a second, and then caught her footing. "Where's Nikoli?"

Gilly frowned. "He's at the front of the float, and he's not doing so well."

"We've got to get to him now," Viv said.

"For more reasons than you know," Gilly agreed.

As the Elders continued to silently murmur their own spells, Gilly, Viv and Evee went over to Nikoli.

Viv's face turned gray when she saw him, saw the blood pooled around his head.

"We've got this," Gilly reminded her. "No worries. Just concentrate. Same elemental incantation for him that we did for you."

"What?" Viv asked. "What's all that noise? I can barely hear you. Are we on a Mardi Gras float? What the hell?"

"More long stories," Gilly shouted. "Too long to go into now. We've got to help Nikoli. We're going to do the elemental incantation for him, but you're going to have to shout your part as loudly as you can so it'll be heard over all this racket."

Gilly, Viv and Evee placed their hands on Nikoli's wounds, and Gilly started shouting her part. She was quickly followed by Evee, and Viv brought up the rear, saying hers so loudly, she went hoarse at the end.

"What is all that noise, though?" Viv asked. "What's making all that noise?"

Gilly sighed. "Cartesians. Hundreds of them, if not more. And they're trying to get to us."

Viv's face went a shade paler than pale. "Oh, no. No way they're going to get us."

No sooner had Viv finished her confirmation than Nikoli's eyes flickered open, and they saw the wound on his head close almost instantaneously. He blinked, looking similar to Viv when she'd been healed, like he'd just woken from a long nap.

Nikoli pulled himself up, resting on his elbows. "Where are we?"

"We're at the Mardi Gras warehouse," Gilly said. "Both you and Viv were hurt badly and brought here. Used as bait by the leader of the Cartesians to bring us all out here. His intent is to collect us all in one place and kill us all at one time."

"I'll be goddamned if I'm going to let that happen," Nikoli said, getting to his feet. "Where are Gavril and Lucien?"

"They are at the far end of the warehouse, at the last bay door. The one we opened to get in here," Gilly said. "There are hundreds, if not thousands, of rifts out there right now, but not a sign of a Cartesian. I think they're hiding just behind those rifts, awaiting a command from their leader in order to attack."

"Some of them have to be out, though," Evee said. "Look at the one that ripped the hole in the roof."

"Some may have sneaked out," Gilly said. She turned to Nikoli. "Gavril and Lucien are trying to close the rifts closest to the building so we'll have a way to get out."

"Where's my scabior?" Nikoli asked, and then padded the right side of his belt, found his sheath and pulled his scabior from it.

"I know you're itching to go out there and kick ass with your cousins," Gilly said. "But how are you feeling?"

"What do you mean? I'm fine. Like I had a long night's sleep. Hell, I don't even remember how I got here." He turned to Viv. "Are you okay?"

She nodded. "Shaken and a bit out of sorts with all that's going on, but okay. I don't remember how I got here either."

"It's the leader of the Cartesians," Gilly said. "We found out who he was. It's Trey Cottle."

"One of the sorcerers?" Viv said, surprise on her face.

"Yeah, if that's what you want to call him," Gilly said. "He's just waiting to give the command to his Cartesians. His plan was to hurt you and Nikoli, hide you out here and have us scrambling all over hell and back to find you. This place is so secluded, I guess he figured it would be the perfect spot to get rid of us all."

Viv's brow furrowed.

"He used you and Nikoli as bait," Gilly explained.

"He knew we'd all come looking for you. Now that we're all in one place, I think his plan is to take all of us out. The Triad, the Elders, even the Benders."

"I'll be damned if I'm going to let that happen," Nikoli said. He got to his feet, blinked his mind back into clarity. "I'm going to help Gavril and Lucien."

"There's a fourth scabior," Gilly said. "Ronan's. If you can charge it, I know how to use it. I used it before. I can help."

"You stay here," Nikoli said. "All of you stay here."

Gunner, standing near the Elders, his eyes closed, his mouth moving as if he were saying his own incantation for safety and protection.

Nikoli's command to stay put went in one of Gilly's ears and out of the other. She appreciated Gunner's efforts because she certainly did not plan to stay put while the Benders fought off all of those Cartesians alone. One more person in the fight might not make that big a difference, considering the number of Cartesians they were dealing with, but it couldn't hurt. For all the right and wrong reasons, Gilly wanted to watch Gavril's back. If any Cartesian came within a hundred feet of him, that ugly bastard would meet its match.

Chapter 23

Although she had been told to stay put, Gilly had never been one to follow directions to the letter, much less be told what to do.

She jumped off the float and told Viv, Evee, Gunner and the Elders, "Stay here. I've got to help the Benders. There are four scabiors. Certainly one more helping to fight these Cartesians can't hurt."

"But you can help better here," Arabella said. "We can do an illusion spell so that the Cartesians will see hundreds of Luciens, Nikolis and Gavrils. They won't know which ones are the real Benders. We can do the same with this building, create lots of them so they won't be able to tell which one we're in."

"But there are so many rifts in the sky," Gilly said. "You have no idea. They can easily get one of the

Benders accidently. There are so many of them, and they seem to be multiplying faster than we can count. If we triple the illusion spell and create thousands of Benders and warehouses, that may work…it may."

"All we can do is try," Taka said. "We've got to at least try that. We've got six witches here. We can multiply the illusion spell until infinity if we wanted to."

"Yeah," Vanessa said. "We'll hold hands, meld our energies together and create as much chaos for them out there as they are creating for us in here."

Gunner, who'd been standing off to one side, said, "May I join you? I don't know the illusion spell, but I can certainly add my energy and intent to have that spell come to pass."

"Yes, please join us," Gilly said, and she held out her hand to him. Once she had hold of him, everyone linked hands with them. And the witches began to chant:

Double, thrice, by thousands shall ye see.
No longer one to be seen my thee.
Thine eyes shall fully confuse thy mind.
Making all evil intentions blind.
Blunder thee, blunder now.
We call upon Poseidon, Tiamat and Apsu.
To bring strength to our command.
So it is said.
So shall it be.

Gilly opened her eyes. They still held hands. Everyone else's eyes were closed, intent on the incantation they'd just cast. The scratching and ripping at the roof came to an abrupt halt, and Gilly only heard an occasional scrape on the roof. She was about to take off from the float to the open bay door to see what was happening with Lucien, Gavril and Nikoli, when she heard a voice from the far end of the warehouse.

"Well, well, well, aren't all of you resourceful."

The sound of the voice made Gilly's blood run cold and sent goose bumps running up her arms. The voice belonged to Trey Cottle. The same voice she'd heard earlier. Only this time, she saw him clearly. This wasn't an illusion, a sorcerer's version of ventriloquism. Trey Cottle was indeed here.

Gilly saw him walking slowly up the center aisle, heading toward them. He was in human form, dressed in black slacks and a white button-down shirt. Sweat had beaded up on his bald head and forehead. His glasses sat near the tip of his nose, as usual.

"You think you're smart, don't you?" he said. "All of you. You're not as smart as you think you are. You might have healed Vivienne and that Bender, and you may have confused my Cartesians, but it won't be for long. I just wanted to make sure I got one last look at all of you before your demise."

"Kiss my ass, Cottle," Gilly said.

Cottle screwed up his face as if the thought of kissing her ass nauseated him. "Be as brash as you wish, little girl. But it's my turn now. Your ancestors ruined my life many generations ago, and I've carried that loathing all this time. Today I get my revenge for what they created when they made me.

They had no idea that this sorcerer, this leader of the Cartesians, had the ability to take over the world, the universe. All it took was a mind like mine. One that is resourceful, powerful, industrious. Your little illusion spell may have confused some of my Cartesians, but when I issue my command, they'll no longer be confused. They've been trained since their conception as to what to do to you when the time came. And today is that day. All of you are exactly where I want you. The Triad, the Elders. The Benders are only lagniappe. I will get my revenge, and I will gain more power than any human or any being from the netherworld will ever be able to control. I will master this world. Your Originals that I set free to wreak havoc over the city, I will take down one by one. Consume every one of their powers."

"I don't believe you," Gilly shouted. "You're just a big talker."

Cottle paused in mid step. "Really? Then why don't you go to the bay door and tell me what you see happening out there right now? Then, once you've seen it, let's see if your belief system changes."

"I'm not going anywhere near you, you ugly asshole," Gilly said.

Cottle tsked. "Such language from a beautiful mouth. It really doesn't matter. Because all of you will be nothing shortly. And I'll take my time with each of you, savoring every morsel of your powers. What was taken from me, my life, normalcy, I will take it back, and in spades. There will be no more Triad, no more Elders. I'll have run of this city, this state, this country. And it will continue until I have control of the very universe. You see, that's been my plan all along. Someone takes something from me, I take everything back, plus more. There'll be such regret, such mourning, such sorrow that the world itself will not know how to deal with it. And the beauty of it all is that I'll never get caught. Just as it took as long as it did for you to find out that I led the Cartesians, I'll never make that mistake again. I'll have no need to, for my powers will allow me to do as I please, when I please, how I please and from whichever dimension I please. Save for the eleventh, of course, since nothing returns from there. But there is no one on this planet strong enough, powerful enough to send me there. That leaves me in complete control."

"I bind you, you ugly son of a bitch," Viv said. "I bind you from coming any closer to us."

"You bind me?" Cottle laughed. An ugly snort of a laugh. "How droll. Do you think your petty little spells can affect someone of my stature?" He took a step toward them, and then another. "How's that for binding? Do you actually think you can keep me from you? All I have to do is keep the Benders busy outside with the Cartesians—if the Benders survive, that is—and I'll have you all to myself. And that is exactly what I wanted. I don't have to depend on my minions to bring you to me. I have each of you all to myself, and there's not a damn thing you can do about it. For you see, even though I'm a Cartesian, I'm still a sorcerer and can bind all of you little snits to the floor of that contraption that you're standing in now."

"You're giving yourself far too much credit, Cottle," Gilly said. "We may be witches, but we do have our powers."

"Oh, I'll agree with that," Cottle said. "But they're so miniscule in comparison to my powers, it's laughable. I can take you down like a flea, and all the others will be able to do is watch as I suck every ounce of power from you until you're left drained, like an empty plastic bag. Dead, drained, owned by me."

Gilly leaned over to Evee and whispered, "We have to say the 'Marsailla Mon.'"

Evee frowned. "I don't know that spell."

Gilly turned to Viv. "We have to say the 'Marsailla Mon.' The three of us."

Worry marked Viv's face. "The 'Marsailla Mon' is so far back in the Grimoire, I don't know that I can remember how it goes."

"Just repeat after me," Gilly said to Viv and Evee. "I saw it today when I went through my Grimoire. For it to work, though, you have to take all the anger and frustration you feel over all that's happened to us in the last couple of weeks and let it bubble to the surface. Let it rise up until you want nothing more than to knock somebody out. Think of the loved ones we've lost, and let love follow those emotions. Mix them together, but let those emotions be your power source, not your brain."

"And what could you possibly be whispering

about at a time like this, you little pathetic bitch witch?" Cottle said to Gilly. "You think you're going to connive some kind of trick to escape from me? That's a laugh. I can take all of you down in one fell swoop. But I just can't help but be greedy and take one at a time, making the others watch, feeling useless, helpless. I want to savor the look of horror in the eyes of your sisters and Elders while I take you down."

"Leave them alone, Cottle," Gunner said, suddenly appearing. He took a step forward. With a wave of his hand, Cottle sent Gunner flying to the opposite end of the float.

"Stay out of this, pissant, before I turn you into a groundhog," Cottle said. "You're taking the side of witches over your own. I never thought I'd see the day."

"You're not my own," Gunner said, getting to his feet. "I don't know what the hell you are, but I don't want any part of it. I'm a sorcerer, not one of your stupid minions. What you're doing is wrong. As sorcerers, we have a code we live by, and you're certainly not living up to that."

"Screw the code," Cottle said. "I'm making up the codes now, and any to come. That's what leaders of the universe do. As for you, I'll simply take the miniscule powers you have and make them my own. Don't want you to feel left out, right? When was the last spell you cast, Gunner? Two years ago?"

"That's because I don't like taking advantage of people the way you do," Gunner said.

"Shut up!" Cottle said. "You don't have any idea what you're talking about, so the best thing you can do is keep your damn mouth shut." Cottle put his fingers against his lips and moved them from right to left, like he was zippering them shut. Suddenly, Gunner's mouth pinched closed, and he couldn't open it to say anything further.

"Grab my hands now," Gilly said to her sisters. "Take all the anger you feel toward that bastard, all of the passion you have for the ones you love—let that be the catalyst that drives this spell. Now hold your hands up. We're going to say this spell twice to make sure it sticks. We'll have to make it quick before he catches on and comes after us."

Gilly studied the Elders. "I know you want to help, but it has to be just the three of us. I'm not sure why. Just something I know."

Arabella nodded. "We understand more than you know."

"The three of you, please do a support spell," Gilly asked. "So that ours can be the most powerful it can be."

"No problem," Taka said.

"Of course," Vanessa agreed.

Gilly turned to Gunner. "I know you can't speak now, but please, in your mind, say a spell that will give extra powers to ours."

Gunner nodded enthusiastically.

With that, Gilly, Viv and Evee, still holding hands, raised them up high.

"What are you up to now?" Cottle chortled. "Going to play 'Ring Around the Rosie'?"

Gilly felt fury roll through her as she thought of how close she came to losing Viv, her missing Originals and all of the humans who'd lost their lives because of the asshole standing in the middle of the warehouse. All the Benders had sacrificed, even one of their own. In that moment, her mind and heart filled with Gavril, with his bravery and determination. With love for him.

Gilly could tell her sisters were experiencing the same emotions, for their grips tightened on her hands.

"Just repeat after me," Gilly whispered to her sisters. Then said loudly,

Hochezamo, conja, marsailla mon.
Elementals far and wide.
Come hither and forgo thy pride.

"Stop!" Cottle screamed.

Bind together one to one.
And shout into the universal ear.
That every power in the cosmos may hear.

"Shut your mouth before I kill all of you right this minute!" Cottle began to transform into a Cartesian, standing at least ten feet tall, his head five times the size of a human's.

Combine thy strength and open thee.
The folds of time to rid us of our enemy.
Hochezamo, conja, marsailla mon.
Let it be said.
Let it be done.

Forever!

With legs that looked like they belonged on a grizzly bear, Cottle was now on his feet, talons fully extended.

"Again!" Gilly shouted.

Having already gone through it once, the Triad spoke the spell in unison.

Hochezamo, conja, marsailla mon.

Elementals far and wide.

"Shut up!" Cottle yelled, quickening his pace toward them.

Come hither and forgo they pride.

Bind together—

"Noooo!" Cottle screamed.

One to one.

And shout into.

The universal ear.

That every power in the cosmos may hear.

Combine they strength and open thee.

The folds of time to rid us of our enemy.

"No! No!" Cottle's voice began to shiver and shake, and he stood in place, his entire body trembling.

Hochezamo, conja, marsailla mon.

Let it be said.

Let it be done.

Then the Triad, the Elders and even Gunner, who was now able to move his mouth, shouted together, "FOREVER!"

As they watched, Cottle rose into the air and blipped out of sight, like a soap bubble that had burst.

They heard a loud popping sound, and then a second one, a third, a fourth; they were up to ten before all went quiet.

"Oh, hell, no, you bastard. Not the tenth dimension. You're going to the eleventh, where you'll never be able to return," Gilly said. "*Hochezamo, conja, marsailla mon.* Let it be said, Let it be done, *now*!"

And for the first time ever, for a Bender, for any of the Triad or any other being listening, there came one more popping sound. Trey Cottle had been pushed back to the eleventh dimension, from which there'd be no return. To a place where he'd be trapped forever.

In that moment, the scritch-scratching against the building stopped immediately. Gilly took off running for the open bay door, with Evee, Viv, the Elders and Gunner following closely behind.

When they reached the door, Gilly saw Gavril, Nikoli and Lucien standing just outside with their scabiors in hand and a look of shock on their face as they looked upward. Gilly followed their gaze and saw that there was not one rift left behind. The dusky sky was a starlit gray with a quarter moon.

"They just vanished," Gavril said. "We were trying to close them up, you know, the ones closest to the bay doors, then suddenly, poof—every damn rift just disappeared."

Everyone looked up at the sky. A normal sky. A riftless sky.

Gilly smiled and looked at Gavril. "It's like you've always said. Chop off the head of the dog, and the rest of it will die. Cottle's gone. In the eleventh dimension. He'll never be back to harm us again."

"How...how did you—"

"We're the Triad," Gilly said with a soft smile. "Had I not looked through the Grimoire earlier, I wouldn't have seen the spell we needed to get rid of him. It saved our lives. The Cartesians are gone. With their leader gone, they've followed him to the eleventh dimension. Like sheep, one runs off a cliff, the rest follow because they're too dumb to think for themselves. I feel it in my heart and soul that we're free of them. We're finally free."

Chapter 24

"It feels weird, doesn't it?" Viv said, as she and her sisters sat with the Elders at Bon Appetite, Evee's café. They'd decided to meet there for an early breakfast.

"Which part?" Gilly asked.

"Which part what?" Taka asked, and then shoveled down a forkful of scrambled eggs.

Vanessa sipped on some orange juice. "She means, all of it feels weird."

"That's what I'm trying to understand," Taka said.

"Oh, for the love of breakfast, eat your eggs and hush," Vanessa said, and then took a big gulp of juice, emptying her glass.

Gilly did her best to help Taka understand. "Viv

is saying that our lives feel weird right now. And I asked which part feels the weirdest."

"Oh," Taka said, dabbing the corners of her mouth with a napkin. "So which part feels the weirdest to you?"

"I don't think there's only one part," Gilly said. "Everything is so different now."

"Right," Evee said and took a sip of coffee. "It got stranger still when the Benders left to tend to Ronan's family."

Viv nodded. "True. But you can't blame them for hurrying out there so quickly. They could have bailed on us right when it happened. Instead, they stuck with us throughout the whole Cartesian ordeal."

"We were very lucky to have them," Arabella said. "If I've ever felt grateful that humans were around, I certainly was for them."

"Well, you'll be seeing more of them," Gilly said. "Gavril told me they'd be back in about a week, as soon as they helped get their uncle's affairs in order."

"Why are they coming back if the Cartesians are gone?" Taka asked.

Vanessa and Arabella gave her a sideways glance that all but said, "You're kidding, right?"

Taka shrugged her shoulders and sopped up the last of her grits with a piece of biscuit. Then she patted her stomach. "I'm so full, I can't even swallow my own spit right now."

"Ugh," Viv said. "Maybe you should have stopped after the half pound of bacon you ate."

"It wasn't a half pound," Taka assured her. "I just

asked Margaret, Evee's manager, to triple the order, which should have been only six slices. She put ten. Can I help it if I like bacon and Margaret likes me?"

Gilly chuckled. "Taka, you crack me up."

"But you don't think I'm like…cracked?" Taka asked.

"Oh, for Pete's sake," Vanessa said. "Do you have to fish for compliments? Of course you're not cracked. A little pitted in a few places, but not cracked. You were a big help during all we went through, and I'm proud of you."

Everyone sitting at the table stopped in midbite or middrink and looked from Vanessa to Taka.

Taka's mouth dropped open, and then she snapped it shut when she realized she'd still been chewing on part of the biscuit. She quickly washed her food down with some water and eyed Vanessa. "You mean that? Like, you didn't even shoot me a comeback. You really meant it?"

"Of course I did," Vanessa said, and patted Taka's hand.

Tears welled up in Taka's eyes. "I'll never forget this day as long as I live," she said.

"I think there are quite a few days we won't forget," Arabella said. "And I've got to throw my two cents in, too. I'm proud of all of you. When things got really tough, not one of you gave up. You simply kept on fighting and hunting like all Circle of Sisters would."

"Well, except for me," Viv said with a smirk. "I evidently decided to take a nap through some of it."

"That's not even funny," Gilly said to her. "You have no idea how hard we searched for you, how worried we were about you. We came so close to losing you." She shook her head. "I don't even like to think about it much less talk about it."

"Then we'll change the subject," Arabella said. "But before I do, I have to admit, and I think Vanessa and Taka will agree. We were wrong about the Benders. I'd hate to think where we'd be now had it not been for them. And anyone who can make the three of you so happy can't be bad certainly." She smiled. "Now, something I've been wanting to know but never found the right time to ask," she said to Gilly, "was, how did it feel to pop one of those suckers back into another dimension?"

Gilly grinned. "Glorious. Once the scabior was charged, it was pretty easy. All I had to do was aim, and the lightning bolt that came from the bloodstone on top of the scabior just seemed to know what to do."

"Yeah, but you had to have a pretty good aim," Evee said. "It's not like the scabior did it all by itself."

Gilly felt her cheeks grow warm. "Okay, so my aim was decent. Now can we talk about something else?"

"You know what feels pretty weird to me?" Viv said. "It's going to the compound and not having to feed any of the Originals. Turning that entire place into a cattle ranch was a decent idea. We're getting some great stock out of there and selling them for premium. Even better, no more wee hours of the morning. I can work eight to five like a normal person."

"I hear that," Evee and Gilly said in unison.

"Those early mornings were killers," Gilly said. "I'd leave the bar and grill around two in the morning and couldn't even take a nap before I had to start corralling the Chenilles for their feedings."

"Want to know what's better still?" Arabella asked.

All eyes zoomed in on her face.

"It's that the Originals all came back, only as human. We don't have them to feed anymore because they're no longer turning into the creatures they were. And that's because of you three."

"As in me, Viv and Evee?" Gilly asked.

"That's right," Vanessa said.

"It's all because of you," Arabella said. She lowered her voice and glanced around to make sure no one was eavesdropping.

Arabella leaned into the table and lowered her voice. "As the Triad, you've been told the story about how the Nosferatu, Loup-Garous and Chenilles came to be in the first place, remember?"

"Yeah," Gilly said. "The first Triad got pissed off at their boyfriends for cheating on them."

Arabella grinned. "Close enough."

"That first Triad was so angry over the incident, they collectively issued an incantation that they had no business messing with. It turned their betrotheds into the creatures you've been responsible for all these years."

"But why did it have to follow so many generations?" Gilly asked. "We didn't have anything to do with it. Doesn't seem fair, does it?"

"I agree," Taka said, and then burped.

"Although it didn't seem fair," Arabella said after giving Taka a disgusted look, "the creatures would never die, and someone had to watch over them. The Elders at the time simply added to the punishment curse that the ones who'd be responsible for them would be Triad, since they were the ones who created them."

"Well, I'm glad things worked out the way they did," Viv said. "It's only been a couple of weeks since this all came down, but I've seen some of my Nosferatu in town in human form. I don't think I've seen them so happy."

"Same with my Chenille," Gilly said.

"Ditto with my Loups," Viv said.

Arabella wiped the corners of her mouth with a linen napkin and placed it on her plate, indicating she was done with breakfast. "Thanks to you, they're all living normal lives."

"What about them?" Taka asked.

"Them who?" Vanessa asked.

"The Triad, ding-dong. Don't they get to live normal lives?"

Arabella studied Gilly's, Viv's and Evee's faces. "Once a Triad, always a Triad," she said. "That's something that can't ever be changed. You were born witches, and you will die witches. The same goes for me, Taka and Vanessa. It's just part of who we are."

"Being a witch isn't such a bad thing," Vanessa said. "You can always use your powers to help others, and for the love of biscuits, there are a lot of people here who can use your help."

"You most certainly can," a man said from beside them, startling everyone at the table.

Taka slapped a greasy hand to her heart. "Gunner, you almost gave me a heart attack!"

"I'm sorry for startling you," Gunner, dressed in a gray-and-black pin-striped suit with a gray shirt and black tie, said. "I saw all of you sitting here and was hoping you'd have room for one more."

"Of course," Evee said, and then got up and grabbed a chair from one of the other tables. She placed it between her and Arabella. "Please have a seat."

A look of embarrassment crossed Gunner's face. "I hope your conversation wasn't private. If it was, please let me know, and I'll be happy to meet up with all of you some other time."

"Not a conversation you can't be involved in, that's for sure," Gilly said. "We've just been talking about how different things are now that the Originals are all humans. Our lives and sleep have certainly changed because of it. How about you? How've you been?"

Gunner settled himself into the offered seat with a huge smile on his face. "Life hasn't been this good since… I don't remember when."

"I'm so glad to hear that," Arabella said.

"How so?" Taka asked.

"Well, first of all, I don't have to worry about Cottle and Black anymore. Both always gave me a hard time if I didn't spend enough time with them. Now, with so much time on my hands, I've been able to open my own hardware store."

"How wonderful," Vanessa said.

"Oh, it's not a huge place," Gunner said, "but it makes me happy. I've kind of always been handy with tools and such, so helping others find just what they need is right up my alley."

"Do you miss hanging out with the sorcerers?" Taka asked.

"Taka!" Arabella reprimanded.

"It's okay," Gunner assured Arabella, and then turned to Taka. "To be truthful, no. I always make a little time in the evening to go over my spells so I don't get rusty. You know, just in case I need to use one or two. But so far, it's only been me, the hardware store and my handful of spells. Oh, and I've started a vegetable garden. Tomatoes, okra, snap beans—things like that." He blushed. "I'm sorry, I'm sure this is boring the heck out of you."

"Not at all," Arabella said. "You sound very resourceful."

"I don't know about that," Gunner said. "But it's nice to be able to share fresh vegetables with my neighbors. In fact, if any of you ladies are interested, I've got a boon supply of tomatoes this season. I'd be happy to bring some to you if you'd like."

"That'd be great," Arabella said. "I love tomatoes."

"You hate tomatoes," Taka said with a frown. "You said they give you hives."

"Only raw tomatoes, dear," Arabella said, and Gilly could hear the restraint in her voice.

"That's very kind of you, Gunner," Gilly said. "Thank you. And thank you for all you did to help us in our many hours of need. Had it not been for you and your car...well, there's no telling how this might have turned out."

Gunner lowered his head for a moment, and when he lifted it, his lips were pursed. "If it's the same to you, Miss Gilly, I'd prefer never talking about that again. I'm just getting over nightmares about it now."

"Me, too," Taka said. "I keep dreaming of clown heads and devil heads and—"

"He asked us not to discuss it any longer," Arabella told Taka with a stern look.

"Oh...yeah...sorry," Taka said.

Gunner gave her a small smile. "Well, ladies, if you'll excuse me, I'm off to the store." He turned to Arabella. "I noticed you were here and just wanted to stop in and say hello."

After they shared their goodbyes, Taka leaned over toward Arabella. "I told you he likes you."

"He sure does," Vanessa added.

"Both of you stop it right now," Arabella said. "He's just a nice man and likes all of us."

"Hmm, I don't know," Gilly said. "He looked to be pretty sweet on you."

"Like sugar on a cream cake," Evee said.

"Don't encourage them, please," Arabella said. "They give me a hard enough time as it is."

Viv chuckled. "It's kind of hard to miss, though, Arabella."

"Well, miss it and move on," Arabella said, and then abruptly stood up from the table and headed out the door.

"Hey, you forgot to pay for your breakfast," Taka called after her.

"That's okay," Evee said. "I'll put it on a tab. Tell Margaret she had cream cake with sugar on top."

With that, the entire table of women broke into side-splitting laughter.

Epilogue

Three months later

She wanted a candlelit wedding, but since St. John's Cathedral wouldn't allow open flames due to fire marshal laws, the wedding planner had come up with a the idea of putting battery-operated flickering flames in five-foot bronze candle holders that stood at the end of each pew.

The front of the altar was adorned with carnations, roses, lilies and a nervous groom awaiting his bride. The entire congregation fidgeted as they waited for the organist to play the right song.

As the organist began the traditional wedding march, the priest walked to the front of the altar.

Everyone in the church let out a little gasp as the bride entered the church. She was beauty personified.

She wore a slim-fitting, floor-length satin wedding dress with three-quarter-length lace sleeves, a high lace collar, and a row of mother of pearl and sequins that ran from her bodice to the floor, down the middle of the gown. A three-foot satin train flowed behind her, and her veil, the front covering her face, was made of simple tulle that reached her shoulders, with rows of baby's breath forming the crown. She walked with her arm linked through that of a handsome young man, who led her to the altar.

There were no bridesmaids or flower girl. She'd wanted a simple ceremony. The only two thing she'd insisted on were the candles and to have someone walk her down the aisle, both of which the planner had managed to accomplish.

As the ceremony began, sniffles could be heard in the audience. The cathedral was nearly packed to capacity. Neighbors, friends—it seemed like the entire community at large had come to participate and wish the bride and groom the best of luck.

When the priest finally said, "I now pronounce you man and wife. You may kiss the bride," Gunner Stern gently lifted Arabella's veil and kissed her softly on the lips.

The entire congregation went wild with excitement. People whooping and shouting, "Congrats!" and thunderous clapping.

As Gunner and Arabella headed down the center aisle, arm in arm, their expressions couldn't have been happier, or their smiles bigger. The moment they reached the steps of the church, the congregation followed, throwing dry rice at the bride and groom for good luck.

The couple jumped into a waiting limousine and was whisked off into the night.

They'd told no one where they were headed for their honeymoon, and Gilly couldn't blame them. So much had happened over the past three months, ever since they'd gotten rid of Trey Cottle, their lives had become so different. Of the Originals that had gone missing, Gilly had spotted many walking the streets in New Orleans as human. They were no longer tied to the creatures they once were. No more hiding in dark corners. No more hidden feedings. They were now permanently human.

The Triad no longer had Originals to feed, but could still enjoy their company. The Originals had been family to the Triad, and they always would be. Just because they'd become human hadn't changed that at all. It all seemed so gloriously strange.

It took the Elders to make sense of it all. They explained that back in the 1500s, the original Triad had turned the men they were to marry into a Nosferatu, a Loup-Garou and a Chenille. They'd held hands and combined their powers, fed by anger to turn them into the creatures that had lasted for so many generations. When Viv, Evee and Gilly had joined hands and issued the spell to destroy the enemy, they did it with the same amount of fury as the first Triad, only fury for their loved ones that have been lost. Fury over injustice. Fury over the chaos that they had to deal with and for the humans who had died because of it. Fury over Cottle and his manipulative ways and his determination to take over the world and the universe. That same fury that started this all in the beginning broke the curse, for its origin was different. No longer were there any Chenilles or Nosferatu or Loup-Garous. There were still offshoots of the Originals, like vampires, werewolves and the like. Those did not disappear. But they were someone else's worry. No longer that of the Triad.

Lucien, who'd been chosen to walk Arabella down the aisle, was grinning like a kid who ate an entire jar of cookies. He took Evee by the shoulders and hugged her close. "I can't wait."

"Me either," she said.

The city itself, people who'd witnessed some of the Originals killing the humans, went silent. It was almost as if they'd had their memories erased. No one ever brought up the incident again. The police no longer bothered the Elders and, in fact, nodded hello cordially whenever they crossed them on the street.

No longer did they have to worry about relationships with another human. And the proof of that would be solidified by the triple wedding planned in the same Cathedral two months from now. Evee was to marry Lucien, Viv had Nikoli, and Gilly had her precious Gavril. Man and wife. Since the traumatic incident with Cottle, they'd become inseparable, each Triad with her Bender, learning the depths of one another. They lived, laughed, loved and craved more of the same.

Never in a million years would Gilly have thought that possible. The entire time she and Gavril had been intimate, she had feared the repercussions of their actions, thinking that, because of their sexual exploits, they had caused things to become worse. When, all that time, it had been Cottle planning his universal domination.

Man and wife.

Finally, without consequence.

All because of love. All because of the fury of love, the passion of love.

As if to prove what she was thinking, Gavril squeezed Gilly's hand, and she glanced up at him as they walked down the steps of the church and down the Riverwalk.

"I love you," he whispered.

"I love you more," Gilly said aloud, and then smiled, knowing she'd never have to fear those words again. Anger and disdain had caused the curse to be issued so many years ago, and it had taken the fury of unconditional love mixed with determination to break it. Love broke the curse. Love bound her to Gavril. And love gave her a new forever.

* * * * *